Love is the Easy Bit

Love is the Easy Bit

MARY GREHAN

WITHDRAWN FROM STOCK

PENGUIN
IRELAND

PENGUIN IRELAND

Published by the Penguin Group
Penguin Ireland, 25 St Stephen's Green, Dublin 2, Ireland
(a division of Penguin Books Ltd)
Penguin Books Ltd, 80 Strand, London WC2R ORL, England
Penguin Group (USA) Inc., 375 Hudson Street, New York, New York 10014, USA
Penguin Group (Australia), 707 Collins Street, Melbourne, Victoria 3008, Australia
(a division of Pearson Australia Group Pty Ltd)
Penguin Group (Canada), 90 Eglinton Avenue East, Suite 700, Toronto, Ontario, Canada M4P 2Y3
(a division of Pearson Penguin Canada Inc.)
Penguin Books India Pvt Ltd, 11 Community Centre,
Panchsheel Park, New Delhi – 110 017, India
Penguin Group (NZ), 67 Apollo Drive, Rosedale, Auckland 0632, New Zealand
(a division of Pearson New Zealand Ltd)
Penguin Books (South Africa) (Pty) Ltd, Block D, Rosebank Office Park,
181 Jan Smuts Avenue, Parktown North, Gauteng 2193, South Africa

Penguin Books Ltd, Registered Offices: 80 Strand, London WC2R ORL, England

www.penguin.com

First published 2013
001

Copyright © Mary Grehan, 2013

The moral right of the author has been asserted

Typeset in Garamond MT Std by Palimpsest Book Production Ltd, Falkirk, Stirlingshire
Printed in Great Britain by Clays Ltd, St Ives plc

A CIP catalogue record for this book is available from the British Library

ISBN: 978-1-844-88311-0

www.greenpenguin.co.uk

Penguin Books is committed to a sustainable
future for our business, our readers and our planet.
This book is made from Forest Stewardship
Council™ certified paper.

ALWAYS LEARNING   PEARSON

For Rita, Denis and John

The sea was calm the day she walked into it. The cold cut through her flesh and into her bones. The pain surprised her.

Black cliffs loomed around her, separating her from the life she was leaving behind. Gulls wove paths overhead.

She had chosen this place with care. She had gone there over the days before, approaching it each time from a different direction, planning her way into it, and out of it, until she was sure.

She was alone with the sea, her hair softly slapping her face, stones in her pockets and a child in her belly, while her husband and boys slept at home, curled tightly into each other. She stopped to remember them one by one, before walking towards her future.

The water wrapped itself around her, through her clothes, between her legs, into every crevice. It was almost inside her. It was just a matter of time.

She turned around to face the cliffs. Then she knelt down as far as she could go.

PART ONE

I

The old man waiting to cross the road makes me turn. Loose hairs fray the edge of his skull and his flesh is the texture of heather. He is, for the briefest of moments, my father.

'Straighten her up,' says Roger. 'Eyes on the road.'

'Sorry.' Behind the wheel everything is a target. Wherever I look, the car follows.

'Right at the next lights. Don't slow down. They're green. Keep going.'

I speed up and move my arms sharply so that all at once my left fist is at twelve o'clock and my right is at six. The car turns and we make it around the corner, which is good, I think, at first, until a vicious little bullet of a thing is heading right for us, its horn squealing at the top of its voice.

'Christ!' *So this is how it happens.*

With one hand, Roger pulls my top fist down to nine o'clock and the car back over to our side of the road.

'Oh, Jesus.'

'You're okay. You just over-extended, that's all.'

'We could've *died.*'

When I was young, younger than my daughter is now, my sister Joan told me I would die. Not straight away, of course. She said it probably wouldn't happen until I was an old woman but it would happen. There was no telling how or when. I worried about it for a while, curling myself deep under the covers at night so that Death would not find me, and when I awoke the next morning, I stayed still for a while for fear I had woken in some other unknowable place. I learnt to avoid all the things Ma said could kill you – oncoming cars, wild mushrooms, strange beasts, the edge of cliffs, the sea.

'But we didn't die,' says Roger. 'We're still here. Relax. Move on. Bring her up a gear.'

With time, thoughts of dying had passed away and didn't return until the night they covered my father's face with a sheet.

'These things happen when you're starting out.'

'Yes.'

'Don't let it put you off.'

'No.'

'It's not like you've ever driven before.'

'Right.'

On my sixteenth birthday, I'd driven my father's Morris Minor giddily around the top field in first gear, through posts he had erected. Later, when I was pregnant, I'd taken to the road with my husband and a set of hand-painted L-plates. That was back in the days when JP and I ate breakfast on the patio and went for evening-sun walks with fingers linked, when we looked out on the world through each other's eyes. My belly was swelling with the promise of new life and the future spread out before us, without the *if*s and *but*s to trip us up.

'We're coming up to a T-junction. Bring her down through the gears and stop.'

We wait, fingers drumming thighs, at a junction beside a school and I let myself breathe again. Roger's left elbow is propped on an open window and his moustache brushes against his brown-tipped fingers, absently sweeping to and fro. He has a good head of hair. Always a cause for suspicion. It rises in white waves from low on his fore-head.

'We just have to hang on here till the traffic breaks?' I say. He's probably a good kisser if you could get past the moustache.

'Yep. Just gotta hang on.'

At traffic-lights in front of a school, a young teacher waits. Her foot lightly hammers the ground. She's carrying a pile of large cardboard folders, full, I reckon, of charcoal drawings of startled faces, still-lives of wine bottles and grapes, and lino prints, the kind churned out by students of a certain age. She inhales on a cigarette before dropping it as soon as the man turns green and stubbing it out with a twist of a foot. I was her once. I turn the steering-wheel towards her, not meaning to.

'We'll be going the other way,' says Roger. 'Don't forget the mirrors.'

The road drains of cars and we take off for the final leg, through the ashen cement of north Dublin housing estates, framing a spectacular sky of gilt-edged clouds that are screening the sun.

I'm almost enjoying myself. This feels grown-up, miles from the shackles of bus queues and the come-and-get-me calls that punctuate my life. Now, for the first time in a long time, there's a sense of the possible. A fantasy of the open road unfolds – Route 66, motels in strange towns, eating alone at sundown.

'Well, allefuckingluia, sister. Woman aged thirty-seven takes to the road. About bloody time,' said Joan, when I told her about my lessons. 'But why now, of all times?'

Why indeed? I guess my resentment of sunshine mummies perfectly manicured, no loose threads or hairs or feelings, finally boiled over inside me. They drive their kids to school in shiny saloon cars, smugly waving back at Kate and me through the rain and their forced grins.

When it's all over, Roger drops me off at the edge of the city centre. I slide out from behind the wheel, cradling my stomach, then remember there's no need – I am not pregnant. My legs are soft and boneless when my feet touch the ground but I'm quietly elated. Roger shakes my hand, assesses my thighs, breasts and face in that order, gets back into the car on the driver's side and is gone.

I bob along the street for a bit until, step by step, my legs become stronger and straighter and my footsteps more solid on the ground. It's like one of those Darwinian diagrams you find in an encyclopedia that illustrate how blobs become fish become reptiles become ape become man. By the time I get to Dame Street I'm a fully formed human being, but people move around me as if I'm invisible. They brake suddenly in front of me, walk backwards into me, and force me to dodge contact. They flank me on both sides and shout through me.

I turn away from them, off the main street, and make my way through the back-streets – left, right, left, left – towards my bus stop, taking a small detour to pass a glass-fronted gallery I've visited many times before. I still crave the smell of paint.

The gallery is shut for the installation of an exhibition. Inside are ladders, pots of paint and a posse of upward-looking men, all dressed in black, swarming like bees on a mission explicable only to themselves.

LOVE IS THE EASY BIT
A. H. DELANEY

is written on the gallery window, followed by the dates of the exhibition.

The letters are large and black, suggesting the arrival of something new, something exciting and life-changing. Once, A. H. Delaney was these things to me. And he was more, so much more. Whatever he has become since, I'm not sure, but the implications are huge.

LOVE IS THE EASY BIT

I read the words again, one by one, amazed by his audacity. In his hands, they are meaningless building blocks, which he has moved around and assembled for effect, to find the best composition.

'Any chance of some change, love?'

I jump and land on the same spot. A man is standing before me, hands deep in his pockets, wearing a pristine pink hoodie with 'Boston' stitched on it.

'It's for a hostel, like.'

His words come out of his nose and his mouth sinks into his skull where his teeth once were. He blinks vacantly at me as I search the bottom of my bag.

'There you go. Now clear off and leave the lady alone.'

The junkie scrambles backwards into the shade and I look up. 'Arthur?'

And there he is, tall and tweeded, combing his fingers through his thick hair. 'Sylvia.' He has the temerity to smile, a wide, guiltless smile that shows most of his teeth.

It's funny the way the hairs on the back of a dog's neck rise when it's angry, or afraid, or both. I always wondered how that happens.

9

'How the hell are you?' he asks.

My hand moves to cover my eye and my body collides with a body behind me. 'Sorry.' Then I rub my arm to flatten out the goose bumps and try to recall what it was my father said about him.

'You haven't changed a bit,' I hear him say. His shoes are long and shiny. 'So what are you up to?'

He hasn't changed either, or has he? If anything, he's even taller than before. His cheekbones are more polished, his cheeks are now in the shade and his jowl is looser. But the eyes are still dark and impenetrable.

'I'm learning to drive.'

When I think of all the things I'd planned to say to him when I saw him again. I crossed the continent rehearsing lines. I scribbled them on beer mats in pubs, on napkins in trains. I made bad poems from them, set them alight and watched them float up into the air. I woke in the middle of the night with new lines, lines that would floor him, lines that would make him crumble in remorse. By the end, there were book loads of lines, squeezed into the folds of my grey matter. Yet now the only one I can come up with is that I'm learning to bloody drive.

Arthur snorts in the way only Arthur can. 'I don't drive myself. Never got around to it.'

Well, of course you don't. Too busy spinning great art around the world.

'It's been so long,' he says. My pumps, flat and scuffed, angle towards each other. They must stay, not move. 'Are you living in Dublin?'

I nod.

'Married?'

'Yes.'

'Kids?'

I swallow painfully. 'Just one.'

'A boy?'

'Girl. Actually.'

'Yes, yes, of course. A girl. I bet she's just like you?'

'She's not.'

A knuckled tapping comes from inside the gallery window.

'I've got to go,' he says. 'Gotta have this bloody show up by tomorrow. It's opening Thursday. At seven. You should come along and bring . . .?'

'JP.'

'JP. Of course. Bring JP.'

Then he turns and leaves me – tremulous and sick – behind him.

Back home I slam the front door shut in relief and lean into the hall mirror for signs of I'm not sure what. Damage, perhaps. The flesh around my mouth points downwards. I force a smile and let it drop again. A vague outline of pink is all that's left of my lipstick and a few specks of mascara darken my lower lids. I lick a finger, wipe them away and smudge some makeup from my cheek to cover the scar near my right eye. Then I sink a brush into my hair and pull it out from the crown to the ends at right angles to my head, watching it fall, strand by strand. Arthur used to love my hair. He called it 'mellifluous', taking care to point out that it wasn't a typical use of the word. He was being poetic.

'There's ten out now.'

When I turn around, JP's standing there, in the middle of the kitchen doorframe, grinning preposterously at me, with Monty circling his feet. His fingers are braided over the crown of his head and his legs are spread wide. 'That's two more than this morning.'

'JP?'

'And they're beginning to turn already.'

'You gave me a fright.'

'You know, Kent was right. That really was the best spot to plant them. Funny the things Kent knows about.'

'I didn't know you were home. It's only three o'clock.'

'Do you know, he covered his strawberries with loads of his old socks for the whole of the winter?'

My husband is in the middle of a passionate love affair with his strawberry bed. He got excited when the hard green berries began to appear a few days ago, as if a fairy had come in the night and left them out especially for him.

'JP?' I follow him into the kitchen. 'What are you doing home at this hour?'

He's at the sink and his back is to me. 'Site visit.'

I study the whole of him, tall, narrow, long-limbed. He hasn't changed much since he was a boy. His mother says he just drifted into adulthood. There was no dramatic turning point, no teenage withdrawal from the world and adult re-entrance. In many ways, he's still a boy in a man's body. He's a handsome man, people say, and his forearms still thrill me. He's a good man too. He cares for Kate. He cares for Monty. He cares for his mother. He cares for his strawberries and, yes, they say, he cares for me.

'Site visit?'

'Yep.'

But I can't read him, not really. I look at his sandy, boyish head, his light green eyes, slightly too close together, framed by creases from too much smiling, and wonder if maybe he's attacking me through his jovial distance. Maybe there's another life out there that must be kept separate from mine. In times of my most vivid paranoia – and they are vivid indeed – I imagine another family, other kids, another home, another JP that fills his greenhouses with strawberries and takes to the open road on a Harley Davidson. But usually, on days like today, I decide there isn't that much going on, that there are no hidden chambers in JP's brain and that I'm being ridiculous.

'JP?' I speak slowly this time in an attempt to stay measured. 'What site visit?'

He turns and looks at me, eyes widened by innocence. Drops of water from his hands land on the floor. 'I had a site visit up on the new bridge. No point heading back into the office now. I'll work from here.'

'Fine.'

And it *is* fine. It might even be nice. It might be nice to siphon off some daytime alone together, like we used to, but I must leave it at that. There's nothing to be gained from opening up old memories.

The door bell goes and Kate's frosted silhouette is jigging about on the front porch. Monty barks, then skids to the door, his tail in full rotation.

'Mam, what's "a-li-en-a-tion" mean?' Kate asks, as soon as I open the door. Then she spots her father in the kitchen. Her schoolbag thuds to the floor and she runs to him, heaving herself up on to his lap while Monty's paws dig away at his knees. In the midst of this group hug, of which I've no part, she drops her new word into JP's lap.

'That's a very big word for a little girl.' He laughs.

'I'm eleven.'

'Are you?'

'You know I am.'

'So who gave you that big word?'

'Brigid. She's always giving me new words. She writes them on little bits of card for me to keep. Today she gave me "alienation". Look.'

Kate goes out to the hall and drags her schoolbag into the kitchen. She unzips the front pocket and pulls out a grubby piece of card torn from a corn-flakes box. 'See?' says Kate, handing the cardboard to JP. 'It says "alienation".'

'So what do you think it means?'

'Brigid said it kind of means feeling alone, that nobody understands you, kind of.'

'So why did you ask me if you already know what it means?'

'I was just checking. Besides, I thought you might know other words that also mean "alienation", other long words with loads of parts to them. I want to be able to give a big word back to Brigid. I'd like one with an *s* in it.'

'Why an *s*?'

'I like *s* words. They sound foreign. Like French.'

'Okay, then. Well, there's "isolation" – I-S-O-L-A-T-I-O-N – as in "feeling alone" or "being estranged".'

'What does "being estranged" mean?'

'"Estranged"? Why don't we get the big dictionary down and look it up?'

I watch from the bottom of the stairs as JP hoists Kate up as far as the top shelf of the bookcase in the front room. I'm invisible in this vignette, like a viewer in a darkened theatre where the only lights are on the stage.

I climb the stairs alone to remove my makeup.

2

A piece of coloured paper lies across the desk in front of me, pale blue like the morning sky.

'Today,' a woman declares, in pulpit tones from the top of the school hall, 'we're inviting all the parents and children to get creative. We've lots of different kinds of materials – watercolour, pastels, pencils, even clay. This is your time to express yourselves and to get to know each other through art.'

She's wearing a loose grey polo neck, over which is tossed a pashmina, an ethnic thing, woven from hand-dyed threads. Silver earrings tremble from her ears and her arms are stretched out like Jesus of Rio's.

'Here you are, Mrs Larkin,' she says, when it's my turn, sliding an open box of oil pastels on to the desk before me. Her voice is low and breathy as if she's trying to hypnotize me. 'There are lots of beautiful colours to choose from. I don't want you to be afraid of the materials. Just go where the colour takes you.'

I accept the box to make her go away.

The colours collude to form a rainbow. Richard Of York Gave Battle In Vain. The Pashmina is circling the hall, a relentless voiceover telling us of her hopes for the afternoon. Something about letting go, being free, no judgement and something about a safe space. I don't feel very safe. I'm glad JP isn't here.

My hand wraps tightly around a yellow-ochre pastel and

pushes it in a number of short directions, not too hard. The stick skates over the paper, leaving its mark on the raised parts only. Maybe I should have told him about this. The letter from the school inviting parents to a 'special event to mark the end of the school year' was addressed to both of us. But I didn't.

The blue of the paper peeps through the mark, which has taken the form of a star. I do another, and another, basic yet elegant. I fill in the spaces between the stars with a crazy orange, enjoying the combination of the marks and the blue beneath. A border in red. I lose myself in the colour, the texture and the smell. Mario, my college tutor, is in my ears. 'Sylvia, you've got to keep going. We need more painters like you. Less ego, more soul.' Back then he encouraged me to paint large canvases in sun-soaked studios, to swim in blocks of cerulean and vermilion, to get drunk on the smell of the oils. Poor Mario. He expected great things of me.

I marvel at Arthur. He didn't need the blessing of the elders; neither did he get it. Yet he has never faltered in ploughing his glorious artistic vision and now wears his emperor's new clothes without a shiver of self-doubt. I lean back to take in all my stars in one go. What would Arthur make of them? I suspect he'd love their 'raw energy', assuming they were some kind of 'naïve art'. They'd be a celebrated feat of creativity if made by Outsider Artists or recovering drug addicts. He'd be horrified to learn they came from me.

'Where's the conceptual basis?' he'd ask.

I'm egged on by Arthur's contempt and decide to dedicate the picture to him, just for the hell of it. I write a caption in crude letters with a red pastel at the bottom of the page.

'Oh, that's nice,' says the red-haired woman in the desk

next to me. 'Look, Carol, isn't that nice?' prodding a woman beside her.

Carol leans over the redhead to take a closer look.

'"Love is the easy bit",' she reads aloud. 'What's that mean?'

'Nothing.' I shrug. Soon all the other mothers are making gasping noises at my stars. I smile mutely.

'You're Kate's mum, aren't you?'

'Yes.'

'Your husband's not here?'

'No.'

I take another piece of paper from the pile at the top of the hall and start again. I'm not sure when I stopped inviting JP along, when I started reducing his lines in the script of my suburban life, when I stopped taking those risks.

The women are back, laughing at each other's jokes. 'You're right there, Sandra,' one calls, over the bent head of her husband, and 'True enough for you, Betty,' says another, nudging a third in a game of communal affirmation. They visit each other's houses for raucous pots of tea in the afternoons during which they discuss their husbands' body parts. I'm not in the club.

I look down at my stars, each like a half-hearted explosion. How did it come to this? Did I know back then I was embarking on a life in which there's more that I can't say than I can, more that I don't say than I do? A life reduced to oil-pastel stars on coloured paper? Did I know I'd be leaving it all behind – conversations accelerated by the onset of dawn, journeys to parties in the middle of the night, painting marathons fuelled by the joy of a beautiful mark? It had been exciting back then, hadn't it?

I had called myself an artist in those days, like Arthur

does now. A. H. Delaney, the artist. He's back in this city, just a few miles from here, the map of his life lying over mine, and that thought makes me hold my breath.

Thoughts of Arthur come with traces of cynicism and fear. And somewhere in there is an aftertaste of awe that says there's still a hunger in me I hadn't known was there, for the ideas, the exchanges, the what-ifs and we-coulds, the trials and the errors, the problems, the resolutions, even the 'poor aristocracy' and the 'colourful Bohemia' – his words, not mine.

But on the third set of stars, I straighten my back and tell myself not to be foolish: that's all in the past and a night of wine-sipping in a Dublin gallery isn't going to rewind history. It's ridiculous to think I could go to Arthur's opening after everything that happened between us and because of us, and pass myself off as one of them. I'm a mother now, for God's sake.

The children are sitting in desks opposite us. Kate's in the front row beside Brigid. I stop to view her, with her wide forehead and gently sloping eyes, in the way you'd view an Old Master, made long ago in a time that has nothing to do with you now.

She's telling the Pashmina about JP. 'He's building this enormous bridge that can carry millions of cars. That's his job, you know.'

'How wonderful. He must be very clever.'

'He is. He built bridges in Australia.'

'Your father lived in Australia?'

'Yeah. Bits of him are still brown from the sun there.'

A pain in my pelvis begins to stir. When she was born, they held her up in the air so I could see her over the curtain. All eyes were on her rubbery body, grey against the green of their robes, not human at all, and everyone, but me, was gasping in wonder. Her head was a bloody scarlet and she scrunched up her face and screamed in outrage, short, angry shrieks, moving her head from side to side in a perplexing motion. Her fingers, like claws, scratched the air, each working involuntarily, randomly, independently of the other. She didn't want to be there any more than I did.

'Gosh.'

'Yeah. He drove on his motorbike all the way up to the place where the people who lived there for hundreds of years live.'

'The Aboriginals?'

'Yeah. Them. Well, he drove up to this big rock where they live.'

They offered her to JP and he took her, touching her head with a painful tenderness. I watched from the outside. It didn't feel as if it had anything to do with me any more.

'He has a motorbike in the garage. Another one. Not the one he had in Australia. He drove Mam all around Ireland on it and they slept in tents. That was before they had me.'

The Pashmina smiles and strokes my daughter's head before moving on, and Kate returns to making animals out of clay. She pulls up the necks and pinches out the ears. Her hair, a sheaf of many golds, falls across her face as she leans sideways to study their profiles. The neck of one of the animals droops and Kate straightens it up. She looks around to share them with Brigid.

Brigid's freckled face is propped up by a fist. She's reading a book through her greasy glasses, which have slipped down her nose. Kate elbows her, and Brigid smiles vaguely at the creature. Brigid's the sister my daughter never had.

'Why don't I have any brothers or sisters?' she had asked,

one morning at breakfast, of no one in particular. Kate's funny that way. Her questions crash-land on you when you least expect them. I looked at JP. He picked up a crust of toast and fed it to Monty.

We used to talk about having children during our evening walks when we were on the countdown to parenthood. We talked about everything back then. We talked about the perfect family we'd have to plaster in the gaps of our childhood. We wanted an even gender balance. We wanted the little boy my father had hoped for and the little girl JP's mother never had. Our boy would look out for our girl. Our girl would look up to our boy. Our family would be a steady four-legged stool. And if a third child got added, we'd have another one to even out the numbers. We talked about getting a second dog for Monty. We liked even numbers. We liked symmetry. We liked balance. And our family would be the image of our aesthetic ideals.

'It just didn't happen,' I said.

JP gave me a look I chose not to read.

Then, without a word, Kate had slipped off her chair, out of the room and up to her bedroom, followed by Monty.

She spends an hour every evening in her bedroom after her homework. I see the results there the next morning – drawings of fantastical outfits and little girls, all with long, straight hair and big eyes, all standing in a row holding hands. Lately, she has started drawing from life – Monty, an egg, herself in the mirror. Her line is tentative but beautiful. She has taught herself everything she knows, and is so much more committed an artist than I ever was. But she doesn't always share it with us. She doesn't need our affirmation. She has her dog.

JP brought Monty home one day out of the blue during

our first year of marriage, a basset hound pup with over-sized ears, and eyes that looked sad beyond their years. We both understood it to be a sort of parenting trial. He was taken to classes to learn how to walk, heel, sit, give the paw and roll over. We got up an hour earlier to walk him, and on Sunday mornings we drove him to the Phoenix Park. His stubby legs struggled to wade through the fallen leaves. He whimpered when he saw the deer. JP and I laughed and congratulated ourselves on how well adjusted our dog was. There was nothing we wouldn't do for our baby. We'd have got him French and piano classes if he'd shown an interest.

Kate took over caring for Monty as soon as she could walk. They shared secrets and a bed. Soon JP and I were outsiders looking in on their relationship. Monty is always civil to us, but it's Kate he waits for behind the front door in the mid-afternoon. It's Kate he leans his body against at the breakfast table. Kate is Monty's mistress and we're just part of her posse.

It just didn't happen. That was what I said. How could I have left it like that, as if having a child was as random as the wind? I look across the hall at her golden, timeless head, not yet chipped away by life. I could slap myself.

It could have happened. If I'd let it.

I drive my oil stick faster in every direction, faster and faster, not even waiting till I re-enter the centre before reaching out again, so that the tips of the stars are connecting with each other. The specks of paper are getting erased by the layers of oil pastel.

A cloud of musk hits me.

'Oh, that's fan*tas*tic,' the Pashmina says, with enough gush to make the whole room squirm. 'Look at all those lovely

stars, all twinkling and bright. What do you think they're saying?'

So this is what it's like to live in a care home.

'Are the stars your dreams?'

She crouches to make eye contact with me. Soft flesh oozes out between her polo neck and her chin. I'm astonished by her nerve and opt for the silence of an artist.

'Hmm?' She's determined not to lose face. 'What would you like to make now?' she asks, gently disarming me of my stars.

I suppose a baby's out of the question?

I freeze for a moment for fear that the words actually made it to the outside. The Pashmina doesn't seem to have heard. I flatten my hands on the child-sized desk, push myself up and shuffle out of it, inch by self-conscious inch.

'I thought this was supposed to be an art session,' I hiss. The Pashmina recoils. 'Not a bloody session on the couch.'

All the eyes in the hall look in my direction. My eyes meet Kate's. Her hands are shielding her animals. I want to get us both out of here, but we're trapped in this charade of family unity.

So I leave the room, not quite knocking over the Pashmina on my way.

3

All around me couples are inclining their heads towards
each other like stag deer entering a fray.

'Yeah?' the waitress asks, holding her notebook right up
to her chin.

'Just a coffee, please.'

'Latte? Cappuccino?'

'Black, thanks.'

'Milk?'

'No milk. Completely black.'

These furtive cups of coffee in unfamiliar coffee shops
are now a habit. No one knows I am here. I can play at being
someone else. I could be that woman from *Brief Encounter*,
in her fur-trimmed coat and gloves, in town on a few errands.
But in truth I have no such sense of purpose. Better to be
no one.

I plan these visits in advance, mould my day around them,
taking care not to revisit places I've been to before. God
forbid I should have to match the faint recognition of bored
waitresses. It's important to remain anonymous, as if I'm
having an affair.

'Just for one?'

I keep my eyes on the door. As if.

'Just for one.'

Everything in this place is brown – brown leatherette
seats, brown Formica-topped tables, brown coffee. Even the
light is brown. A brown interval between one world and

another. After this, I will go to Arthur's exhibition. I don't know why. A tiny bit of skin juts out from the nail on my little finger, which I manage to get between my teeth. I pull until I taste blood. I shouldn't be here. I should be getting things ready for the annual trip to Waterford, measuring out two weeks of socks and underwear, paring our lives down into travel-sized containers. We go to Ma's every year for a fortnight. That's our summer holiday. It's in the family contract. A tried and tested formula, a given protocol that spares any negotiation of alternative how-abouts or do-you-fancies. We don't fancy. We go to my mother's. Everybody knows that. And in between our going to Ma, she comes up to Dublin for Christmas and Easter and family occasions dreamt up by my sister.

For the past couple of years we'd brought Brigid with us to Waterford because, as Kate pointed out, she doesn't have a sister and Brigid has too many.

I should turn around now and go home, leave my plain black coffee behind and head back to my husband and daughter. It'd be the right thing to do. I sink deeper into the corner of my booth, putting the whole finger into my mouth to suck away the blood. My husband and daughter are perfectly complete without me. They'll be wrapped up in each other on the sofa at home, legs entwined, slowly unpicking the latest plot twist of my daughter's little life – Brigid didn't come to school today – in between the spelling tests and the long division.

Kate had blurted out her news after tea.

'Miss Kavanagh said it's because of "personal reasons",' she said, in a kind of protest. 'Dad, what are "personal reasons"?'

'Well, it can mean a lot of things,' said JP. 'Things that are personal to you might be things you don't want other people to know.'

'But when I went up to Brigid's house after school, her mother said she had a "special visitor" and couldn't come out. She didn't say anything about "personal reasons".'

'Well, having a special visitor can be a personal reason.'

'No, it can't. Personal reasons are more important than that, like really important. Like maybe she has consumption like the woman that wrote *Wuthering Heights*. She lay on the sofa until she died.'

'I doubt it very much.'

'No, she did die. Brigid told me. She's always going on about her and about *Wuthering Heights*, about how Heathcliff and Cathy – they're in the book – fell in love with each other when they were very young and then, after that, they stuck to each other for ever even after Cathy died. Then, when Cathy died, Heathcliff became a real monster because his heart was broken.'

'Did he now?'

'Yeah. Did terrible things on everyone. Brigid says she wouldn't like to marry a man like Heathcliff but it's better than marrying Edgar. That's the man Cathy married in the end.'

'What's wrong with Edgar?'

'Oh, he had a very nice house and all that, and that's good, but Brigid says he was boring, and boring is the worst thing ever. But Brigid says her mother says it would be better to marry Edgar because Edgar was reliable and every woman needs a reliable man.'

JP broke into a massive laugh, surreal in its sound, the kind of laugh only Kate can induce. 'Let's ask your mother.'

I was pouring the dishwasher powder into its place. It

missed the mark and scattered around the door of the machine, like the first flakes of snow.

'What do you think, Mrs L? Do you think a woman should marry Edgar, safe, reliable Edgar, with a nice house and all his pension contributions up to date, or should she go for drama and passion and marry Heathcliff, dark, brooding, dangerous Heathcliff?' He moved his fingers like the wicked witch when he mentioned Heathcliff.

'How should I know?' I slammed the dishwasher shut, twiddled the knobs and left the room. My bus was due in ten minutes.

'Kate, my darling,' I heard JP say, from the hall mirror where I ploughed a brush through my hair one last time. 'I'm pretty certain Brigid doesn't have consumption. The reason she wasn't in school today will come out in its own good time. It always does. You wait and see.'

I listened to the silence of their hug. When I turned around, JP was hanging like a baboon from the kitchen doorframe, surveying me.

'You look nice.'

'Thanks.'

'Kooky.'

'Kooky?'

'Isn't that what they say?'

'Is it?'

'I think it's meant to be a compliment. So, whose exhibition are you going to anyway?'

'No one you know.'

'Right.'

'I've got to go.'

'I like your stars.'

'What stars?'

'The ones hanging over the Unilions on the piano. Kate said you did them.'

Kate was beside me by then, explaining that her clay Unilions were a mix between unicorns and lions. Apparently the name had been Brigid's idea and it had been the Pashmina's idea to make two, as in Noah's Ark. She dragged me into the front room to point out the unicorn horns and the lion hair and ask me if I liked them and to tell me she was going to bring one down to Gran because Gran was always asking her to make something that she could stick up in the house. But I was too busy yanking my stars off the wall to reply.

'Mam? What are you doing?' she cried.

'They're embarrassing, Kate. I can't bear to look at them.' I scrunched the paper into a ball and bounced it into the fire grate. 'Your animals will be much better off without them.'

'What did you do that for?' asked JP, flatly.

'They're just a load of scribbles, JP. It's no big deal.'

I'd left them standing there, staring at the Unilions, while I tripped out of the house towards the bus stop.

The inside of the gallery is a concrete box, insulated from the city around it. Unlikely sounds are bouncing against the walls – the sounds of speeding through tunnels, the sounds of Sellotape being pulled sharply, the sounds of metal doors slamming on you never to be opened again, the sounds of chains. I circle the gallery once, but there's no escaping the sounds, so I choose a spot in the middle of the floor within range of the main exhibit: a cloud-like form, made of a strange, translucent material. People are mingling above me on a glass mezzanine, examining the cloud from a loftier level. The sight of them suspended mid-air, with the soles

27

of their feet forming patterns above my head, makes me queasy, so I stay where I am on solid ground, transfixed by the cloud, until I remember that I am also on view.

I move on to the next piece, tucked away in a dark corner. A large male mouth opens and closes in slow motion. The tongue is swollen and moist. Air bubbles surface and burst on the pink flesh, leaving a wetness that makes me swallow.

I scan the piece of paper in my hand.

This work propagates the absenting psychologies of violence. In particular, disenfranchised notions of passion and love. Cognition is searching endlessly for an absented referent. This restless searching speaks of isolation. Searching is marked by anxiety and collapsed into waiting. Time emerges as the flux of anxiety and the site of displacement. The transparency of nature, spatial penetration and the ubiquitous flow of air and light instilled in the urban space and the transitory conditions of the environment that constitutes it create a transgression of form.

Oh, to be a child again, like Kate, at that boundless stage when you don't have to know it all and questions are considered endearing. I need a square of corn-flakes box to bring my new words home on, the kind that JP cut out for Kate for her to write her 'isolation' on as a present for Brigid, leaving the poor cockerel without a beak.

'Sylvia?'

The man in front of me is gleaming in a shiny navy suit. Silver-coated hairs are sprinkled through his crew-cut.

'Smoke?'

He has the advantage of having those teeth that converge towards the tongue. They make for a nice smile.

'I'm sorry,' I add quickly.

I can't recall if Smoke was his official nickname or a behind-his-back one. Every night he hung his clothes in front of the hearth in his mother's house so that by day he smelt of turf fires, the kind you might want to curl up in front of. I kissed him once, for six hours, just to get closer to the fire. He was a terrible kisser, despite the nice teeth.

'How the hell are you? You haven't changed a bit,' he says.

I breathe in discreetly. The turf smell is gone.

'What are you up to, these days? I never see you around,' he tries again.

'Trevor,' for that's his real name, 'what does "absented referent" mean?'

'I don't know.'

'What does "flux of anxiety" mean?'

'Jesus, Sylvia, I don't write this stuff.'

'Who does? Arthur?'

'Probably.'

With that, Arthur steps into the ring, smelling of cologne and wine. Smoke slips away, as if dismissed.

'Sylvia. You came.' His smile blots out everyone in the room and releases a terrifying pleasure in me that makes me want to run away. But before I can, he reaches forward to kiss me on the cheek. I divert my head slightly so that I receive and don't give. The kiss lands at eye level. He doesn't notice.

He looks around the gallery.

'Where's . . .?'

'He couldn't come.'

He registers this with eyes looking up, before turning

back and taking me in. He moves through my face, to my hair, my earrings – silver studs from the Grand Bazaar – my mouth, my eyes, the scar. There's no avoiding the scar. He moves down to my blazer, jeans and shoes. I took care to wear clothes that say little about me and makeup that aimed to be invisible. He reaches forward to push back a loose strand of mellifluous hair. His fingernail scrapes my ear. I hold my place.

'"Is she kind as she is fair? For beauty lives with kindness",' he says, half to himself. I smile. Arthur had a line for every occasion.

We barter a few thoughts, abstract, academic ones, not grounded in the reality of our lives. I make vague comments about his work, followed by a quip on his illustrious career, and he has the decency to look embarrassed. It's easy to talk to Arthur. It shouldn't be, but it is. I'd forgotten how easy.

'Great title,' I offer.

'Sorry?'

'Of the show.'

'Thanks.' He's forgotten that too.

He stops and frowns so that his eyes are tucked back in under his brows. It's strange meeting someone you once knew intimately after a long period of absence. 'Ah, yes, the eyes were just like that,' or 'Yes, that's how he used to frown,' you say to yourself, almost surprised by the familiar.

'Sylvia, why did you leave like that?' he asks, with an unexpected seriousness. I begin to shuffle backwards. 'So suddenly. In the middle of the night, practically. We could've . . .'

A woman with scraped-back hair and geometric bones approaches and introduces him to an old lady in a Chanel suit. I step further back. I know now that I came for a hearing of some kind, to voice my outrage or prove to him the hurt he caused, even to cause him pain, if only in some way to be understood. I came to make a point, but there's none that can be made without the ground cracking open under us to reveal a never-ending well of points, each more imperative than the previous. I re-enter the sounds of chains, but not before Arthur reaches forward and hands me his business card. It's small, white on grey, infinitely tasteful.

'Call me,' he mouths, holding a fist up near his ear.

Then he turns to blast La Chanel with his most artistic smile.

My mobile rings on the bus home.

'Hello?'

'My plane is delayed, and I'm due for an event in London in just over an hour.'

My sister Joan only ever phones when bubbles appear in her airtight plans.

'Oh. Hello, Joan. Nice to talk to you too.'

'And you can't get a decent cup of coffee in this hole of an airport.'

'That'll make headlines.'

'Funny. What are you up to?'

'Nothing.'

'I tried to get you at home but JP said you were out.'

'I was at the opening of an exhibition, that's all.'

'And JP didn't want to go?'

'No, why would he?'

'I thought he was interested in learning about that arty stuff you go on about.'

'That was years ago.'

'Huh. So how's the driving going?'

'Okay, bit scary.'

'Are you going to drive to Ma's?'

'You must be joking.'

'Why not?'

'I'd get us all killed, that's why.'

'At least for part of the way? JP'll be with you.'

'Actually, JP doesn't know about me driving.'

There's a silence, the judgemental kind.

'Well, I haven't driven in years.'

'So? Why don't you just tell him, Sy?' It annoys me the way my sister shortens my name to a sigh, as if she's too busy for all the syllables. 'I don't get what the big secret is. Really, I wonder about you sometimes.' It annoys me the way my sister wonders about me.

'Joan?'

'Yeah?'

'Who did you marry?'

'What?'

'Edgar or Heathcliff?'

'Edgar who?'

'*Wuthering Heights*. Remember?'

'Oh, Sy, you don't believe in all that crap, do you?'

'No, of course not.'

She sighs. 'Men aren't as simple as Edgar or Heathcliff and all that baloney.'

'I know that.'

'Good. Well, I married Edgar, if you must know. Why do you ask?'

'No reason.'

'They're announcing my flight. Gotta go. When are you off to Ma's?'

'Saturday.'

'Be nice to her, Sy. Gotta go.'

She hangs up, leaving me leaning against the cold of the bus window, looking out on the wet night, its streetlights becoming stars through the prism of raindrops.

4

We follow a cloud to the south, a bulbous cumulus, brilliantly white and optimistic on top, with a dark underbelly, like a romantic exercise in tone. It bursts forth in all directions, losing bits and gaining bits in the course of the journey, but holding on to the same heart.

I never figured out what it is about clouds that makes them so intriguing. Maybe it's their elusiveness, the way that you can't put your arms around one and bring it home, wrap it up, put it in a scrapbook and keep it for ever. Or maybe it's the contradiction of the audacious exterior and the blurred greyness inside. I said so to Arthur, sort of, at his launch, and he snorted.

'Oh, yes, I forgot that clouds were your thing,' he said. 'That and the sea.'

He hadn't forgotten, not for a minute. He used to tease me about my obsessive cloud sketches in paint, one after another, fast, ever-changing, in keeping with the rhythm of their movement. He called me 'Constable' for a while and told me I was born a hundred years too late. 'Look, Sylvia, you've missed one,' he'd say, pointing with mock urgency at a wispy tuft of white in the sky.

Arthur never really got it.

Clouds were there from the beginning. As a child, I followed my father across the fields in the evening, my short legs running to keep up with his stride and braking when he'd stop for a reading of the sky, his fingers knotted over the top of his stick. Da knew the quirks and tics of each cloud. He could second-guess them. He knew when rain was on the way or when the clouds were just teasing him.

One evening, they wouldn't let me go with him.

'Why can't I go with Daddy?' I screamed, all the pain in my heart turned on full.

'No, Sylvia,' my mother said. 'There are storm clouds on the way.'

'I want to see the storm clouds. I like storm clouds. Why can't I see the storm clouds?'

'No,' she said, like a door closing in my face.

I had to settle for watching my father walking into the storm alone, his split-second silhouette made by the lightning through the kitchen window. The clouds growled from a distance, as if throwing a tantrum of their own, and I worried for him. My mother dragged me from the window and sprinkled me with holy water.

'*Nooo*,' I bawled. 'I have to see that Daddy's okay.'

In the end, she let me stay on the sofa opposite the window until my father came home. Only he didn't, and when I awoke the next day, the morning sky was pale and innocent through my bedroom window.

So I worked at re-creating clouds. But no matter how hard I peered, how deftly I moved my brush, I could never make one. Arthur's sculpture, dangling and shimmering in the middle of the gallery, matched me in my failure. Clouds will always defeat us.

And, of course, Arthur's right. When I wasn't painting clouds, I was painting the sea, as vast and unknowable as the sky. I viewed them interchangeably, one or other of them dominating a canvas at any one time. When I wasn't looking up, I was looking down, and rarely, it seemed, looking straight ahead.

But when Kate was born, clouds disappeared from view for a while. She was three or thereabouts before I noticed one again, a faint-hearted little fella that blended with the sky on one of these annual trips down south. For the whole journey, I followed it as if it were a new discovery, afraid that it would disappear or, more to the point, that I'd lose sight of it.

JP turns off the motorway and joins a local road with houses where real people live, surrounded by washing lines and wheelie-bins and bored dogs that chase cars, pretending they have a job to do. I reach into the top pocket of my blazer and feel the corner of Arthur's card.

'You don't paint clouds any more, do you?'

It's JP who's speaking, not Arthur, as if he'd been wandering around inside my brain, knocking on doors, checking for signs of life.

'Sorry?'

'I used to love the clouds you painted. They were so sort of lively.' His smile is hopeful.

'I don't paint any more, JP. Full stop. You know that.'

His eyes return to the road ahead. One hand is on the gear stick, the other draped over the steering-wheel. His veins run like rivers down his arms, splitting off into smaller tributaries, pulling the flesh up with them. For a while, he hardly says a word, not even to Kate, who's sitting alone with Monty in the back.

Brigid couldn't come on holidays with us this year. Her father had turned up in her life after an absence of eight years and managed to persuade her to go with him instead to his parents' house in Meath. Kate was inconsolable when Brigid told her. In a scene fuelled by rage, she unpacked all her clothes and flung them into every corner of her room, sobbing out her refusal to go to Waterford. I'd struggled to calm her with every argument I could think of – 'Brigid's grandparents haven't seen her in eight years. Imagine if you didn't see your grandmother in all that time,' and 'He's her father, Kate. Of course he wants to spend time with her,' and finally, 'Your father has booked his holidays, you're going and that's that.' It wasn't until JP got home, mashed up a banana, brought it upstairs to her and stayed there for at least an hour (I don't know what was said) that she gave in.

I should speak now, lighten the mood, make noises about the landscape or try to tell a story. I know it's expected of me. I could tell them both about Arthur's exhibition. But I'd have to be careful not to let anything slip. I could tell them about my driving lessons, but as soon as I rehearse the script in my head, I know I won't broach that either. Suburban drives with Roger are mine, like the sneaky cups of coffee and the business card in my blazer pocket.

I used to have so many stories for sharing when I was out in the world, one for every occasion. I was a working girl, an art teacher. I had staff-room rivalries, angled insights into family lives, the occasional amazing use of paint by a student, encounters at parent meetings when my words were listened to as if they had meaning. I could afford back then to share these with JP because the next day would bring more. But now my scraps are so rare that all I want to do is to wrap them up and preserve them.

And yet I know that all those little unsaid things are accumulating over time and gathering into an enormous heap of debris between JP and me that could take years to excavate. Their secrecy gives them a significance they don't deserve.

This morning, the invitation to Parents' Day lay open and self-conscious on the kitchen table. I don't know how it got there – I'd thought I'd put it away. I slotted it quickly into the letter rack and waited for the questions, but they didn't come. Just another unsaid thing for the heap.

When I turn to face Kate in the back seat, she looks smaller without Brigid. Together, they'd provided a soundtrack for these past few trips that is now lacking, but this year even the sound of her aloneness doesn't propel me into talking.

'Don't worry, Kate. I know you miss Brigid,' says JP, 'but we'll only be gone for two weeks and you'll be able to write her long letters, telling her everything you get up to. You like writing Brigid letters, don't you?'

'Not really.'

'No?'

'I just write them because Brigid likes getting them.'

'But Brigid's dad is back now. That's good, isn't it? You must be happy for her.'

'I didn't even know she had a dad.'

'Kate, everyone has a father.'

'That's what Brigid says. "Even if you don't see him, he's still there," she says. But I don't see how she could know she had a father. He never phoned or wrote to her, apart from a Christmas card that always arrived on Christmas Eve and only said "Love, Dad" at the bottom.'

The dogs on the street know about Brigid's bounder father taking off to Scotland with the twenty-year-old student. Ever since, her mother, Ingrid, has been discussed in reverent tones at the school gates, as if she had been beatified for her suffering.

'Brigid thought he must be an anto . . . Dad, what's the name of the person whose job it is to live with people in wild tribes?'

'An anthropologist?'

I never understood the sainthood that goes with single parenthood. Apart from the money bit, surely Ingrid O'Sullivan's better off without her skirt-chasing man.

'Yeah, an anthropologist living with the tribes in Papua New Guinea. That's why he couldn't write letters because the post isn't very good over there. That's what she thought. But it turns out he's been teaching English in Scotland all along. He has a new daughter called Sarah. He never even visited Papua New Guinea.'

'So he was her special visitor?' asks JP.

'Yeah. He's like a spotted animal.'

'What?'

'He's got all these freckles, and Brigid says they're evenly spaced all over his body. They're on the back of his neck, in between his fingers and inside his arms.'

'I see. So is she glad she met him?'

'Dad, she doesn't even like him.'

'What makes you think that? Did she say so?'

'Well, she can't, can she? The Christmas card was between all of them. No presents or nothing.'

'Maybe it was hard for him.'

'That's what Brigid says.'

'Yeah?'

'Well, she says he said he had a partner – that's what they call a girlfriend in Scotland – who wouldn't let him write to his family at all. He had to send the Christmas card when she wasn't looking or otherwise she'd go nuts.'

'There you are. There's usually an explanation.'

'Yeah, but why does he want to see Brigid now suddenly?'

'I don't know why, Kate, but he does. He's her father and that means he has every right to see her.'

Kate's silence is not approving.

JP pokes his nose towards the rear-view mirror to catch her eye. 'Kate, do you remember that game we used to play with Brigid in the car?'

'Which one?' she mutters.

'The one where Brigid and you used to guess what would be on the other side of the hill or around the corner.'

'Mmm.'

'How about we play it now? What do you reckon is around the next corner?'

'Dunno.'

'A giraffe, perhaps? Or a kangaroo on the run?'

'It's not the same without Brigid.'

'Come on, Kate. You always loved that game. Mrs L, will you play? What do you think is around the corner?'

As long as I've known him, JP has been asking me this question. On our honeymoon he had me guess what might be at the top of Croagh Patrick or on the other side of Conor Pass. We travelled the country on his motorbike and he'd shout over his shoulder, 'Next corner?' as we approached a sharp bend. He liked impossible answers.

'I haven't got a clue,' I say, with a sigh I fail to suppress.

Silence falls on all three of us and I check back in with my cumulus, but its heart dissolved when I wasn't looking. It's strung out now and the blue of the sky is taking over.

Blue, the colour of infinity. Gather a lot of nothingness together and it always makes blue.

5

The road to my mother's village twists and turns, shifting the view from close trees to distant hills. We turn a corner and there's the blue of the estuary. It surprises every time. With every new corner, it overtakes the green a bit more until the estuary, slow, grand, with presence, fills our view. Clusters of houses on the other side of the water stitch the land into place.

Another turn and, finally, there's the village. Houses, unchanged in the last hundred years or so, are slowly choking each other. Thin curls of smoke smudge the boundaries between them. The village wraps around the rocky hill that rises up over it. The goats are on the road to greet us. Usually they stick to the upper, thrill-seeking edges at the top.

My mother's house sits demurely in duck egg blue at the outskirts of the village, like an afterthought. You're halfway up the hill and out of the village before you come across it. Ma has lived there all her life, as did her mother before her. The house has passed through the women, from generation to generation. The men either died too young or were not born at all.

It takes some minutes for Ma to answer the door to us, enough time for me to sketch out the profile of a stranger in my head, the lover who, while we wait, is being stuffed under the bed, a travelling salesman perhaps, with a penchant for poetry.

'Ah, Sylvia, you're here at last,' says Ma, as she yanks open the front door. Her left arm is around a pile of folded towels. Her hair is drenched in olive oil and wrapped up in a clear plastic bag. A rope of cotton wool bandages her skull to seal the bag, but despite it, the oil dribbles down her forehead, mixing with the kitchen sweat. I'm impressed by the absence of vanity. No lover, then, not this time. She wipes her forehead with the corner of her apron. Its pockets are filled with bunches of keys that weigh her down and deform her matronly shape.

'Well?' she says, as a suitcase falls from my stiff hands.

'Well.'

'You made it.'

'We did. Nice to see you, Ma.'

'Yes, yes. Go up to the bathroom now and wash your hands. And you'll have to get that case out of here. We'll be falling over ourselves. Bring it up to the gable room. I've made the bed up there for you. Kate's in the blue room. When you come down, you can keep an eye on the bacon while I wash this out of my hair.'

She scrutinizes every part of me with an internal tut-tutting as she rapid-fires the orders.

Monty squeezes through my legs and Kate shuffles in behind him.

'Ah, Kate, my pet, how are you?' Ma places the towels on the stool beside the coat-stand where my father used to sit to lace up his boots in the mornings. She encloses Kate in her arms with a tight, uncompromising love. 'Stand over there and let me take a look at you,' pushing her back at arm's length. 'My goodness, how you've grown since I saw you last. It's quite the young woman you're becoming, isn't it?'

JP's in the house now so I step out of the frenzy of greetings, the pointless questions about the journey, the traffic leaving Dublin, the hour we left and how we made good time, to look around the house for changes, of which there are few. The rooms are soaked in unnameable smells from long ago. They move with the wind or the corner you're standing in, but they always come back.

The heart of the house is a kitchen with a table covered in a fading oilskin and a stove that's always on no matter what the weather. Over the stove hang sheets and towels like heraldic flags. To the right of it is the Sacred Heart, with eyes that never quite leave you alone. At the end of the hall, the parlour is filled with relics of the past, all smelling of polish. This house is a museum to my childhood. I can't look at the spaces between the curtains and the windows without seeing Joan and myself, aged eight and six or thereabouts, taking turns to hide.

'Sylvia, are those bags still here?' calls out Ma to me.

'Okay, okay.'

'And, Sylvia . . .'

'What?'

'Would you ever stop biting your nails?'

I climb the steep staircase and drop my case in the middle of the mothballed gable room at the end of the landing, which every year is assigned to JP and me. It was Joan's bedroom once and I took it over when Joan left home. I flop on to the bed. It's as lumpy as ever. Ma won't change the mattresses. 'Sure what's the point at this stage?' she says. 'I'd never get the wear out of them.'

Over the bed hangs a painting, a tricolour of sorts – dark grey clouds on top, a cold green blue sea on the bottom, and in between, a still white nothingness. It was painted with urgency long ago, at home, when evening clouds were bursting with rain, but it could've been anywhere. On the back is written 'To Dad, from your loving daughter, Sylvia, June 1985'. It's the only painting of mine that he seemed to like. It reminded him of his childhood. I think that's what he said. It's one of those flukes that you later try to re-create but never do. It's funny the way bits and pieces of my painting are dotted throughout the house. They got stuck up while not quite dry and quickly became invisible. If something was to happen and the village was suddenly evacuated, they'd be able to trace this house back to me and me to it by virtue of these clouds, my mark.

Back downstairs, JP is in the orchard hunched over something. It's not really an orchard – there's only one old crock of an apple tree whose fruit rarely make it to adulthood. It's a garden with a couple of trees at one end, vegetables at the other, and flowers squeezed between the onions and the carrots.

Ma and Kate are studying one of the clay animals Kate made at Parents' Day, which travelled in a shoebox on her lap all the way down from Dublin. Ma is rotating it in her palm, making the poor creature dizzy.

'That's beautiful, Kate, really beautiful. What's it supposed to be?'

'It's a Unilion,' says Kate.

'A Unilion?'

'Yeah. It's a cross between a unicorn and a lion.'

Ma places the Unilion on the windowsill beside the statue of St Francis of Assisi. 'And what made her come up with that?' she asks me, as if the Unilion should be a cause for concern.

'Ma, it's just a piece of clay. There are no great hidden meanings.'

She goes to speak but the words stay inside for now.

6

JP and I step into the spotlight of the forty-watt bulb in Manning's and all the punters turn towards us, holding their breath. Then, one by one, they breathe out and return to their drinks. They know right well who we are, and we know them, but it'll take more than a couple of drinks and a polite few words about the weather to return us to the back-slapping familiarity of our wedding day, when JP and I stopped off for 'one' after our vows. That was fourteen years ago.

Five men sit at the bar in a row, arms folded, elbows holding themselves into position, just like their first day at school. Mossie Keogh Junior, who bought the farm from Ma with his Holy Communion money, is there, as is the hunchback postman Tommy Carroll. It's hard to know if he was born with a hunch or whether it developed from the years of staring down into his pint. I must remember to ask Ma. Thady Walsh sits offside, stonily erect, staring ahead. If you didn't know better, you'd say he was blind. A half-drunk pint sits on the table in front of him.

My father's stool is beside the cigarette machine. An arrogant young pup is perched on it, telling anyone who'll listen about his time on the oil rigs.

'It used to rock so badly that when you reached dry land you'd still be rocking away. Rock, rock, rocking away. For days, you'd be rocking away, not days it was, but weeks.' The others take no notice. I want to slap his face, tell him to have some respect or get off the stool, but I don't. Instead I take a seat in the corner at a red-topped table. JP steps up to the bar, casting a shadow over the locals.

'Are you down for long?' Mossie Keogh Junior makes a sideways approach. He's older than me, but gets younger-looking every year as his face becomes more inflated. His wet black curls stick to his crimson neck. His fleshy lips pull right back when he speaks, revealing a perfect set of equine molars, museum quality. He's a prick.

'A fortnight,' says JP.

'And will ye do a spot of fishing while you're here?'

'You never know. I might just give it a go.' JP picks up his drinks and leaves. Mossie's eyes bulge as they follow him across the room. They don't like outsiders in this place. Still, JP gets a warmer reception than I do when I head up later. Seamus Manning takes my money without a blink of recognition. He might've been my brother-in-law once.

It wasn't my idea to come to Manning's. It was Ma's. She ordered us out just as we were recovering from an obscenely large dinner of bacon, cabbage and potato. It's the same every year. She arranges a mountain range of mashed potato and cabbage in the middle of our plates and tops them with slices of bacon. If we don't finish everything, she plays the starving children of Biafra card, just as she did this evening.

'Ma, there's no such place as Biafra any more.'

'Well, Ethiopia, then. Or Mozambique. One of those places out there. They're all the same. What do you think, JP?'

JP's mouth was full of bacon by the time Ma roped him in. She waited patiently for his swallow.

'Well, Kathleen, it's true what you say. There are starving

47

children all over the world and the thought of them should make us all the more grateful for what we have.' Then he quickly inserted another square of meat.

Ma pounced on Kate after that. 'And where is little Brigid this year?'

Kate spoke quietly and deliberately, as if delivering grave news. 'Her dad came back.'

'Oh? Back from where? Where had he gone?'

'From Scotland.'

'I see. So why . . .?'

'Brigid has to go on holidays with him to Meath.'

'Meath?'

'Yeah. She didn't want to go. She wanted to come here.'

I avoided Ma's eye, her head shaking with judgement, by studying the spines of the three tomes on the shelf beside the Sacred Heart picture, over her head. There's something on the sinking of the *Titanic*, Irish fishing disasters and, just for a bit of variety, the bottom one is a collection of black-box recordings from air crashes.

'And what has Brigid's father been doing in Scotland?'

'He's been teaching English in a boarding school. He ran away when Brigid was four. She doesn't remember him. She thought he was in Papua New Guinea.'

'Did you know about this, JP?'

'Kate told me.'

'Well, that's very strange. Why would he turn up after all these years and why would he stop Brigid going on holidays with her best friend? Isn't that a terrible thing to do to a girl altogether?'

After dinner when, with well co-ordinated industry, we washed and dried the dishes, wiped down the kitchen table, put the leftovers in clean bowls, covered them in tinfoil and left them on the worktops to cool, after Monty had scanned the floor for last-minute crumbs and Kate had come downstairs and presented her hands for her grandmother to smell the soap, I folded myself into my father's armchair and reached for the local paper. It was opened on the page that said 'In Loving Memory' across the top. Grainy smiles of people who had once lived and were still loved were scattered over the page. Below them stretched long poems of nostalgia and longing. They rhymed beautifully.

We think of you in silence
And often speak your name,
All we have are memories
And a picture in a frame.

It was kind of comforting to be in the old house again. Any minute Da could come through the back door massaging his hands in a soapy lather and ask me to pull up his sleeves. Sometimes in the evenings, I'd wander down to his workshop at the back of the orchard. His tools still lie about the surfaces in busy disarray, waiting for his return. I'd mooch from shelf to shelf, grazing with my eyes over the collection of objects, like a museum visitor on a Sunday afternoon, calling up bits of him, the raw bits of knuckles, the wry smile, the involuntary dimple.

Ma was having none of it. She snatched the newspaper from my knee. 'Away down to the pub with you now.' She flapped her hand in the air, back and forth, as if getting rid of a fly.

'What? Manning's? I thought you boycotted that place?'

'I might have. But you don't have to. Sure can't you bring all the goings-on back to me? I've precious little supply of news, these days.'

'But what about Kate?'

Kate was sitting on JP's knee and he was brushing her hair with long, slow movements.

'And what about Kate? The two of us will spend some quality time together. Isn't that what it's called?'

Kate half smiled without meaning to. Monty's tail drummed against the leg of the kitchen table. It was all stitched up.

JP carries a pint and a brandy over to our table and raises his glass to meet mine. This is what normal couples do. Brandy for no other reason than to take pleasure in the company of each other. Time out from work. Winding down. Relaxing. Rejuvenating. Restoring oneself to a previous position. It's a strange notion for one who has little to wind down from. Nor do I know what previous ideal position two weeks beside the sea is meant to restore me to.

The annual holiday at Ma's has been reduced to a series of procedures we both understand and carry out. JP takes Kate and Brigid off to the beach after breakfast and swims and plays with them there until lunchtime. I hang around the house with Ma, helping her with the lunch. In the afternoon, I take over looking after the girls and JP goes off for a hike on his own or helps turn hay or fix tractors for Batty Power, who owns eighty dairy acres up the road, or he works in Ma's orchard, tending the vegetable patch. Most times I sit and read my book on the beach while the girls race baby crabs that they caught with JP that morning, or build large sand and shell sculptures. We all come together again at teatime.

The clean-up takes most of the evening and then us adults watch Ma's favourite news programmes. You might say it was idyllic, if you were standing outside the kitchen window looking in.

I'm not sure how long JP and I have been running our marriage like a relay race. I can't remember the last time he asked, in that casual way of his, 'Want to come?' as he slipped on his jacket, or reached for my hand to pull me into step with him. I guess I have only myself to blame. In any case, things are now so neatly mapped out, we're safely buffered from each other. The lines of demarcation are clearly drawn. It's probably for the best. There's little danger we'll find ourselves with nothing to say and no third party to distract us.

Of course, that's all under threat this year. The absence of Brigid could turn us back into a two-legged stool. This year it'll be JP and Kate, Kate and me and now me and JP, thanks to Ma. I wonder what her game is. I cradle the brandy glass in my hand, watching the alcohol coat it, and try to recall what I learnt in science class about it.

'It's a pity Brigid couldn't come this year,' says JP, as he pulls a stool between his legs.

'Yeah.'

'Kate misses her something terrible.'

'I know.'

'So, what do you think? Is Ingrid going to get back with William?'

'Ingrid?'

'O'Sullivan. Brigid's mam.' He stops short of 'of course'.

'Oh. Do you know William?'

'Yeah. Didn't we play footy together? Short, red-haired guy. Freckles.'

'You did?'

'Yeah, wasn't he in the house loads of times? Years ago. You remember him?'

JP's studying me closely but I focus my stare at a painting of the local coastline hanging on the wall above his head. I struggle to replay the tape to the time before Ingrid's husband had done a bunk but I can't be sure if the half-drawn images I see are real or imagined. Did we even know them then? Was Kate friends with Brigid? For that matter, how and when did Kate and Brigid become friends?

'I don't remember.'

'It was when Kate was very young,' he says, by way of a cautious explanation. I keep my eye on the painting. The brushwork is flat and self-conscious.

'Sssylvia?' JP has a habit of extending the hiss on my name when he's building up to something.

'What?'

'Are you okay?'

'Yeah. Why wouldn't I be?'

'It's just you seem a bit . . . distracted.'

He doesn't mean distracted. He means something else but is afraid to say it.

'I do?'

'Yeah. In the car on the way down here . . .'

'Just because I don't feel like pretending there's going to be a unicorn around the corner.'

'Oh, it's nothing to do with that, Sylvia. That was for Kate's sake.'

'I know that, JP. And it's not my fault that Brigid's dad walked back into her life out of the blue and whisked her away up the country leaving Kate on her own here, stuck with the pair of us for company, like an only kid.'

'I know it's not. Look, I'm not trying to get at you here. I'm only saying . . .'

Just then, the pub door jangles open. I turn around. At first I don't recognize the shiny skull that walks in.

'Orange juice when you're ready,' the man says to Seamus.

Seamus places the juice in front of him (Old Manning would have refused) and inclines his head bitterly in my direction. The man spins around, not sure at first where he should be looking, until his eyes settle on me.

'Well, well, well,' he says, approaching our table. 'Of all the bars in all the world, if it isn't Sylvia Keane.'

'Bo.' I stand up suddenly, knocking over my stool. 'When did you get back?'

''Bout a year ago now. Just in time to throw the sod into the father's grave,' he says, with a smirk.

'I'm sorry.' I'd always liked his irreverence.

'Ah, sure, the old man wasn't going to live for ever now, was he?'

We survey each other. He hasn't changed. The smooth flesh of his face has sunk into his skull a bit more, folding over his cheeks, like a thick rug, and two ear studs sparkle against the gloom of the pub, but the lower lip still protrudes slightly, just as it always did.

Then I remember. 'Bo, this is my husband, JP.' I exhale suddenly, thrusting an arm towards JP. I almost gag over that word 'husband'. It seems so big, so permanent, so institutional, like a classical temple on top of a hill, bigger than me, indestructible, non-negotiable, but I manage it anyway.

JP stands up slowly and holds out a hand. Bo shakes it

firmly. They look each other over without discretion, absorbing the details, in the way dogs sniff each other on the street, sniffing and backing away at the same time.

Bo returns to me. 'Well, good to see you again, Sylvia Keane. I might see you around so.' With a procedural nod to JP, he's gone into the lounge beyond.

7

I lie poker straight in the dimness of the gable room with pictures of Bo stagnant in my head. Arthur too. Arthur and Bo, two encounters from a previous time, who would not recognize me now, close up, so close I could make out the pores of their skin, the hairs growing from their earlobes and their unspoken speculations about whatever became of Sylvia Keane.

Of course, it was Arthur who had made the deepest mark, shifting something inside me, somewhere down in my stomach, or deeper still. He's released into my veins at regular intervals, like a quiet drug. There's an image I can't shake, of a ceiling fan circulating our words around the room as we lay on our backs with just a sheet to cover us. Our fingertips tracing over the edges of each other. The soft dryness of his lower lip. But there's always a bitter residue that can't be avoided.

I roll over to face the dark contour of the man lying beside me. This is the man I married, the man I bound my life to, and that was not simply a question of timing or convenience or need. I married out of love. Yes, I can say that. Love.

Now, many years on, how much of love is habit? Or duty? Or promise? How much is it born of fear, fear of what another kind of life might be? I listen to his breathing, consistent, deep and tender. I want to curl up next to his ribs, fit my head under his chin so that he can breathe for both of us, but I don't. I breathe in as he does, pause slightly, then turn a corner and out again, in time with him. Breathing: the only thing that separates life from death. My father's last breaths, each slower and further apart than the previous, heralded his retreat from this life. The silences between them grew longer with time. I tried to hold on to the breaths back then. I tried not to hear his silences, but he retreated, like a train backing into a tunnel, going back, back, back to the place whence he had come and, in time, the silences claimed him for the other side.

My father. He wrapped me up in love when I was a little girl. He carried me across the fields on his broad shoulders, breaking into a gallop until I squealed with fear and joy. He lifted me on to his knee at Mass. I'd fall asleep on him during the Our Father. 'Our Father, who art in heaven' – I learnt those deep bass notes with my ear pinned to his chest.

All remembering ends with my father.

When the sky becomes pale, JP gets up and dresses noiselessly. Then he disappears, pulling the front door behind him with a gentle thud a little while later. I roll into the hollow he leaves in the bed and breathe him in before falling into another world.

A boat heaves from side to side as waves wash over it. I'm on the deck, getting wetter and wetter but am unable to move. A man's hand reaches over the side of the boat from the sea and grasps my forearm with a strength that brings pain and relief. I catch a half-smile as he pulls me towards him. Another wave comes from nowhere and the hand slips away from me. I wake in the shadow of fear.

Ma is fixing her curls in the hall mirror. The top ones fade in the light of the window. She takes up the hairspray, covers her eyes with one hand and sprays her head from every angle.

'About time you're up,' she says. 'I thought I was going to have to come up there and get you.'

'Where's JP?'

'I have a curl here and it won't sit down for me.' She attacks it again with the hairspray.

'Ma?'

'He brought Kate up to see Moriarty's horse.'

'Right.'

'She loves that horse, bless her, but I'd be awful afraid it could turn around and give her a kick one of these days. You heard about that girl in England. She's lost without that little Brigid.'

'Who? The girl?'

'No. Kate.'

Ma follows me into the kitchen and watches as I scoop porridge out of the pot on the stove and let it plop rudely into a bowl.

'Strange the way her father turned up out of nowhere like that, wasn't it? What do you think happened there?' she asks.

'I don't know. None of my business.'

'Hmm. I don't suppose there was anyone in the pub last night?'

'Seamus was behind the bar, and that prick Mossie Keogh Junior was in.'

'Sylvia, must you talk like that?'

'Well, he is. And Thady was there in the corner. Does he live in that place?'

'Well, there's not much keeping him at home any more, God love him.'

'Oh, and Bo Quirke is back, looking very cosmopolitan.'

57

'Bo?'

'Robert. Robert Quirke.'

'Is he now? Were you talking to him?'

'Not for long. He came back for his father's funeral.'

'Of course that's why. But I didn't think he'd stick around.'

She's putting on a jacket over her Mass outfit, pulling her stomach in and sticking her butt out as she fastens the over-sized buttons.

'Ma?'

'I mean, I always thought this place would be too small for him.' She plucks pieces of fluff, real and imagined, off the sleeves.

'Ma?'

'He always seemed to have bigger fish to fry. Is this jacket okay? I haven't worn it with this dress before.'

'*Ma.* I want to visit the grave.'

She stops for less than a second, then resumes her plucking. 'And what's brought this on all of a sudden?'

'I want to visit the grave every year.'

'But you never actually do.'

'That's because I'd have to get someone to bring me. And before you ask why doesn't JP, I'd rather not, thanks.'

She picks her silk scarf up from the back of the chair, lassoes it over her head and lets it land on her shoulders. She knots it in front and tucks the tails neatly into the V of her jacket.

'Well, don't expect me to be driving you when your husband has a perfectly good car lying idle outside this house.'

Then she busies herself with putting the last of the breakfast things away, as if she's not waiting for an answer.

It annoys me the way she says 'your husband', as if he

were a duty I should be fulfilling, and she knows that. That's the whole point. I scrape up my porridge and take my dish to the back kitchen without looking at her, while the church bells toll in the distance.

8

Ma likes to be seen leading her brood to Mass so it's easier to go than not, just like at home in Dublin it's easier not to go than go. We all traipse up the hill after her and I think of what Joan would say.

'For God's sake, Sy, why don't you just tell Ma that you don't believe in God any more?'

'Because, Joan, I don't know that I don't. That's why.'

'And you don't know that you do either.'

'Well, how do any of us know for sure?'

'Oh, Sy dear, when are you going to get off that picket fence of yours?'

I envy the glorious certainty of my sister's world.

The priest presents Mass in the booming voice that sounds like the wind howling over the Irish Sea. He doesn't use his pedestrian one, the one that pops in to see how you're getting on and stays for a cup of tea, only if you're having one yourself and just the tiniest sliver of apple tart, thanks very much. It wouldn't have the necessary authority. This voice has a direct line to God.

I spend Mass in a state of readiness, scanning the crowd with head down for the sight of one of my former classmates before they see me. For the most part, we've managed to dodge each other since the goodbye hugs that followed our Debs dance. Our mascara was smudged and our taffeta dresses stank and we believed we meant it when we promised never to lose touch, ever.

My eyes stay prayerfully closed as the Holy Communion queue shuffles past. When I open them, they are level with the piano fingers of Sally Ann Power, stretched over a child-filled bump. *Shit*.

Once Mass is over, I take the contraflow lane up to the altar to light candles in front of the Virgin Mary. I like lighting candles. I like watching the flames bend and straighten, like dancers. I light one for my father and one for my mother, and one each for Joan, JP and Kate. I warm my fingertips over them until the heat makes them withdraw, and then, just for devilment, I drop an extra coin into the brass box and light one for Arthur.

The church has emptied and I can't hide any longer. I walk down the aisle and step into the glare of the sun and the viewfinder of Sally Ann Power.

'Sylvia. Hi.'

'Hi.' Already she's too close to me and her cow-like lashes are fanning my face. Her neck is long and balletic and her hair is pulled back into a bun, the kind that air stewardesses have to take classes to learn how to make. Joan and I used to marvel at the other-worldliness of her delicate face. But at this intimate distance, it's possible to make out tiny red veins criss-crossing her cheeks and the eyelids weighing down on her lashes. Yes, even Sally Ann Power has been marked by the years.

'Are you down for the holidays?' she asks.

'Just arrived yesterday.'

'Oh, what a shame. Bob had to fly to Boston this morning for work. I'd love you to have met him.'

By all accounts the American Sally Ann married is gigantic and loaded.

'Pity.'

Then suddenly she says, 'As you can see, I'm with child,' spreading out her fingers on either side of her bump. 'We've been trying for years. We went for IVF in the end.' Her facial muscles stretch in all directions as she mouths, 'I-V-F'. 'And now we're expecting a *baby*.'

'Right.'

She glances around in all directions. 'Sylvia, don't tell anyone.'

'About the baby?'

'About the IVF. Mammy doesn't know.'

'Right.'

'It's just that I don't want to burden her with my, well, com-pli-ca-tions.'

'Okay.'

'The problem was with me, not Bob.'

'Of course.'

'She'd probably blame Bob.'

'She won't hear it from me.'

She lays her fingers on my folded arms. 'As you say, Sylvia, you were so lucky.'

'I was?'

'Yes, it happened first time for you, more or less, right?'

If only it hadn't. Not then.

'I remember your mother telling me when you were expecting Kate and your daddy was ill. She said you were so happy. Not about your daddy, of course,' she laughs, 'but to have found JP after, you know, everything, and then to be expecting so soon.'

Maybe the pregnancy hormones are skewing her world-view, turning tears into smiles, pain into joy. It must be some kind of biological phenomenon that God designed to ensure the future of the human race.

'You know, I haven't seen you since the funeral,' she goes on, 'but I get regular updates from your mother. She's so proud of you.'

I look around for a crack in the crowd through which I can slip away. Ma's shaking hands with everyone, furiously. You'd swear she was up for election.

'Is that your daughter?' asks Sally Ann, pointing to Kate, who's hovering at the edge of the crowd with JP. 'She's so like you. You know, I think it's wonderful that you didn't go back to work after she was born, that you were, as you say, there for her. It's the greatest gift any mother can give their child.'

'Right.'

'Here, let me introduce you to Fred.'

'Actually, Sally Ann, we'd really better be going.'

'It won't take a minute. You'll love Fred.'

Sally Ann steps over to her mother's gang and says something into the ear of a boy whose head is sprouting metallic red hair. He follows her back over to me.

'Sylvia, I want you to meet Frederick Larsson, my stepson.'

The boy blinks in slow motion. He looks like a young Jesus Christ, apart from the hair.

'Pleased to meet you, ma'am.' He shakes his head to move a wave of hair out of his eyes.

'Pleased to meet you, Fred.'

'Fred, what did I tell you about meeting new people in

Ireland? You must shake hands.' Then Sally Ann whispers over Fred's head, by way of an explanation, 'Fred is Bob's son, from a previous relationship. He was brought up in Arizona.'

Fred pulls a hand out of a pocket. It's warm and dry, just like his homeland, but the handshake is brief. When Kate comes over and tells me that Ma wants to go home now, Sally Ann pounces. 'Hi, Kate. I'm Sally Ann.'

Sally Ann opens and closes her mouth as if Kate has a hearing problem and needs to lip-read. I never really learnt how to talk to children but I can't help wondering if this is necessary.

'Oh, my, it's impossible to believe you're eleven years old.' Her palm slaps her chest three times as she utters Kate's age. 'Where do the years go?'

Kate looks to me for the correct answer.

Sally Ann bends down towards my daughter and lowers her voice. 'Kate, I am an old, old friend of your mother's, and this is my step-son Frederick Larsson.'

Kate and Fred face each other, waiting for the other to speak, but before either does, Ma summons us into line and we head back down the hill in a carefully choreographed formation. Ma and Mrs Power are on either side of JP, leading the way, Sally Ann, her bump and me after them, and the children at the end. Sally Ann is telling me about her birthing plan. I try to switch the channel to Kate and Fred.

'Have you ever read *Wuthering Heights*?' Kate is asking Fred.

'No. Have you?'

'No, but it's my best friend's and my favourite book ever.'

'Well, how can it be your favourite book if you haven't read it?'

'Brigid told me all about it.'

'Who's Brigid?'

'My best friend.'

'I don't read novels,' says Fred, in a soporific drawl.

'Why not?'

'I don't read fiction. I read factual stuff with lots of diagrams.'

'Like what?'

'Well, right now I'm reading about the Enigma Code that was used in World War Two.'

'What's that?'

'You wouldn't understand.'

'Do you know anything about nuclear weapons?'

'Sure I do. What about them?'

'Do you know anything about nuclear weapons and the Third World War?'

'Of course. In fact my father reckons that World War Three is just around the corner and we should've bombed the asses out of the other side when we still had the chance. Why?'

'Just wondering.'

9

A man and a girl are down on the beach building a fortress from sand and shells. The man is digging a moat with a regular garden shovel. His shoulders glimmer in the midday sun. The girl is pouring water from a sandcastle bucket into the moat, but with every pour, the sand swallows the water. She goes back to the sea to refill the bucket. The fortress is a large mound of sand covered with shells. A seaweed flag is stuck into the top and a piece of wood lies over the moat to act as a drawbridge.

I'm supposed to be down there with them, doing my bit. They asked me along but I said no, muttering something about getting the Sunday papers. I continue up the hill towards Moriarty's shop at an accelerated pace.

On my left, the sun makes sequins on the water's surface. The land in the distance is painted soft blue. There's a feeling of being surveyed, and sure enough, when I look up, the goats, with their silhouetted horns hooked on to the sky, are gathered at the top of the hill staring down on me disapprovingly.

Before, Moriarty's was a musty old grocer's and draper's where the bales of cloth lay across jars of sweets. These days, it's a modern mini-supermarket with a franchise. There's a deli counter with shrivelled-up sausages and slices of quiche, a magazine rack and freezers full of ready meals. Some of the stock from the original shop has slipped through – balls of twine, cards of buttons, even cotton shirts with wartime rationed sleeves. Arthur used to love rummaging through the old place, collecting indigenous objects for his next art installation.

Mrs Moriarty is behind the counter, keeping watch. I don't think I ever saw her anywhere else. She's wearing the same navy housecoat she always wore and her face is embalmed in a look of blank virtue. It's hard to put an age on her but she looks younger to me now than she did when I was a child.

I fold a newspaper under my arm and slide some coins across the counter towards her. She straightens herself to get a good look at me.

'It's the youngest Keane girl, isn't it?'

'It is.'

She shakes her head. 'I remember when you were just a tot in your daddy's arms.'

I look down at the five-cent jelly snakes on the counter, all swimming in the same direction.

'And how's your mother doing?'

'Fine, thanks.'

She drops my coins into the till from a height. My change stays wrapped in her hand while she looks at me some more, her mind moving back through the years. She knows stuff, I can tell.

'You're so like your daddy, God rest him,' she says, as the coins tinkle into my hand. 'You're the spit of him.'

The sun warms my back on the way down the hill. I'm working on a plan to disappear, to read my paper somewhere in the village where I can't be seen, as if by not being seen, I'm not held to account.

A red Mini pulls up beside me. I look in from the

passenger side. It's Bo Quirke, spruced up in a pin-striped suit.

'Are you getting in?'

The car door is stiff and the heat of the leather seat pricks my flesh.

'So, we meet again, Sylvia Keane,' he says, with an infectious smile. 'Did you miss me?'

'Madly.'

'What're you up to?'

'Nothing much.'

'Sounds good.'

'And you?'

'I've just been spending some quality time with my aged grandmother in the hope that she will think fondly of her faithful grandson when she meets her solicitor next week.'

'Old Birdie? Is she still alive? God, she must be ancient.'

'And she sends her warmest regards to you too. Now, my dear, as you're up to nothing much, why don't we drive to the headland and do nothing much together?'

'Just like the old days?'

'Just like the old days.'

During our final summer at home, just after we'd finished school and in preparation for the huge world that beckoned, Bo and I used to play-act our fantasy futures by going for drives on Sunday afternoons in his father's car. I'd pinch some ham, cheese and bread from the kitchen at home and borrow my mother's old polka-dot swing skirt with matching hair band. Bo would wear the tank top Birdie had knitted for him from scratchy wool and carry his unopened copy of *Ulysses*. We'd share a picnic of domestic bliss somewhere along the coast. We made a good couple, Bo and I.

'More ham, dear?' I'd ask, while Bo lay propped on one elbow flicking through the fashion pages of my magazine.

This time is different. I have a husband, a child and a mortgage in the suburbs. This time the joke isn't funny.

We drive away from the village along the coast. It doesn't take much probing to get Bo to tell me why he didn't go back to London, why he's still here doing feck-all. He was working too much, then drinking too much, doing everything too much, poppers, cocaine, out all night, down, up, down, until he was going up and down so fast that one day he couldn't get up.

'I was the true emigrant cliché,' he says. 'My father died at just the right time, bless him. I had to come home and dry out, the hard way, under the eye of the mother.'

'Are you going back?'

'To what?'

'Your friends?'

'You mean my drinking buddies? The ones who stood me rounds so they wouldn't have to drink alone?'

'But what about the business?'

'The business is long since gone and the bridges are burnt. One by one. Every bridge I had in London. Even the half-built ones. I'd be lucky to get a job in a burger joint now.' He shrugs in defeat.

'Oh, for God's sake,' but I stop as quickly as I start. I can hardly preach.

We drive the rest of the way in uncontested silence, reflecting, I suppose, on our great expectations back then. He stops the car in the usual spot and we get out. It's seventeen years since I last saw Bo. He must be reading my thoughts for, all of a sudden, he asks, 'Do you remember the last time we were up here?'

'Should I?'

'You were with that prick from college.'

'Arthur.'

'Yeah. We all came up here with a bottle of vodka one Good Friday. You, me, Joan, Seamus and that prick.' Bo spits out the word.

'What was wrong with him?'

'He used to begin every sentence "The trouble with you, Sylvia, is . . .". I never understood how you could stick him.'

'I guess I was in love.'

'Or lust.'

'You were just jealous, that's all.'

'You mean I probably fancied him?'

'Weren't you going out with Miss Perfect Tits 1983 at the time? Now, what was her name?'

'I was just trying to be the hetero man for the sake of my parents and my rich granny.'

'I bumped into her today after Mass.'

'Who? My granny?'

'Sally Ann Power. Your sweetheart. How you broke that poor girl's heart, Bo. She's "with child" now, as they say. God, there's something about that woman that gives me the creeps.'

'Ah, Sylvia, don't be like that. She's not the worst, quite harmless, really.'

'Precisely.'

Bo grins to himself. 'So what happened with you and Arthur?'

'We went to Istanbul after college for a summer. It all got a bit intense. I came back and did my teaching diploma.'

'And Arthur?'

'He didn't.'

'Didn't come back?'

'Didn't come back.' I clasp my knees to my chest, lift my feet off the ground, roll back on to the bones in my bum and hover like that for a while, staring out to sea. Bo pulls out a box of cigarettes still in its plastic and unwraps it with tenderness. He points a slender white fag towards me. It smells of temptation. I shake my head. 'I quit.'

'Oh?'

'That's what having a baby does to you. One of the many things.'

The tip of the cigarette somersaults in slow motion through the air into his mouth and he lights up.

'He's back now, I think. Arthur. In Dublin. And his career is in the ascendant.'

'And you, my dear Sylvia? What about you? Are you in the ascendant, as you say?' The words float out with the smoke. 'You're still painting, aren't you?'

'Bo, you know how it is. The world is choking with bad art. It doesn't need me to add to the pile.'

IO

IN LOVING MEMORY OF JAMES KEANE
1925 – 1990

It's the only name on the gravestone. I stand facing it, feet together, head bowed, hands wringing. That's how it was. Incessant wringing. The mournful affectations of the priest. Strangers who were sorry for my trouble. Under my chopped-down nails lodged the remains of a sod of clay. Incense in my nostrils. The vicious kick of the baby in my belly. Its impudence hurt me. It should've had more respect.

The baby grew inside me in time with the tumour in my father's stomach. Both shared the same waiting room before that switch-over between death and life, life and death. It was as if the conception had caused the rot in my father. If only I hadn't got pregnant when I did. We could've held off. It was I who pushed for it, impatient as ever, always rushing to the next stage. And Sally Ann's right. It happened so easily, first time trying, whatever that means. A real textbook case.

The line turned blue on the same day as they diagnosed my father. My mother phoned late that night. We both had news, only, of course, I had to go first. She didn't tell me then. She didn't want to infect the baby with death.

She continued to keep the news from me for the months

to follow. Maybe she was expecting me to ask about what was obvious to all but, of course, some things are just too big to see. And so, in the end, I only had those last few countdown days with him, when Death was knocking on the door. If only I had kept my mouth shut.

Those dying days and nights, soaked in the pink smell of sanitized sleep and hospital chemicals, were painfully long and never long enough. Soggy tissues littered the bed. The oxygen hummed in time with his breathing. It was the only thing left of him – the only thing he did. We witnessed every hopeless breath with dread while the baby kicked inside me, warming itself up for life. God forgive me, I would've swapped those kicks for one more walk across the fields with him.

And what then? Wellingtons at the doorway. Unfinished medication. Empty glasses case. A dented mattress. The memory of a feeling.

My father's all alone in the grave, still. He was the first one in, leading the procession towards death in a place that was not his place of birth. He had maintained no connection with County Clare. His brothers were nothing more to us than names at the end of Christmas cards. Ma said her father, Christy O'Connor, had all but adopted Da when he first came to work on the farm at the age of fifteen. He just turned up one day, she said, with the clothes on his back and an eagerness to work.

He never returned to Clare, apart from that time when his father died. I must've been about Kate's age, maybe a year or two younger. One white-sky November day, I came home from school and he wasn't there, not in the kitchen, not in the yard, not in his shed, not in the fields. His car was gone too. I ran around the house and yard, like electricity in a circuit, looking for him. Ma had come downstairs with a hugful of washing.

'Where's Da?'

'He had to go to Clare. It's his father. He's not well.'

'When's he coming home?'

'Well, I don't know, love.' As if the question was unreasonable. 'It depends on his father.'

Da was gone for three days. I hardly ate in that time, and no amount of coaxing could get me away from the window. It was my job to look after my father, to make sure that nothing bad would happen to him. I found Clare on a map, a triangle of pink sticking into the Atlantic, and *The Photographic Guide to Ireland* on the bookcase in the parlour showed pictures of tall black cliffs, with sheep grazing near the edge, fields made of rock, and caves with deadly spears hanging down from the roofs inside them, which, it said, were all part of the 'fascinating geology of the county'.

When he returned, my father was clean-shaven and wearing his black suit and tie. He changed into his work clothes and went into the yard. We didn't see much of him for the next few weeks but I was happy that he was back.

I pull a dock leaf out of the gravel and lay a bunch of sweet williams from Ma's orchard on the grave. Then I help myself to a graphite-coloured pebble with a white streak running through it, about the size of a grape, and plop it into the pocket of my jacket.

The other gravestones are carved with names belonging to people who are lovingly remembered by their wives, husbands and children. Death whitewashes them, erases their creases, makes them benign. Life moves in to fill the spaces they've left behind. They used to live in the village, salute us when driving past, talk to Ma after Mass, tell me I was a grand girl, but it's difficult to imagine them alive again. Even my father. I close my eyes but can't give him a role in my life, much as I try. I can't get him to brush Kate's hair or have a pint with JP, or even nod vaguely to me when I enter the house.

In the beginning, I used to get angry with him, although less and less now, for not being there when Kate was born. His hand slipped away from mine long before I was ready to let it go, and a knot of grief still sits like a bubble of compressed air in my chest, like a cry that has no voice. It just lodges there, refusing to burst or dissolve.

I walk away from the grave with steps that barely leave the ground.

Bo's leaning against the bonnet of his car outside the cemetery gates.

'Well?' he asks.

'Well?'

'Well, how did you get on?'

'We had a great chat.'

'Good.'

'It was okay . . . well, a bit weird, actually. I guess I realize why I don't come here much any more.'

'Why's that?'

'It never feels, I don't know, satisfactory.'

'Isn't it about "paying your respects" and all that?'

'But what does that mean?'

Bo shrugs. I take my place beside him against the bonnet.

'Fancy going for a jaunt along the coast before we bring you back to the bosom of your family?' he says suddenly.

'Ah, yes, the family.'

I circle the ground underfoot with my right shoe until a perfectly symmetrical circle, like a big scream, is carved out in the earth. It's the kind of scream Munch painted when the mouth couldn't be made big enough to let it all out.

'Sylvia, you would tell me if something was wrong, wouldn't you?'

'What do you mean?'

'Well, tell me to mind my own business and all that but you seem, I don't know . . .'

'Distracted?'

'Something like that.'

I plunge my hands deeper into my pockets and speed up my circling. I wish Bo wouldn't look so alarmed.

'I don't know. I don't seem to be able to do this family thing, that's all.'

'What's there to "do"?'

'I don't know . . . clap loudly at school plays, join in egg-and-spoon races, whoop in delight, jolly along, do the group thing, go where everyone else is going, do what everyone else is doing, be grateful for it.'

'Is that what having a family means?'

'I think so. I can never seem to do the things they expect of me, Bo. The more they want, the more I screw up. And being down here with Ma around, it's like being a lab specimen. She looks at me looking at JP and looks at me looking at Kate and looks at them looking at me. JP and Kate went to the lighthouse today. I should've gone with them. I go every year but I just can't fake it any more. I know it's bad. It's really bad. *I*'m really bad.'

'They just want you to be happy.'

'Happy. Yes, they just want me to be happy and I can't even give them that.'

We stand there for a while, propped up by the Mini and wedged between the sound of birdsong and the smell of freshly cut hay, while I swim about in my badness and the absence of happiness. Bo dangles his car keys in front of me.

'Want to drive?'

'I'm sorry.'

'For what? Come on, it's a beautiful day for a drive in the country.' He dangles the keys some more.

'I can't.'

'Why not, Sylvia Keane?' He laughs. 'Will the grown-ups not let you?'

'No, I can't drive. Or, at least, I'm learning.'

'Okay. So you can't drive. And you're learning. Well, do you want to learn with me?' He bends his knees to look directly at my face, in the way adults do to sulking children to get them to look up.

I erase my circle with a flat foot. 'Okay.'

I like being with Bo. For whole moments at a time we can put our grown-up bags into storage and be seventeen again, with all the possibility of the world wrapped up in a parcel yet to be opened. I take the keys, slide on to the driver's seat and root around for the lever to haul the seat closer to the steering-wheel. I adjust the mirrors, all the time recalling Roger's instructions. I check the gear stick is in neutral, look over my right shoulder, and turn the ignition. Then I drive west, away from my father and my family.

We take the coast road, winding through corridors of stone walls, past green fields dotted with monochrome cattle and black and yellow signs predicting the future. I translate each sign aloud – 'Road to the left ahead', 'Road to the right ahead', 'T-junction ahead'.

Bo laughs at my pidgin road signage. 'Don't hog the road,' he says, so I concentrate on skirting the stone walls while not making contact with them, in the way you might dance with a boy at the school disco, close but not touching. We pass through tunnels made by trees arching over us. The sunshine through the branches makes diamonds on the ground. Then we're out on the open road again, where the sea is filling the margins of my view. It tries to lure us over to it but I focus on the white stripe that divides the road into two. Finally, there's a row of parked cars ahead. I brake, drive a bit, brake, drive and brake until the car is almost standing still. I pull in beside the other parked cars. We're at a scenic viewpoint, where the sky is high and black cliffs frame the sea on both sides. It's the kind of place carved out to help tourists photograph their memories of Ireland. We get out.

''Tis a grand country all the same,' says Bo, in the voice of his dead father.

Gulls criss-cross above us towards a congregation on the cliff ledges. Their squawking, like urgent warnings, gathers force as more arrive. My eyes are led down to the lonely beach below. It feels as though I've been there before but I can't recall. The cliffs begin to move sideways before me so that they're swapping places with each other, moving faster and faster, spinning outright, until the sea is erased by darkness. A sickness rises to my throat, my forehead is cool with sweat and I grab Bo's arm to steady myself.

'Are you all right?'

'Let's go back.'

We take the same road, this time in silence. As we approach the graveyard, two figures are at the gate, a man and a young girl with golden hair standing on the bottom rung. Her arms are slotted through the bars and folded over. She throws her head back and squeals with joy as the man pushes the gate open. I accelerate around the corner.

I I

Back at Ma's, Mrs Power, her daughter and step-grandson are gathered around the kitchen table. My parting from Sally Ann after Mass was a ridiculous jumble of promises to meet up again, and reassurances from her that she and Fred were staying around for a while and would call in for a proper catch-up, as if we hadn't got along before they entered our lives and now, suddenly, we desperately need each other. And, sure enough, Sally Ann is as good as her word.

Mrs Power is a regular Shirley Temple, with curls that bounce when she talks, chubby cheeks and a proclivity for petulance. You can tell how long she's been in Ma's by the amount of space she's taking up. It grows in direct relationship with time. Today it seems she's polished off a chicken, half a sliced pan and an apple pie, perhaps with help from the others, and the remnants have spread to all four corners of the table. During their marathon exchanges, she and Ma update each other on every person they ever knew, their children, grandchildren, parents, siblings and distant relatives.

Mrs Power is in the middle of telling Ma about a funeral she went to the week before. They both love a good funeral. They scan the death notices in the local paper the way you'd check out what's on in the cinema. The younger the deceased, the more orphaned children, the better. Tragedy is their genre.

'It came very sudden in the end, Kathleen, very sudden altogether.' Mrs Power's curls quiver with every 'very'.

'Oh, there you are, Sylvia girl. How are you, girl?' She perks up when she sees me. Sally Ann, too, is smiling brightly in my direction. It must be tiring to smile like that, in a never-ending way.

I sit down at the vacant side of the table and pour myself a mug of stewed tea. 'I'm very well, Mrs Power. And how are you and Batty?' You have to give her the attention she expects. Minimal responses lead to bad press.

'Are JP and Kate not with you?'

'They headed over to the lighthouse for the day.'

'And you didn't go with them?'

'No. That place makes me feel queasy. All those positive ions.'

'I see. Well, isn't it great news about the baby here?' Mrs Power inclines her head towards Sally Ann's bump.

'Great news altogether.'

'It's been a long time coming but it'll be worth the wait, please God.'

'Mammy.' Sally Ann loves the attention. It makes her bloom like a gaudy pink rose.

'What, girl? Amn't I only saying what we all think? We're all delighted about it, Sylvia girl, and she'll make a great mother. She's a natural. You should see her with Fred here.' She nods to the boy who's constructing something long and narrow out of Ma's coasters.

''Tis the same for Joan,' says Ma. 'She took her time on starting her family, but she's taken to it like a duck to water.'

Mrs Power ignores her. 'And, hopefully, now that Sally Ann has the hang of it, she'll keep going.'

'*Mammy.*'

'I'm only saying, Sally Ann. No need to go all touchy on me, girl. You weren't tempted to go again, Sylvia?'

'No.'

'Oh?'

'I couldn't follow the diagram.'

'Sylvia.' Ma is more embarrassed than cross.

We're all saved by the sound of JP, Kate and Monty coming in the back way. Soon the kitchen table is surrounded by bodies, and the rigmarole of musical chairs begins. Those who are sitting make moves to stand and persuade those standing to sit down. Those who are standing insist that, no, really, they'd prefer to stay standing and those sitting should stay right where they are. Only Fred and I make no attempt to move and, in the end, everyone's back where they started.

'Hello, Mrs Power. How are you?' says JP, with an overstated grin.

Kate reaches across the table for some bread and jam.

'Kate? Did you wash your hands?' I say, deciding I need to be a 'natural' in front of the Powers, but before Kate can answer, Mrs Power is back in the prosecuting role.

'So, Kate, what happened to your little friend Brigid this year?' As if she hadn't been briefed on that too.

'She couldn't come. Mam, the waves were up around the lighthouse higher than ever before.'

'Oh, Kate, child, I hope you didn't go near them?' Ma drums her chest with a white fist.

'We went for a walk around the top of the cliff near the lighthouse and looked right over the edge.'

'Oh, Jesus, Mary and Joseph,' intones Ma, as if Kate's body were crashing through the air into the sea before her eyes.

'It's fine, Kathleen, really,' says JP. 'We kept well back.'

'Then we stopped at this enormous old house on the way

home. It looked just like Wuthering Heights, all lonely by itself in a big flat field.'

I marvel at Kate's ability to hold an audience. Even Fred has put down his coasters and is listening.

'There was a sign on the pillar that said "Keep Out".'

'JP?'

JP puts his finger to his mouth to silence his mother-in-law.

'I thought there was going to be a big, vicious dog with loads of teeth. So did Monty. He kept stopping and turning around to make sure we were behind him. But there was no dog, just this enormous house with hundreds of chimneys and windows covered in wood.'

'I think I know the place,' says Mrs Power. 'There's talk of it being haunted, you know.'

'Yeah, and Dad said people went to balls there, old-fashioned balls where they did the waltz. They came from miles and miles away. Mam, you could just imagine them holding up their dresses to go up the steps, just like a fairy-tale, and the butler letting them in.'

'Did you get inside to see the ghost?' asks Fred.

'No. We couldn't get in 'cause all the doors are covered with wood too, but we went into yards and barns and old sheds around the back that were full of useless stuff. They were brilliant. They smelt like someone with bad breath.'

Sally Ann laughs and nudges her mother.

'No, they did. We went around the gardens. There were these big walls all around them that you couldn't climb over and they were all grown over with huge weeds.'

'Isn't it a disgrace?' says Mrs Power. 'And the money that lot have.'

'There was this summerhouse,' says Kate, 'like a hut that

was beautiful even though it was falling down. Dad said that's where the lady who owned the house read poetry. Oh, and Mam, we found this for you in one of the sheds.'

'What is it?'

Kate's delving into her backpack on the floor and pulling out a tatty photocopied piece of paper, the corners of which have been burnt away.

'"Who is Silvia?" By William Shakespeare' is written at the top of the page. She hands it to me.

'It's a poem all about you,' says Kate, as proudly as if she had written it herself.

'Oh, I love a good poem,' says Mrs Power.

'Kate, will you read it out for us?' says Ma.

'Ma, she's not a performing monkey.'

'Be quiet, Sylvia. Let the child read.'

Kate takes the piece of paper back from me and affects a little cough.

'"Who is Silvia? What is she" . . . ' Her words are tentative at first. '". . . That all our . . ."' She points to the page. 'Dad, how do you say that word?'

'Swains,' says JP.

'That all our swains commend her?
Holy, fair, and wise is she;
The heaven such grace did lend her
That she might admired be.

Is she kind as she is fair?
For beauty lives with kindness.
Love . . .'

She points again to the page.

'Doth,' says JP.

'Love doth to her eyes repair,
To help him of his blindness;
And, being helped, inhabits there.

Then to Silvia let us sing. . .'

Kate directs all the words to me and the audience follows her eyes. I'm busy studying the pattern of ducks in flight that covers the tablecloth and there's a heat rising up through my body, starting from the feet and moving up and through to every fingertip.

'. . .That Silvia is excelling;
She excels each mortal thing . . .'

Every year, the ducks are missing more bits of wings and beaks. I probably only know they're ducks because I remember what they looked like once.

'Upon the dull earth dwelling.
To her let us garlands bring.'

The sound of palms on palms fills the room.
'Well, Dolores, did you ever in your life hear anything so gorgeous?' says Ma.
Even I am clapping because I don't dare not to. Sally Ann Power puts her manicured hand on my arm and says, 'You must be *so* proud of her.' They're all waiting for my response, but I'm too embarrassed by this attention on Kate and me, this very unnecessary attention. Besides, I'm confused. I

can't understand why Kate is telling us about the lighthouse, the cliff walk, the old house and now this bizarre poem, and not telling us about the most important thing of all. Is this some kind of game that is being played on me? I look to JP for a clue and he's looking back at me, funny.

'Well done, Kate,' I say, and pull my lips back towards my ears. JP squeezes Kate's shoulder and Ma gives her a theatrical hug for the audience's benefit. Kate beams.

Then, before I can think of a reason to leave the room, Mrs Power says, 'I won a prize there a couple of years ago for my millennium poem, didn't I, Sally Ann?'

'Yes, Mammy.'

'Do you write poetry, Mrs Power?' Kate asks.

'I do, child, I do. You know, it's quite easy, really. Anyone could do it. You just get a thought, something you want to write about, and you think of two words that match. You make sure you put the matching words at the end of the line. Of course, people don't like poems that rhyme any more. They like what they call "blank verse".'

Mrs Power's forceful utterance of 'blank verse' makes Fred's structure come crashing down.

'Oh, Fred,' cries Sally Ann, in dismay. Fred stares motionless at the coasters scattered over the crumbs of the apple tart.

'What are you making there, Fred?' asks JP.

'A bridge, sir,' says Fred, still staring at the coasters.

'A bridge?' Kate moves towards Fred. 'My dad's building a bridge. Dad, tell them about your bridge.'

'Not now, Kate. We have to have our tea. Some other time. You'd better run upstairs and wash your hands, like your mother says. And bring your bag up while you're at it.'

'Yes, indeed. We'd better be going, too, and let you get on

with it.' Mrs Power sways from side to side until she is standing. She is followed by her crew.

Fred has neatly piled up the coasters and is handing them to Ma with a polite 'Thank you, ma'am.' Mrs Power's telling JP that he must come over some evening to see what Batty has done with the dairy. Sally Ann is telling me that Fred is delighted to have a new friend in Kate, and she has only four weeks to go, can I believe it, and in the middle of the commotion, I hear my daughter telling my mother that they went to my father's grave on their way home from the lighthouse.

'You did, child? Wasn't that a lovely thing to do?' Ma tugs JP's sleeve. 'Whose idea was it to go to the graveyard?'

'It was Kate's, really. She's been asking a lot of questions about her granddad lately. It was a spur-of-the-moment thing.'

'Yeah, and it's really nice there, Gran,' says Kate. 'There were flowers on the grave, the purple and pink kind with the white edges, just like the ones that grow in the orchard.'

'Sweet williams? They were your granddad's favourite,' says Ma, sending her words through the crowded room towards me.

I 2

The typeface is dense and the dialogue is earnest. It's an anti-quated story of a woman stifled by marriage who falls in love with another man, a younger man, not her husband, not the man she is permitted to think of. The emotion is sin-cerely described, right up until the last paragraph when she cuts herself loose and swims naked far out into the sea to a point of no return. It comes as a surprise. The story seemed too polite for so violent an end. I read again the final page to reassure myself that I hadn't imagined it, and there it is, the drowning, said all the more loudly for not being said.

I close my book and look around, satiated, wishing to share the sadness of the ending with another while wanting to preserve my own lonely obscurity on this rock that so perfectly fits the curve of my spine.

JP's walking up the beach towards me, but when I look around I realize it's not me but Kate, Monty and Fred who are waiting for him. A pile of twigs and seaweed falls from his hands, and his knees bend until they land on the sand.

'Ladies and gentlemen, in today's lecture, I will present to you the principles of building a bridge, not just any kind of bridge but a bridge that is light in weight, can hold up heavy loads, withstand strong winds and even, ladies and gentle-men, yes, even earthquakes,' he proclaims to his audience of three. 'In fact I can say, without fear of contradiction, that this will be the most beautiful bridge in Ireland.'

Kate giggles.

He quickly breaks bits off one twig and holds what remains up in the air so that it pronounces itself a Y. He takes out a penknife and cuts a slit through the foot of the Y. Then he tears narrow strips of seaweed off bigger strips and wraps them around the foot, wedging the end into the slit. Kate and Fred kneel before him, wide-eyed. Monty examines the leftovers. JP pulls a flat piece of wood from the back pocket of his jeans and holds it up, turning it around like a magician so that all sides can be viewed.

'This, ladies and gentlemen, is what is known as the deck of the bridge.'

He places it carefully on the sand. Then he gets the Y and puts it upside-down over the deck, driving the arms into the sand until it stands up all by itself. He makes use of Fred's fingers to pin the strips of seaweed into place on one side and Kate's on the other.

'These are what are known as the cables.'

The Y begins to wobble.

'We could do with one more finger,' he says, while his index finger stands in for the time being.

'Mrs Larkin, we need your finger,' calls Fred.

I pretend not to hear and bring my right hand up to defend my eyes from the sun. My lashes flicker against it, like butterflies in a cage. Something small is wandering aimlessly around the soft flesh between my T-shirt and jeans, creating a barely there sensation. Arthur and I spent our first night together following each other's contours with fingers so light it was hard to know if the touch was real or imagined.

'Mam.'

They're all looking at me now, expectantly, all apart from JP, that is. I look down on myself. It's an ant that's traversing my belly, lost and frantic. I blow him away, straighten my legs and lever myself into sitting up. 'What is it?'

'We need your finger to hold the bridge,' instructs the mighty Fred.

I resist the temptation to tell Fred to get lost. As usual, there are too many people involved. I slide off my rock, crawl the few steps towards the group and place a sullen finger on the tip of the twig. It steadies itself.

'Good,' says JP, to the class. He takes an exaggerated step back and thrusts forward his hands. 'Ladies and gentlemen, I present to you, da, da, daa, the bridge. Have you ever seen a bridge like that before, Fred?'

'I have.' Kate sticks her hand as high as she can into the beach-blue sky and with that her cables become limp. My finger loses its grip and the Y falls on its face. 'I saw it on your computer, Dad. It's the bridge you're building, Dad, isn't it?'

Fred considers the mess of twigs and seaweed.

'It's the bridge Dad's building in his work,' Kate repeats, for Fred's benefit.

'I know,' says Fred, scornfully. 'Sir, I've been on the Golden Gate Bridge in San Francisco.'

'Really, Fred?'

'Yeah. Lots of times. More times than I can remember.'

Kate looks at Fred as if he's speaking a foreign language. She decides to ignore him. 'But, Dad, I don't understand. What's all the seaweed for?'

JP takes out an old envelope and a pencil from his jeans pocket and sits down on the beach, legs long in front. Kate and Fred arrange themselves on either side of him as I blunder my way to my feet. I look over at my warm, safe rock but decide to stay put for now. I get to work on the nail of my little finger. I don't know what I'm doing here. I blame Fred. He turned up at Ma's house after breakfast with a lunchbox of crustless sandwiches and a bottle of orange juice.

'Good morning, Mrs Larkin. Sally Ann said could I join you and your family on the beach today?'

What could I say? *Well, actually, Fred, I was planning to escape my family today, spend some time alone, hiding behind the apple tree in the orchard with my book, only don't tell your step-mother like a good little boy.*

JP draws the elevation of his bridge, the deck and the tower with its legs out wide, in a series of assured moves.

'Bridge Man,' cries out Kate in recognition.

'What's Bridge Man?' asks Fred.

'It's that,' says Kate, pointing to the tower. 'I've seen it before. It looks like someone who plays puppets. You wait and see.'

JP draws several straight lines from the top of the tower to the bridge.

'See?' says Kate. 'They're like the puppet strings.'

'They're suspension cables,' Fred corrects her.

'Well, yes, they're like suspension cables,' says JP. 'We'll make an engineer out of you yet, Fred.'

Kate and I are redundant in this master class but Kate's not giving up. 'It's like a picture Miss Kavanagh showed us of *Gulliver's Travels*. The little people tied Gulliver down with rope so that he couldn't move, just like Bridge Man is tied into place there.'

Kate's analogy stirs no response. JP continues to draw lines in downward movements.

'What are they for?' Fred asks JP.

'Basically, the cables hold up the bridge. They're anchored

beyond the end of the deck. The force pulling inward is equal to the force pulling outward.'

JP hands the boy the envelope. Fred seems pleased, as pleased as Fred gets. He sits motionless, studying the inward and outward forces. He's a weird child. I'm not sure if it's his strangely hooded, almost prophetic eyes that make me nervous, or because wherever there's a Fred around, a Sally Ann is not too far away.

'I'm going for a walk,' says JP, out of the blue.

'Can I come?' asks Kate.

'No, Kate. You stay here and keep an eye on things.' He turns to me. 'You can manage here all by yourself, can't you?'

My lips tighten. I know I'm being tested.

Monty follows JP down the beach for a few steps. The rest of us keep our eyes on him as he heads towards the horizon line, stopping from time to time to skim the water with stones, until his silhouette merges with the rocks. The tide is far out and his bare feet crack the glassy sand. The water is still and carries downward all the colours of the coast, the light green fields, the dark green hedgerows, the white bungalows dotted around so that reality and reflection are almost indistinguishable, apart from the soft focus of the watery image. Arthur once said it was as if an artist had taken the wet colours and blended them with a soft, flat brush. Or was it I who said that? When I look back for JP, he has turned the headland. The blood from my nail tastes of metal. I plonk myself down on the sand and wait to be given my lines.

'Mam?'

'Yeah.'

'Why has Dad gone off on his own? Why didn't he take us with him?'

'I don't know, Kate. Maybe your father needs some time

to himself to figure out how to build the most beautiful bridge in Ireland.'

Kate seems satisfied with this. Fred reaches for his lunch-box from under a neatly folded jacket.

'What do you have?' asks Kate.

'Peanut butter and jelly.'

She watches as he peels away the lid. 'Did your mam make them for you?'

'No.'

'Oh?'

'My mom lives in the United States.'

'Why?'

'Why what?'

'Why does she live in the United States?'

''Cause that's where she lives. That's where I lived before I came here.'

'So is Sally Ann not your mam?'

'She's my step-mom.'

'So why did you come here?'

''Cause my father wanted to spend some time with me, that's why.'

'That's just like Brigid.' Kate kneels up suddenly in excitement and points her finger at no one in particular. 'My best friend Brigid. Her dad ran away when she was four but then he turned up and said he wanted to spend time with her and so she had to go off on holidays with him instead of coming here with us, like she always does. Did your dad run away when you were young too?'

'My parents divorced when I was five, if that's what you mean.'

Fred takes a full-on bite of his sandwich and chews it rhythmically.

'That's *just* like Brigid. Only Brigid was four. So do you have any brothers or sisters?'

Fred shakes his head.

'But Sally Ann's going to have a baby?'

'Kate!' I try to silence her but it makes her speed up.

'So the baby will be your step-brother or step-sister?'

He shrugs.

'You'll have a new brother or sister. I wonder what that'll be like.'

'Kate.' I raise my voice this time. 'What's with all the questions? For heaven's sake, let the boy eat his sandwiches in peace.'

Fred shrugs again and opens his mouth to speak just as the bread and peanut butter and jelly have mixed fully in his mouth to become a mottled pale brown. 'It's just a baby. It's not like it's going to do anything.'

Kate lands back on the sand and we sit in silence as Fred chews and swallows and chews and swallows his sandwiches. She and I stare gloomily towards the bit of the horizon that swallowed JP, waiting for him to reappear as a speck that will grow into a father and a husband, so that we can return to Ma's as one complete family.

13

Every night about nine Ma discharges JP and me to Manning's. It's her crude form of marriage guidance, as if two brandies and two pints will absolve us from ourselves and bring us back to some previous time when smiles were natural and kisses were damp on the back of my neck. I can't be bothered arguing with her any more. Ma won't be seen in the pub herself, apart from the odd funeral. She has never forgiven Old Manning for his liberal hand with the whiskey bottle.

In many ways, it's good to have this recipe for being together. No risk, just a shared assumption. We can talk in Manning's at a steady pace, in the style of a happily married couple, if we stick to the same menu of topics – his work, where the next job will be, the house, concerns about his mother living alone, concerns about my mother living alone. Anecdotes from the files of fellow drinkers also keep us going for a while.

We don't talk about Kate.

JP is easy to talk to when I want him to be. He laughs readily. Sometimes he even says I'm funny. I can simulate interest in things I know little about too. I can ask timely, prompting questions. It comes from my teaching days, I think.

But something closed off a couple of days ago, the day he went to the lighthouse, and now he rations his word count. It's up to me to compensate, to fill the spaces and to steer us back to the make-believe of harmony, at least while we're here under Ma's roof.

'Fred really loved your explanation of the bridge today,' I start, as soon as JP places his pint and my brandy on the table between us.

'Yeah?'

'Yeah, really. He kept studying the drawing you did. Funny kid, isn't he?'

'Is he?'

'Well, maybe not. Maybe it's just me.'

'Sssylvia?'

He's looking at me in the strange way I'm beginning to recognize, where his close eyes seem to get closer. He wants to ask a question, but I'm not ready for questions.

'What was that you were telling Fred about the inward and outward forces?' I ask.

He sighs and peels back the top layer of a beer mat. I scrabble around for a pen but he's there before me, pulling one out from his shirt pocket and embarking on an elaborate Open University-style diagram. He warms up once he gets going and moves the mat around, scribbling words with his big left hand along different axes. I smile and nod heartily and this encourages a proliferation of arcs and arrows, so that soon he's looking around for more beer mats and I supply them, relieved that the moment has passed and the question has dissolved.

The door of the pub clatters open on the third beer mat. JP and I look up just as Bo Quirke steps down into the room. I haven't seen him in Manning's since the first night of the holidays. Bo clocks us in the corner and throws me an incriminating half-smirk before moving on to the bar beyond. When I turn back to JP, his eyes are closing in. He snaps his pen into its cap, stands it upright in the breast pocket of his shirt and pats the pocket. Then he pours the end of his pint down his throat, plants the spent glass on his beautiful diagram and stands up. I watch the arrows melt into each other. I want to rescue them, but instead I knock back my brandy and follow him out of the pub.

The house is asleep when we get home. JP takes my father's seat under the lamp of the Sacred Heart and massages his forehead with a veined hand. The red light flickers on his skull but it's impossible to make out his face. The clock is ticking louder than usual.

'Is everything okay?' I ask eventually, sliding out of my shoes and folding myself into my mother's chair. The game's up, I know. There's no running from this one.

'You tell me, Sylvia. Is everything okay?' He's glaring across at me. His pupils are huge and the irises are no longer touching his lids. So this is what his anger looks like.

I tighten the embrace of my arms around my knees and say nothing. I can only say nothing.

'What the fuck is going on, Sylvia?' he demands.

'There's nothing going on.'

'You're making a fool out of me.' He presses the palms of his hands into the arms of the chair, levers himself into a full standing position and steps towards me. 'I'm supposed to be your husband, for fuck's sake.'

I feel the shadow of him over me. His arms hang loosely by his sides. My hand rises to my eye. 'Arthur's just a –'

'Arthur? What has Arthur got to do with it?'

'Bo. I mean Bo. Bo's just a friend. He's gay.' I laugh a shaky laugh.

'I don't give a fuck about him. It's *you*, Sylvia.'

97

My name is a strange, sibilant sound.

'Do you think I'm some big fucking eejit? We saw you out driving with Bo, or whatever his name is. Since when have you been driving?'

'I'm entitled to drive.'

'Of course you're entitled to drive. No one says you're not entitled to drive, Sylvia, but since when is it this big secret? You'll do anything, *anything*, to get away from me and Kate. You just want to run off and do your own thing, like a teenager with your own secret life. You're now even driving around in secret.'

'I didn't think you'd be interested.'

'You didn't think I'd be interested? Do you always just assume that I won't be interested? As if we have nothing to do with each other any more? As if we're not married? You never even told me about that thing in the school. Did you think I wouldn't be interested in that either? Or are you just ashamed of me?'

'You would've hated it.'

'Let me decide if I would've hated it or not. I suppose all the other fathers were there?'

'Just a couple.'

'Don't patronize me.'

I stare down into the dark well between my thighs and my breasts while he circles the kitchen table.

'And you wouldn't come to the lighthouse with us. You don't even come to the bloody beach any more, for God's sake. How do you think that makes Kate feel?'

'I came today.'

'Big deal. You came today only because Fred embarrassed you into it. Do you expect a medal?'

'You were the one who went off walking on your own. Even Kate asked why you wouldn't take her with you.'

'Oh, don't try that on me. I was just hoping to get you to face up to your responsibilities as a mother.'

'My responsibilities as a mother? Don't you lecture me about being a mother.'

'Look, Sylvia, I know it's been hard on you and I've tried to understand, I really have. I know losing your father –'

I'm on my feet. 'My father? Don't you dare bring my father into this.'

'I'm just saying –'

'Well, don't say. Don't say. Don't you dare say a word about my father, because you don't know. You've got no idea.'

'I'm your husband, for God's sake. I love you. I want to take care of you. Why won't you let me? Why won't you trust me? What are you afraid of? What do you think I'm going to do? I'm not like –'

His hands reach forward and he goes to place them on me but I dart away before they make contact.

'– him.'

Rage is rising through my innards and trembling through me. A huge cavernous fury from another time, another place explodes. Words burst out in all directions – 'My father loved me' – like missiles – 'like you never could' – words I don't know the meaning of – 'You don't love me' – destroying us both – 'You're suffocating me' – spilling out from the depths – 'You're killing me' – just below the surface. They all merge in a scream, a terrifying scream I can't hear. I can only feel jaws stretching wide, neck straining back and ribs being forced apart.

And then something breaks.

Panting. Snorting. Spent.

'I don't know you any more, Sylvia,' he says, with absolute clarity. 'God knows I love you and God knows I've tried. I really have.'

'Why don't you just fuck off . . .' My voice is deadly quiet, shaping each word slowly and deliberately and placing it in the space between us. '. . . and leave me alone.'

I'm accelerating towards the unthinkable.

'Go,' I say.

It's not too late. I can still stop now.

'Go away, JP.'

'What?'

'Go away. Just fuck off if it's so hard, if you've tried so fucking hard, if . . .'

'Sylvia, don't say that unless you mean it. Don't say it just to scare me.'

'I'm not trying to scare you. I mean it. I really mean it. I've never meant anything more in my life.'

He stands there like a little boy who has just wet his pants. It's too late.

The thud of the door rings around the room, hitting every wall like a frenzied drummer. I stare at the back of it. It holds my stare. I wait. For it to open again. For him to come back in. For the tape to be replayed. For us to rewind to the moment before.

But he's gone. Not stopping to pack a bag, grab a coat. He just leaves, with nothing but a strangely moulded grimace of expanded nostrils and protruding chin.

The door doesn't open. And when it doesn't, I look around and Kate's Unilion is staring up at me, bewildered. I reach instead for a vase filled with lush sweet williams sitting beside the creature, purple and pink with sharp white teeth. I wrap my fingers around the neck. The scent tries to hush me. I step forward into the hall. My stomach clenches and, with a grunt, I lift and hurl the vase in the direction of the front door.

It doesn't make it. Instead it collapses mid-way with the abruptness of a fighter plane. I feel water fill the spaces between my toes. My body slackens. I go to my knees, bringing my arms up to shield my head from myself. The moans are coming in spasms, each with a cadence of its own, primitive, primal, pathetic.

Two arms smelling of hairspray and onions are around me. My mother's holding me tightly to her and rocking me back and forth, back and forth, like a new-born mother. When I look up, my daughter is standing at the top of the stairs looking down on us.

14

Bloodshot dogs lie in the shade. Oranges and apricots are piled up on market stalls. Old men in long raincoats and skull caps are trailed by scarved women. They smile at me with beady eyes set like jewels between their wrinkles. A row of men are fishing from the bridge. Their catches live out their last hours in basins at their feet. The smell of the sea oozes from the fishermen's clothes. Cargo ships sail up the Bosphorus, and minarets dot the hillscape, like sentry guards. The honking horns and warbling prayers never cease. There's no quiet in this city.

Arthur is near me. We don't speak. We don't touch. I just sense him. But when I turn to face him, it's JP who's looking back at me, JP with his single-spaced eyes.

I wake up.

I'm alone in the gable room. It's somewhere between darkness and light. The smell of mothballs hangs in the air and the pillow is a massive boulder under my head. The sheets, once stiff and bleached, are now soft and polished by the sweat of dreams. A faint knowledge sits in my head.

JP is gone.

It isn't long, a matter of hours, but it feels like it has always been so. Somewhere in sleep a curtain was drawn between then and now, and this is now. This is how it is and how it will be. Now and for ever. Alone.

I fold back the duvet. A scar frowns up at me. My feet enter my jeans mid-air and I hoist my pelvis skyward to pull them up all the way. The scar is zipped over. A jumper stretches over my head and my feet fit into a pair of old sandals. I pad my way downstairs.

All shards of broken vase are gone. The sweet williams are choking in a milk bottle that stands on the windowsill in the hall. JP's anorak drapes like a deflated balloon from the coat-stand, gently kissing the floor. A life on building sites has washed the colour out of it. The cuffs are frayed. My hands skim the lining until I find the plastic-covered birth cert on the inside. 'Dillons of Roscommon. Made in Ireland,' it reads. A smell of dried-out wet days calls him up. I reach into a pocket and pull out his mobile phone. It's switched off. I reach in again and fumble about, not knowing what I'm looking for until I find it. There it is, a button, covered with a gentle tweed. Blues and greens run through the warp, peach through the weft. Yet together they don't merge. It's like looking at an Escher print. Your eyes can only see it one way or the other, not both at the same time.

I know this button. It comes from a more innocent time when women dressed up for Sunday drives with their husbands, who wore knitting-pattern cardigans. It belonged to the jacket of my mother's honeymoon outfit. She loaned it to me for my honeymoon. The jacket hung from my shoulders as JP and I wandered, necks strained, fingers linked, through the Sistine Chapel. It was JP who noticed the button on the floor, fallen between the fingers of God and Adam. He crouched down to retrieve it, saying he'd hold on to it for me. And he had, all this time.

I stroke the button, a genie's bottle of memories from that time – God makes Adam, lips blot a moist forehead, a finger dips into the font of my collar bone. My fingers curl around it and I drop it, along with the phone, back into the coat pocket it had come from.

The cold dawn gushes in through an open front door. I grab my jacket from the stand where it hangs beside JP's, like the Queen beside the King on the chessboard, and leave.

The sound of goats pulls me up the street and around the corner towards the beach. They're gathered for breakfast near the bottom of the hill. They stop and look at me with contempt. I keep going. I hear the croak of a single magpie. I walk faster for fear of seeing it. A few yards ahead on the upper road, a man stares out to sea. It's said that Thady Walsh keeps vigil at sunrise every morning – as if time spent looking and waiting will reverse his loss – but I never saw it for myself until now.

The tide is in but that doesn't stop me heading down the beach. I find a route over the crowns of rocks, zigzagging from rock to rock. Not far in, my heel slips out of a sandal and my ankle twists painfully. I raise my leg, point my toe and lower the foot to the next rock, raising my other leg behind me and testing the weight of my body on the injured foot. It works. I could break my leg on these rocks and be made a prisoner here. 'Be careful,' my mother used to say. 'Things can always get a whole lot worse.' Well, let them. Let them get worse. There comes a point when the various shades of darkness just fuse into one pervading grey, when there's no better and no worse.

I keep going. Short distances take a lot of energy. I have a lot of energy.

The sea is divided into smallholdings by the foam, as if the tide is undecided, working one way and then the other. The sound of it makes me shiver, causing goose bumps like tiny mountain ranges all over my body. I walk faster. I arrive at a piece of field that has fallen on to the beach. A wild bush grows out of it. If I walk around it, I'll walk into the sea, and if I walk into the sea, I might never come out.

So I crawl instead up on to the raw earth on hands and knees, clutching the bush as I go. On top, something slips from my jacket pocket, something hard and heavy. I look down and my mobile phone is lying on the rocks below, twinkling up at me in the morning light. I sit, slide down to the other side and keep going. I don't need it any more.

On the other side is an angry crow, perched on a rock. I pull up a finger, point and shoot but he doesn't die. He just walks away.

'I'm supposed to be your husband, for fuck's sake,' JP had said. 'Why won't you let me be?'

I feel the water lick my feet. Fear covers me with a damp film.

Why didn't he fight for me? Arthur would have fought for me. It was different with Arthur. He wouldn't have slipped away like that. Isn't that why I went to Istanbul? He sold me a dream, a dream of Bohemian adventures, of an artist's life. We were going to take the road less travelled. His vision was unwavering. It carried me to the other side of Europe and would have carried me further had things been different.

I keep going. The rocks turn to pebbles. I no longer have to plan every step.

This is what you want, Sylvia, isn't it? Otherwise you wouldn't have let this happen.

Bit by bit, the earth rises to greet the sun. My throat is dry and my head throbs. I'm on the other side of the headland. The emptiness of my stomach feels solid, like a tumour. There's a track up to the road above and I take it. Once on solid ground, I keep my head down and make for home.

A dead rabbit stops me. His legs are sprawled wide and his pelvis is stripped back as if on the operating table. His ears stick up straight, fluffy enough to touch, and his gut trails randomly across the road. Blood outlines his two front teeth. His eyes ask me for help. It seems indecent to leave him here. I look up and around, and there, high on the bank above me, is Fred, his red hair flashing in the morning sun. His head is resting sideways on his folded legs. We look at each other for too long until I step over the dead animal and walk. Fred's eyes follow me all the way down the hill.

The kitchen is empty when I get back. The breakfast dishes are washed and lined up on the dresser. Ma is giving orders to Kate in the orchard. Monty is walking restlessly between the outdoors and the indoors and his separated loyalties.

I take a cracked mug from inside the dresser and throw a teabag into it. The water splutters and hisses as it hits the mug. I force the teabag down to the bottom with a spoon until all the life is wrung out of it, before scooping out the remains, squeezing them against the inside of the mug and leaving them moulded into the spoon like a small, monumental sculpture on the kitchen table. I'm stalling, I know.

Flashes of orange appear through the window as Kate pulls carrots from the vegetable patch in slow, vertical motion. She's squatting into the ground and her bottom is scraping the earth. She feels my eyes on her and turns to face me. There's a frown between her brows, just like on the first day, when they tried to get me to hold her. They said I should, it was important, but my body was beaten and raw and I was gone beyond. I turned my head towards the wall and, after a while, they took her away.

The memory is never far from me – the frown, the pink

head and scrawny body, the nails like little squares of paper, the blood, the pain. They said that, in time, the pain would pass, that I'd heal. But they were wrong.

It wasn't meant to be this way. It was meant to be my daughter and me making daisy chains together. I didn't hold her that first time and now it's too late.

Ma comes in from the back kitchen and closes the door behind her. I wait. I know I'll attack if I have to.

'Where have you been at this hour?'

'On the beach.'

'Have you eaten?'

'No.'

She gets bread out of the bread bin and cuts two thick slices. She takes a plate, knife, butter and jam from the dresser and arranges them on the table beside JP's keys. I go to pocket them but am caught mid-grab by my mother.

'JP didn't come back last night, then?' She leans backwards against the stove. I take my place at the table.

'No.'

'So where did he get to?'

'I don't know.'

'His car is still out the front.'

'I told you. I don't know.'

It's true, so why does it feel like I'm lying?

'That's very strange altogether. You'd better phone him.'

'He left his phone here.'

'Well, are you going to go and look for him?'

'Where would I look? He's a big boy. He'll come back when he's good and ready.'

'Sylvia, things may be bad now but they can get a whole lot worse. I'm going to phone Ed. Something might've happened to him.'

'Ed? The police? You're the one who's always on at us about not washing our dirty linen in public, and now you want me to hassle Ed about my marriage? Ed couldn't track down a missing sheep. Besides, JP's done this before. He'll be back.'

I have no choice but to lie.

'He's gone off like this before? For how long?'

'Yeah, Ma, you think you know him.'

We hear the back door open. She leans into me, speaking in urgent whispers. 'I told Kate that her father had to go back to Dublin for work.'

'She's not going to buy that.'

'Well, for crying out loud, Sylvia, what in God's name was I supposed to tell the poor child?'

I concentrate on my silence.

'You have to give her some bit of hope.'

Kate's on the other side of the door.

'Of course she wanted to know why he left without saying goodbye and how he got to Dublin . . .'

The door opens. My knife sinks into the soft butter. It feels like I'm beginning a sentence that will last a lifetime.

15

The drawer in the dresser is full of junk, always has been –
envelopes of used stamps, elastic bands that break when
stretched, blue tailor's chalk that makes everything around it
blue, loose shoelaces wrapped around the arms of bug-eyed
sunglasses. That's what I'm looking for – the bug-eyed sunglasses.

Ma has popped over to Mrs Power with a jar of jam. Ma
never pops over to Mrs Power with jars of jam, or jars of
anything for that matter. It's Mrs Power who does all the
popping. But Ma's playing a new game and insisted before
she left that I stay in the orchard to keep an eye on Kate. She
says she's worried about her.

I find Ma's sun hat hanging in the back of the shed, put it
on and take shelter in the deckchair under the old apple tree.
Kate is hunched up on a stool, her legs bent like a grass-
hopper's, on the other side of the orchard where she's
plucking petals out of a daisy. She pulls every petal with a
violent jerk and drops it on the ground beside her for Monty
to sniff.

He Loves Me. He Loves Me Not. He Loves Me. He
Loves Me Not. Finally, the last petal falls. She sits staring at
the yellow heart of the flower for a while before getting up
and walking towards me with Monty at her heel. A bed of
flowers blocks me on one side, a bed of vegetables on the
other, and Kate looms over me, shading me from the afternoon sun.

'Mam, will I go and pack now?' Through the brown of the glasses, I can barely make out her brows coming together.

'Pack?' I struggle to sit up, to bring my eyes more level with hers.

'Yeah. We've got to go home now that Dad's at home.'

It's said as an order, so outlandish an order I almost laugh.

'And how would we get there?'

'You can drive us in Dad's car.'

'Drive? But, Kate, you know I can't drive.'

'Yes, you can.'

'What makes you think I can drive?'

'I saw you.'

'You did?'

'Dad and I saw you that day we went to the graveyard. There was a man with no hair in the car too.'

'Bo?'

'Maybe. I'm going to go and pack now.'

'No, Kate. We can't go home.'

'Why not?'

'Because I don't have a driving licence or insurance or anything.'

'So?'

'Kate, it'd be breaking the law. Besides, I can't drive. Not really. I was only learning that time. I could get us both killed.'

'We'll take the train.'

'We can't leave the car behind. We'll have to wait here till your father comes and gets us.'

'But that could be ages. Dad's at work the whole time. He can only come down at the weekend. We can't wait that long. We have to go now.'

'No, Kate.'

'Why not?'

'We can't go home just yet.'

'Why not? We have to go. Dad needs me.'

'We just can't. That's it. Final. I don't want to hear another word on it.'

'Mam. I have to go *home*.'

I can't bear it when she screams. I can't carry the weight of her demands. Never could. When she was a baby, she'd scream and kick with a force that terrified me. I'd cling to the side of the cot and the room would rotate around me. I couldn't pick her up.

'She doesn't love me,' I cried to JP.

'Of course she loves you. And you love her.' That, too, felt like an order.

I tried repeating it to myself aloud – 'Of course I love her and she loves me' – but the voices inside were louder. She didn't love me. I didn't love her, and I hated myself for it.

And so I learnt to cry alone, curled up in a foetal position beside the cot. I cried until it felt as though my eyes had been scrubbed with steel wool. At first I told myself I was crying for my father and then, as the months went by, I was simply crying. I cried as she fed, on to my breasts, feeding her salty tears. Then I got an infection and couldn't breastfeed any more.

I was terrified to be left alone with her and the fear of what I might do, but aloneness was easier than the testing questions that all amounted to the one question: 'What's wrong with you?' All I could do was shake my head. Every day they asked was she sleeping through the night, as if they couldn't see my wretched face. 'If you need me, just call,' they said, on the way out of the door. As time went on, their voices became more distant. Alone, I could let my true madness reign, indulge the horror I could enact. I could get a prescription. Walk under a car. A train. I choreographed it all in my head.

The pain travelled through my smashed-up body, entering and leaving through my scars like a knife-edged band of light. I took to walking in small, deliberate steps, doing everything with an exaggerated awkwardness as if to prove to myself that there was something wrong with me. I was malformed. It was no wonder I was the way I was.

In the end, I agreed to go to the doctor, confess my failure and take the medication.

'I have to go home,' Kate screams again. 'I have to go *tomorrow.*'

I dig my heels into the grass and dive out of the deckchair, stumbling a little. A snail is smashed beneath my feet. The sunglasses fall off my head on to its body, followed by the hat.

'I'm sorry, Kate.'

I don't know where I find that 'sorry' because I'm not sorry. How can she think that we can go back to JP, play happy families, as if nothing has happened?

'We're staying on here.'

I wait in the back kitchen for Ma to return while Kate sobs out her grief upstairs.

'I have to go,' I say, as soon as she opens the door.

I march up the beach again, fuelled by a fury that propels me forward like the burning end of a rocket heading into space. The wind tries to push me over but I march on in its face.

Church bells summon the parish to evening Mass, but

I'm not for being summoned. My daughter hates me. I always knew she didn't love me, not really, not in the way she loves her father, but now she well and truly despises me, with a determination you'd have to admire. I can't be around her any more. I know I'm a bad mother. What's the word they use? Unfit? That's it. I'm an unfit mother. I know I'm supposed to put my child's needs first. Isn't that what child-birth is all about? Subordination. As soon as you hear that first raw cry of life, that's your cue to go underground. You become the roots that allow them to blossom. If you don't, you risk becoming a parasite, sucking the life out of your baby. Of course, they don't teach you that in antenatal class. It's one of the things that are too obvious, too primal, too wrong to say.

I know I'm letting her down. But right now I must keep dog-paddling at the surface, directionless but afloat. I can't risk going under again.

The tide is on the way in so I keep to the narrow corridor of stones between the water and the cliff face of mud.

How can Kate think we can climb into JP's car and drive back to him? Doesn't she realize that our so-called family unit is now broken? He did this. He trampled into my life, got me onside, made me feel safe, safe enough to marry him and have a baby, only to abandon us now like wretched pups on New Year's Day. He sold me a dream, made me a promise – what were the words? 'Till death do us part' – only to crush it to pieces underfoot as he ran out of the door. He doesn't want us. He has no intention of coming and getting us, and I've no intention of asking him to do so. He's left us. He doesn't need us. He's more complete without us. He loves us not.

I wish he were here on this beach, right now, so that he could feel the heat of my rage.

I know what it is I must do.

I U-turn around a rock and march home along the beach to avoid colliding with any of the pious posse heading to Mass. I reach the end in record time, head over the grass and down the steps to the road.

'Well, well, well, if it's not the elusive Mrs Larkin.'

I jump. I didn't see Bo Quirke pull up beside me in his car.

'And what, Sylvia, are you up to this fine Sunday evening? You'll be late for Mass if you don't hurry.'

'I'm not going.'

'Not going to Mass? Did you go this morning?'

'Of course not.'

'And what does your mother have to say about that?'

I lean right into him so that there's only the smell of his cologne between us. 'Piss off, Bo.' Then I walk away, feeling his smirk on my back.

Monty seems pleased to see me when I turn the key in the front door. Poor deluded mutt. Ma and Kate are in the back kitchen. The main kitchen is empty and dim, like a stage set waiting for action. It'll have to wait. I take the stairs two at a time and head straight for Kate's room. Her bed is perfectly made. The crocheted quilt stretches over the rise and dips of the mattress and a manic-eyed teddy bear is hiding in the shadows. I recall long nights lying on this bed, with Joan on the other, trading secrets we hardly dared know, deciphering the noises and silences below. I miss Joan sometimes, despite everything about her.

At the end of the bed is a pile of drawings. The top one is a crude effort of four figures and a dog, obviously from Kate's head. She's capable of doing better than this.

I go to the old wardrobe and open it to where Kate's

clothes hang side by side. Her shoes point neatly towards the back, like ladies in waiting. I scan the shelf above. With one foot on the bottom of the wardrobe and my hands gripping the upper shelf, I haul myself up. Two cardboard shoeboxes lie, one on top of the other, in the corner. I inch them out and lower them through an invisible shaft to the floor. A layer of dust and hair unsettles itself. Slowly I lift the lid of the top one. And there they are, just as I left them in that week of hellos and goodbyes between finishing college and flying to Istanbul. Hardback notebooks filled with earnest scribbles. A box of chalk pastels. A watercolour set. Tubes of oil paint. Brushes with hardened bristles. Graphite. Charcoal. Pencil sets. A box of oil crayons. This was my favourite. I open it and inhale the warm smell of the oil. I greet each of them like old friends. They haven't changed. I hold up the stub of a Prussian blue crayon. At one time I'd had an urgency to push it and shove it around in pursuit of something significant. I can't remember what.

I carry all the materials up to the gable room and lay them out on the floor, opening the notebooks and smiling at my innocent tufts of clouds. But this is no time for nostalgia. I return to Kate's room and pull out a large sketchbook from behind the wardrobe, not doubting for a minute that it'll be there.

Then, back in the gable room, I sit on the floor, legs at sixty degrees, and begin.

The paint in the tubes is hard and beyond use. I've been silent for a long time. I like the 'bad art' excuse I used on Bo. It makes me sound more ideological than lazy. Now, as I roll up my sleeves, a new theory is forming.

I find a clean page in the sketchbook. I take a charcoal

stick and begin drawing the eyes, nose and mouth. Then I smudge them into oblivion with the soft part of my fist. The image is building up in front of me despite myself. I need no photograph or live model. I know this subject intimately, but I have never drawn it. It hangs before my mind's eye, constantly. Erasing. Drawing. Erasing. Drawing. The eyes are too big. I know it. But I can't help it. Those eyes that are slightly too close together, encased in jolly wrinkles. I force the charcoal into them and blow away the excess. They're dark, so I make them darker. The relentless smile. The convex skull. The slightly hooked nose.

There's no flattery in this portrait. This face is one of obscure deceit. It knows something I can't read. Did I ever really trust it?

I rip out the page and start again. Same face, same angle, same expression, at a speed I never knew I had in me. What was it the Pashmina said? Something about being free, expressing ourselves, something about a safe space. The curtains are drawn. I'm invisible in this room, and safe.

I start again. Another page. Another pair of eyes. I see JP picking the strawberries one by one. I push the charcoal around the page with force. I make marks with my left hand and erase with my right fist. Did he go home? I cement the lines with a saliva-coated thumb. Is he angry? I darken the shadow thrown by his lids. Or sad? I pull down the corner of his lips. Or indifferent? I smudge his grimace. I stand up and push my hair back with a right-angled arm. I see him in the garden, smiling to himself at the growth of the summer. He's lovingly reunited with his strawberries now. They'll have greeted him warmly with their ripeness. I line up the triptych and step away.

I've been silent for a long time. I had nothing to say. Loss had no image. But now I draw, not to remember JP but to forget him. I open a fresh page and start again.

16

We're on a train, entering a tunnel. He hovers close. The call to prayer seeps through the carriage. We're compressed by those around us. Eyes look down. Mine are level with the channel of his neck, the fount of his smell. A single drop flows from it. My tongue reaches forward to taste.

Daylight.

'I have to bring Mrs Power into town.' Ma's yanking back the curtains. She comes to the side of the bed, stepping over the drawings of her son-in-law with convincing indifference. 'She's doing up the front room and I promised I'd look for a carpet with her. She's always saying I have a very good eye. I wouldn't mind but I was in town last week and I could've done it with her then.'

I pull the quilt up closer to my eyes.

'Kate wants to come with me. I'm not sure it's a good idea. She'll be bored senseless but she insists. Do you know she was up at five o'clock this morning? I found her standing inside the front door in her nightie. She was perished, poor thing. She got an awful fright when I woke her. She's not herself at all. Did you say something to upset her, Sylvia?'

I keep staring over the top of the quilt.

'No, I didn't think so. But she's very peaky altogether. She'll be missing her father, God love her.' She tugs at the other end of the quilt. 'Come on now, Sylvia, get up and make yourself busy.'

I don't want to get up. I don't want to have to deal with Ma, Kate, any of them.

'Oh,' she throws in from the threshold. 'I tried phoning your house again. Either your husband's not there or he isn't answering. I've tried every different time of the day and night. I don't know what's going on with you two.'

His silence is pointed.

'And Joan rang again. Would you ever ring her, Sylvia? She says she's been trying your mobile non-stop.'

He must truly despise me.

'We'll be back in time for lunch. There's stuff in the fridge left over from last night's dinner. You can use that up.'

My husband hotfoots it out of here and I'm supposed to continue as before, as if nothing has happened. He knew. He knew more than anyone. He was there when Kate was born. And now, after all this time, he leaves. Why didn't he leave back then, when it as good as made no difference? For that matter, why didn't I leave? Wouldn't that have made things so much easier for everyone?

I slide out of bed and on to the damning portraits. His eyes give me a jolt. It was as if someone else was moving my arm. And yet, with some quiet satisfaction, I take pride in the menace of the stare, in the revenge of the artist.

I look around the room for remnants of him. There aren't many – a handful of shirts and jeans in the wardrobe, four sandals under them. I open the second drawer in the chest. Some T-shirts and a couple of jumpers lie there demurely, neat bunches of socks beside them. A book sits on the bed-side locker. A pair of binoculars atop the dressing-table. Then I remember the laundry basket. JP's socks mingle with mine at the bottom. It's as intimate as we've been for a long time. I reach in and scoop them up.

Ma is bellowing from the hallway: 'We're off now, Sylvia. Your breakfast is on the table.'

When she's gone, the breakfast – a Daddy Bear bowl of gelatinous porridge – slides into the bin. I wash JP's socks one by one in the sink. I scrub the bottoms of them together, enjoying the mindless frenzy of it. The truth is I'm not here in my mother's house washing my husband's socks. I'm back in Istanbul.

There's no particular memory, just a slide-show of images rotating before me – domes upon domes springing up like mushrooms, the peach light of the morning sun, the Galata tower edging its way between buildings, the other-worldliness of it. It's strange how my mind is going back there now, of all times, and yet it's not strange at all.

Once the socks are hanging in devoted pairs on the line, I return to my studio in the gable room, take out my old watercolours, fill a jam jar from the bathroom sink and brush on strips of clear water over the page with soft, flat brushes. Dots of sepia, burnt umber and ochre of the East prick the water and ooze into each other. I hold the page up and the water takes over, carrying the paint around the page, making lush washes of evening skies that later I overlay with domes and towers. JP's charcoal eyes fix themselves on me as I work.

'Hi.'

'Fred? What the hell are you doing here?'

'Where's Kate?' The boy steps down into the gable room. His hands puff out the pockets of his chinos and he's looking idly around, like a miniature Great Gatsby.

'She's not here. How did you get in?'

'Did she run away?'

'No. Of course not. She's in town with her grandmother, if you must know. Now, what are you doing here?'

'When's Mr Larkin coming back? I made my own bridge out of sticks and wire and stuff and I'd like him to take a look at it.'

'He's not.'

'Excuse me?'

'He's not coming back.'

'Is he dead?'

'No, Fred. He's not dead. We broke up.'

I separate the three words out for effect but the boy seems unaffected.

'People break up. *You* should know that, Fred.'

I know I'm going too far. He's only twelve and I'm bigger than him, but there's something about the boy that makes me want to shake the swagger out of his walk.

'So what are you doing up here on your own?'

'What business is it of yours, Fred?'

'Just wondering why you're always alone, that's all.'

'I'm not.'

'Whatever.' His eyes focus on JP's. 'Is that Mr Larkin?'

'Yes.'

'Cool.'

'Fred? Fred? Are you here?' The voice from downstairs is one decibel short of hysterical.

'Oh, God. Who is it now?'

'It's Sally Ann,' says Fred.

I go to the top of the stairs – 'He's up here, Sally Ann' – but she's already halfway up and out of breath. Hairs have broken away from her bun and are smudging the outline of her face.

'I knew he'd be here. I just knew it.' She marches down to

the gable room to Fred, who's systematically picking up and examining each item on the dressing-table – the wooden jewellery box, the hairbrush, the bottle of makeup – as if he's about to make me an offer. He moves over to the bed and picks up a damp watercolour.

'Where's this?'

'Istanbul.'

'Frederick. Can you go home now, please, and wait for me there? I'll be over shortly.' I swear she'd have belted him had I not been there.

Fred puts his hands back into his pockets and squeezes past his step-mother's bump. Sally Ann's eyes follow him as far as the stairs with obvious disdain. She turns to leave but her eyes land on the drawings and she stalls. Then, after too long, she faces me. Her eyes are glassed over and her nose is a delicate shade of pink.

'What is it, Sally Ann?'

'Oh, Sylvia, they're just so . . . beautiful.'

'Sorry?'

'They're so like him.'

'Oh, they're useless. I was just playing around.'

She's not listening. 'Sylvia, do you mind if I sit down for a minute?'

Her face is a moist white with a brown gloom around the eyes. I clear the watercolours and paints off the bed. The mattress sinks deep under her weight. Somewhere, in the midst of my irritation, I recognize her exhaustion.

'I'm sorry, Sylvia.'

Tears are sliding down her face now. Crying is a messy, intimate affair, as messy and intimate as sex. I've known Sally Ann for more than thirty years yet never before have I seen her chin become undershot when she cries or her nose turn into a snout when she pushes the top of her hand against it to catch the snot.

'Bob says it's the hormones. The hormones!' Her laugh is muffled by soggy tears. 'Thank goodness for hormones. We can blame everything on hormones.'

'Indeed,' I mutter.

'Truth is, Sylvia, I'm terrified. I mean, what if it all goes wrong? What if I can't take the pain? What if it dies? What if I die? What if they make Bob choose like they used to do in the old movies? Who would he choose? He may as well choose me because there's no way he's going to be able to look after this baby without me. What will happen to it if I'm not around? Oh, Sylvia, I can't stop thinking about it. What if they can't get it out? I'm not big down there, you know. What if they rip me open and they can't . . . I'll never be the same again.'

With this, she lies back on the bed and curls her legs up into a foetal position and cries into herself – 'I'll never be the same again.' Then she winds herself into a smaller ball and repeats the mantra of her grief. 'I'll never be the same again.'

Each 'never' is quieter than the one before until she is silent and still.

I sit beside her and wait in hopeless silence, absorbed by my own memory of blood and bleeps and metal on metal. It's only when we hear voices downstairs and Sally Ann becomes abruptly upright that I realize she had fallen asleep.

'Fred?' she says, pushing the loose hair away from her face. 'Where's Fred?'

'It's okay. He's gone home.'

She gets up and goes to the dressing-table, pulling her mottled cheeks taut in the mirror. Specks of mascara have travelled through the creases around her eyes towards her cheeks.

'Sylvia? Are you up there?' Ma calls out, with a jollity that says there are visitors in the house.

'Yeah, Ma, I'm here.'

'Come on down, why don't you? Mrs Power is here with Fred. And Kate received a letter in the post.'

'Oh, no,' says Sally Ann. 'I've got to get out of here. I can't face them like this.'

'Don't worry. I'll get you out.'

I go downstairs and pull over the kitchen door into the hall. Once the front door is open, Sally Ann makes her way down step by heavy step. I hold my breath at the loose fifth stair but the murmur of voices from the kitchen continues unbroken. She mouths, 'Thank you,' on the way out. I close the door on her and look down the corridor to see Kate in the parlour reading her letter.

There's something about the picture of her standing in front of the window, carefully holding her letter with both hands, that calls to mind the painting by Vermeer. It's the way the light falls from the window on to her brow, her almost closed lids and her quietly assured pose. It takes me away from here for a short, sweet moment.

When she sees me, her mouth narrows. She reaches for the parlour door and closes it to blacken out my view.

17

'Kathleen, this is only gorgeous,' gurgles Mrs Power. Crumbs from Ma's rhubarb pie dangle from the outer reaches of her moustache. 'How do you get your pastry so light? Fred, eat up your crusts now, like a good boy.'

'I'm not hungry, Grandma.' Fred's eyes are fixed on me.

'Sylvia,' says Ma, 'have you been up in your room all this time? Sit down and talk to Mrs Power. Have you had your lunch?'

'No thanks, Ma. I'm not hungry,' I say, holding Fred's stare.

'I was just telling Mrs Power about JP having to head back to Dublin at such short notice.' Ma keeps her back to all of us as she pours tea from the pot on the stove. 'That's a very demanding job he has on, Dolores. He's got an awful lot of responsibility with this new bridge coming up. You know, they can't really get on without him.'

Fred starts coughing. I turn to Mrs Power, full on. 'Mrs Power, JP hasn't in fact gone to Dublin because of work, like my mother says. The truth is we don't know where JP has gone.' I extend my hands wide to prove my ignorance. 'We had a row. He walked out.'

I return to face Fred, as if I'd taken on the dare and now he has to pay up.

'Sylvia, why are you saying such a thing?' Ma would slap me if she could.

'There's no point pretending, Ma. I guess, Mrs Power, it's what they call' – she swallows in anticipation for what she's about to hear – '"unlucky in love".'

The door opens and we stiffen. Kate appears, pale and hostile. Ma swoops in on her. 'Kate pet, who's the letter from?'

'Brigid.'

'Who's Brigid?' asks Fred.

'My friend. The one I told you about.'

'How's the poor girl getting on?' asks Mrs Power. 'Did she say anything about her father?'

Like Ma, Mrs Power likes the Brigid story. She's riveted by the messiness of a broken home – the processes of dividing assets, children and love – as long as it doesn't encroach on her own circle.

'Not really,' says Kate.

Ma leans down so that she's eye level with Kate. 'Kate, would you like to read the letter to us?'

'No.' The word is out before I can stop it and they are all looking at me.

'Ma, we're not the bloody Von Trapp family.'

'But, Sylvia, I don't know what your problem is. She's such a lovely reader. You'd like to read it out, wouldn't you, Kate?'

'Not really.'

'I'll read it,' says Fred, and before I can protest again, he's on his feet and sliding the letter out of Kate's hand. He solemnly clears his throat. 'My dear Kate.'

He reads slowly and deliberately to secure our attention and clears his throat a second time.

'My dear Kate,

*I trust this letter finds you and your family in good spirits. I am
very well, thank you. I find myself staying in a large farmhouse
in County . . .*

'. . . What's M-E-A-T-H?'
'Meeed,' says Ma, sulkily.

'. . . *Meeed. It belongs to my father's brother, his wife and their
three children. Two dogs and three cats reside here too. My father
is staying here momentarily. My mother and all of my sisters are
at home in Dublin. My father's parents, whom I hardly remembered before I came here, live in a little house nearby.*'

Fred's slow Arizonan accent is mangling Brigid's words,
making them lean over to one side when they were written
to stand up straight.

*'They are eighty-four and eighty-five years old and my poor grandfather
is almost blind. Many an afternoon is spent reading aloud to him. He
enjoys Dickens and Hardy, especially* David Copperfield. *My
father's mother cried incessantly when we met. It was most strange.*

'How old is your friend?' Fred turns to Kate, who's half
hiding against the side of the dresser.
'Twelve. Why?'
'She sounds really old.' He clears his throat again.

*'Everyone has been most kind to us. From time to time, my father
borrows my uncle's car and we go on a little excursion. We have been
to the lakes nearby and even went and saw St Oliver Plunkett's head.'*

'Why his head?'
'That's all that's left,' says Kate.

'My uncle's farm is a delightful place. It is surrounded on two sides by woodlands. I enjoy taking walks in the woods, although at first I was quite fearful. The trees lean towards each other and the branches gently kiss.

'Can trees kiss?'
'Yeah,' says Kate.

'My uncle has three sons – Danny, aged fourteen, Richie, aged ten, and Angus, aged nine. Richie and Angus play interminable war games. They cover their faces with mud and run around with wooden sticks that are supposed to be guns. Thankfully I am spared these games. Danny, on the other hand, works with his father on the farm. He drives the tractor, helps save the hay and milks the cows. His eyes are like big dark pools. Sometimes I feel I will drown in those eyes. Kate, I know you will find what I am about to tell –'

'Stop.' Kate jumps out from the shadow of the dresser. 'Stop it.'

'– you quite extraordinary but I really think –'

Kate's in front of him now. 'It's private. Gran, stop him.' Monty growls and Fred raises his voice without looking up.

'– I am in love –'

128

Kate snatches the letter from Fred. She freezes to the sound of ripping paper.

'Wow, the girl's in love. That's quite something,' says Fred, victoriously waving the remnants of the letter above his head.

Kate looks as if she might punch him but instead she turns, twisting her shoulders and hips, to slip between Fred and Ma like water. The back door crashes behind her.

I'm on my feet. 'Fred, shut up.'

Ma throws Mrs Power a nervous look. She's thinking ahead. This could have repercussions for years to come, two tribes battening down the hatches, the dissolution of alliances. An apology is needed, a formal, insincere apology, and soon.

When it's clear there'll be no apology, not today anyway, Mrs Power stands up, frees her skirt of crumbs and makes to go. 'Come along, Fred.'

I leave the room before her and take the stairs two at a time. The front door slams as I reach the gable room. I slide on to the bed, face down into the pillow. I've had enough of this game. I've had enough of having to act like a good mother, a devoted wife, a respectful daughter. I've had enough of acting. I think of my father. What would he have done? He had no time for Mrs Power and didn't pretend otherwise, and she, being a coward at heart, hardly ever crossed the threshold when he was alive.

The negative of his face, his sloping eyes and half-smile, hang in the cross-hatched blackness before my eyes. I didn't draw him often, and when I did, it was only ever in black ink. His forehead called for a strong line. There might still be some Indian ink left in the wardrobe. I haul myself off the bed and into Kate's room in search of it.

A bright pink mass, ominous in its pinkness, sits on the

upper shelf of Kate's wardrobe. It's her backpack, the one she packed for her holidays – it wasn't there the other day. I pull it out and down and unzip it in one arc. Inside are small items of little girls' clothes folded neatly on top of each other. I unzip the front pocket. The zip snags halfway through. I pause and stretch my neck to check the silence is intact. The eyes of the teddy bear catch mine.

'It's okay. I'm her mother,' I tell him.

I tug at the zip and it gives way. Inside is the tattered photocopy.

Who is Silvia? What is she
That all our swains commend her?
Holy, fair, and wise is she;
The heaven such grace did lend her

I shove it back into the shadows of the pocket. It meets something hard. I pull out a small notebook that's covered in cheap blue velvet. The remains of 'My Diary' in gold script are on the cover. I recognize it instantly. It's the diary Da handed to Joan at breakfast on her eighteenth birthday. Ma and I watched agog as she pulled it out of its brown-paper bag. With my adult eyes, I wonder how a farmer who rarely made a trip to town could get his hands on such a piece of feminine frivolity. I did little to hide my jealousy back then but I was assured that I, too, would get something equally pretty when I reached eighteen. I didn't.

I breathe in and open it.

18

When I told Ma that Seamus and I are back together again, her response was 'don't tell your father'. According to her, Dad thinks Seamus Manning is a distraction at this crucial stage in my studies. I don't know what Dad's worried about. It's not as if I didn't get all honours in the mock exams.

I'm back on my rock on the beach with Joan's diary. I had to get out of the house. Demarcation lines were quickly drawn after the showdown with Mrs Power. I stayed upstairs and Ma downstairs, but I couldn't take Ma's singing any more. She always sings when war is declared. It's a kind of morale-boosting exercise for her internal troops, and a way of showing the other side that she won't be beaten.

As far as I'm concerned, I'll be out of here by September and I'm not going to let Seamus Manning or anyone else get in the way of that. No indeed! He said he wants to do the things I want to do, travel the world and all that, but it's all words. It's so tedious! He'll never leave this place. 'One foot over the Waterford Bridge and he'll be crying for his mammy,' Ma said, and she's right. Sy said Da has probably figured out something is going on. She said he has this way of knowing things. She would.

The diary is a virtual Joan, as real as if she were here before

me, eyebrows arched, nails polished. There's no preamble –
it dives straight in, just like my sister, spanning the period
from her eighteenth birthday on 5 March 1980 until the end
of December.

I remember that year. Joan and I would brush our hair
forward and fling our heads back, competing on how big we
could make ourselves (Joan's curls always won). We'd sing of
glittering futures into our hairbrushes. Joan was good at
talking big, as big as her hair. She was gonna get out of this
dump and never come back. She was gonna make a difference, a big pow-wow difference.

Sure enough, she flies high, these days, writing for news-
papers on both sides of the Atlantic, from her chic dockside
apartment, and delivering lectures in established educational
institutions. She can be found pacing from room to room,
talking into her Dictaphone at six in the morning as the poor
nanny tries to coax her two-year-old into his clothes.

Sy has gone and joined the debating society on Wednes-
day evenings – God knows why! It's not like she has ever
shown any interest in oration up to now. The funny thing
is Sally Ann Power has started debating too. It's hilarious
because Sy can't stand Sally Ann. She wears twinsets and
pearls and has pert tits like in the Playtex ads and she
always does whatever Sy does.

Joan always reckoned that Sally Ann idolized me. According to my sister, Sally Ann wanted to be me. I'd forgotten
about that.

Sy keeps practising her arguments in favour of 'Nuclear
weapons are our only insurance against a Third World

War' on me. She is driving me nuts. I told her I don't care if they all blow each other up, and that shut her up for a while.

I'd forgotten, too, about my venture into debating. In the beginning it terrified me, but soon the feeling of speaking words pumped by adrenalin became addictive. I can't imagine standing up in front of a group now and demanding their attention to my rambling opinion. The picture of Fred clearing his throat comes to mind. I rotate a little towards the last bits of sun to shake it away.

Seamus Manning is in love with me!! He declared his love on the beach tonight. You should have seen his face. He was so serious. It made me want to laugh but I managed not to because he would have got really upset.

When I look up, the golden top of Kate's head is moving at a pace away from the village and towards a red-topped Fred, who's waiting for her at the point where the upper road turns out of sight. Kate stops when she reaches him. I wonder have they made up or is it about to happen.

He is one year older than me but you would think he was ancient. Yesterday he asked me where did I see myself in five years' time. Five years' time??!! I said I didn't care as long as it's as far away from this kip as possible.

Maybe Ma doesn't know that Kate is out and about and meeting up with Fred at this late hour, in which case she'll be worried and I should go after my daughter and bring her home. It'd be the right thing to do. What does Fred want from Kate anyway?

I return to the diary with the compulsion of an addict who needs to keep the buzz going.

I think I'll have to break it off with him again to put him out of his misery. Ma said that he'll thank me for it in the long term. It's a pity because he's a really good kisser.

The diary was in Kate's bag but she'd hardly have read it, would she?

Ma said Seamus will be better off without me. He'll find a nice girl that he can marry (a Colleen or a Sarah or someone like that) and they will have lots of kids together. He'll take over the pub and then he'll be stuck here for ever. Come to think of it, I think he should marry Sally Ann. She would be perfect for him. I remember once when she was eight years old and I was ten she said she wanted to have 100 kids!

Poor Seamus. No wonder he won't even look at me in Manning's. Joan dumped him every month or so and was forever trying to fix him up with someone else to dampen her guilt and remove the temptation to go back to him. She killed off that poor boy's heart, bit by heartless bit. I told her so once. She laughed.

I told Sy what Seamus said about being in love with me. She said I was very lucky to have him. She was deadly serious. I wonder about my sister sometimes.

Oh, here we go. Joan is always wondering about me some-times, as if I'm some kind of fascinating case study that challenges given theories. She probably presents me to her students for discussion. I bet she squeezes a good two les-sons out of me and all my foibles. I wonder does she have the decency to change my name.

She has these moonlight and roses fantasies about love.

Oh, come on.

She has quit her debating career (no surprise there!) and is now painting more. She dreams of going to art college and becoming an artist. She will live and paint in a light-filled room in Paris or New York and she will sleep in her dunga-rees and will get out of bed in the morning to start painting again, picking up where she left off the night before. That's what she says anyway. I don't think she knows what she wants. She'll probably end up as a housewife living behind a white picket fence and baking apple pies. Sy is the one who cries when Laura says to her father, 'I love you, Pa,' in Little House on the Prairie. She did it again on Sunday and I told her to cop herself on. It just made her worse.

Bravo, Joan. You win. I'm living behind the white picket fence and am covered with flour from baking pies. You were right all along.

Da's in one of his moods again! He hasn't spoken to any-one for a week or more. He doesn't even talk to the dogs when he gets like this.

I reach into the pocket of my jacket and rub the hard-soft pebble from Dad's grave.

He stays out late in his shed and doesn't come in for dinner. Then he disappears and doesn't show his face until after midnight. Ma and Sy are always trying to humour him. The worse he is, the nicer they are to him. It makes me sick. I wish they would leave him alone! – that is what he wants. I'm not going to tiptoe around him any more. They are sitting down in the kitchen right now, waiting for him to come home. They don't even speak to each other when they are waiting like this. We all know where he is but nobody will say it. It's like one big conspiracy. In the morning he'll go out before we get up, and tomorrow evening another dinner will be spoilt and they'll wait for him again. Sometimes I wish he would just stay away for good.

The selfish bitch. She'll use anything for a story, even her own father. We know she learnt her craft in the School of Life. That's what she tells her students, isn't it? It makes me choke. Since when did the School of Life involve skewing the family history for dramatic effect? Is nothing sacrosanct?

I scan most of the diary as the sun turns around the corner of the earth and a chill moves into the rock – the mind games with the poor Manning boy, the ambitions, the classroom politics – and I stall on the four of us: Da, Ma, Joan and me. It isn't just narcissism. This is my story too, even if it's told from Joan's warped perspective. Memories etch themselves differently from brain to brain. Everyone knows that, but Joan is spectacularly wide of the mark.

I think I'm going to scream!

And they used to say I was the highly strung one.

He's outside the front door right now and he's trying to get his key into the lock. He's pissed out of his skull. I heard Tommy Carroll shout from across the street, 'Good man, Jimmy.' Smart bollocks! I wanted to go downstairs and knock the smile off his face. He's in now at last. I am staying up here in my bed – I'm afraid of what I will do if I go downstairs. I know exactly what's going on – I have seen it all before. Ma and Sy are jumping up to attention. They're taking his boots off. He's kicking them across the room – he always wanted to be on the county team! He's sitting at the end of the table with his knife and fork in his hands and they're bringing out his shrivelled-up dinner. They give him lots of spuds with gravy and mugs of strong tea. They're like a pair of nervous rabbits watching him in case he pukes. He's so pissed he thinks he's drinking porter. They're going to put him to bed and tuck him up as if he were a baby. I can hear them now. They're trying to coax him. I can hear his drunken bullshit. Jesus Christ, I wish they would lock him out for the night and then we could all sleep in peace!!

We all know Da used to enjoy a few pints and, yes, Ma and I used to wait up for him from time to time. I needed to know he was okay. I don't know why Joan was so angry about it. It didn't affect her or her studies or her toying with the Manning boy. It had nothing to do with her. She made that clear at the time. I can't help thinking this rage was for effect, so that her diary would be a more compelling read.

She was probably – what was it she used to say? – 'developing her voice'.

Do they think I don't know what's happening down there? Do they think I sleep through the whole thing? Do they think I am some sort of eejit? Does Ma think that we don't know that she sleeps in the kitchen when he's like this? I don't know what they think and I don't care. All I know is that it takes every breath in my body to stop myself going down there and telling him what I think. The sooner I get away from this kip the better!! Then they can all drown in their sea of misery. It is this diary, this pretty little diary that he gave me for my birthday (oh, the irony of it!!), that keeps me from going insane.

My father appears in split-second vignettes. Opening the gate and letting the dogs out before him. Slicing his knife into his potato with exactitude. Gravy drooling from the side of his mouth. Sure he kept to himself at times but it wasn't all mopping up and tiptoeing around him like Joan says. That's just the way he was.

I sit up and look around me. It's that violet time in the evening, when the light has quietly slipped away without saying goodbye. The upper road is empty and I haven't seen Kate return. My rock is almost entirely surrounded by water and is now a lonely island. I look down at the water, which is close, too close. It would not take much to make a union with it. No one is going to rescue me from here. How far out to sea would I be by the time they realized I was gone? There'd be a bit of disruption for a while but the hole I'd leave behind would be filled in.

I take my sandals off, roll up my jeans and disembark. The water is inhospitable.

I return through the front door to avoid entering the kitchen. Ma and Kate are in there and the news is blaring from the telly. Ma watches news programmes back to back. When one is finished, she switches channels for another one, taking care that a whiff of fiction doesn't seep through the cracks. From the other side of her ironing-board, she tells the newsreader what's coming up next. Natural disasters are her speciality. 'Sylvia, have you seen the floods in England?' she'd say, all excited. 'Fifty people were put out of their homes.' Maybe Joan's craving for fiction came from a childhood absence of it.

Through the window from the hall into the kitchen, I see Ma and Kate folding the sheets, meeting and parting again like a *céilí* dance, while behind them, somewhere in the world, people are carrying themselves and their belongings to drier land.

19

'This'll be our special secret,' says Tommy Carroll, tapping the side of his nose as he passes the letter to Kate. He winks at her over a glass eye that's looking in another direction. Tommy has been making secrets where secrets don't exist with kids in this village for as long as he's been delivering the post. Kate stands in the one spot for the length of time it takes him to hand over the brown envelope. Nothing else would keep her in the same room as me for this long. Then she takes it to the pen jar on the dresser and withdraws the letter-opener with the tortoise head.

'She's a great little girl altogether, isn't she?'

My teeth are closing in on the last bit of protruding nail on my left thumb.

'And getting taller by the day?'

I bite and swallow.

'And her little friend couldn't come with her this year? The little one with the glasses?'

'Her name's Brigid,' says Kate, as she pricks the corner of the envelope with the opener and saws through it slowly. Tiny bits of paper curl away.

'I hear JP had to go back to Dublin for work?'

It's a week since JP walked out and Ma's white lie has travelled around the village, colliding with the truth on its journey.

'That's right.'

'And you're staying on here for a while?'

Kate stops sawing.

'That's right.'

She resumes sawing.

'Sure it's great that you're both getting to spend this time with your mother.'

'Yeah.'

'She misses you, you know.'

'Mmm.'

'She'd never let on.'

'No.'

'She's not around this morning?'

I shake my head. I don't know where Ma is. She shoved me awake this morning with a fresh set of orders to get up and mind Kate as she had to go out. It was a malicious 'out'.

The envelope is open and Kate's pupils darken as she tugs at the letter inside. Tommy's body swivels towards her. His head can't turn by itself. Never could. It has to travel with the mass of his hump. 'Is it from anyone nice?'

Kate's grinning at the single piece of heavy white paper she has unfolded.

'Is it from a secret admirer?'

But she's gone, out of the back door and into the orchard with Monty in tow to read Brigid's letter, leaving Tommy and me facing each other, Tommy in Da's chair, me in Ma's.

'Good man, Jimmy,' Tommy Carroll called to Da, from across the street. That's what Joan's diary says. I didn't know they drank together, but all the men in this one-pub village are thrown together in a crucible of induced merriment sooner or later. My memory of Tommy is of him perched at the end of the sofa with a mug of strong tea in his hand when I got home from school. He and Ma would be quizzing each other at a furious pace as if time were running out. Ma said Tommy was like a bumble-bee, picking up titbits of gossip in one household and bringing them to another. She was careful what she fed him.

He'd never sat in Da's chair, like he's doing now, apart from the night he brought Da home, slumped over his hump, from Manning's. He dropped him on to the sofa because that was nearest to the door and then he dropped himself breathlessly into Da's chair.

I stand up quickly, startled by the memory.

'Are ye all right there, Sylvia?'

What was it he'd said that night?

'I'm sorry, Tommy. I'm going to have to get on.'

Tommy leans his top half backwards so that the last of his tea slides into him. Then his tongue moves frantically around his mouth to locate a stray tea leaf, which he spits into the mug.

'Oh, right you be.' He rocks from side to side as he rises. 'Far be it from me to keep anyone from their work.'

He's pissed out of his skull. I heard Tommy Carroll shout from across the street, 'Good man, Jimmy.' Smart bollocks! I wanted to go downstairs and knock the smile off his face.

Joan's writing sprawls across the pages on to my lap. Like her, it's too big for this book. The words press so deeply into the paper, they rise up from the page on the other side. I close my eyes and lightly stroke the pages as if the writing were Braille and I were blind.

'He's not getting any lighter, Kathleen.' That's what Tommy Carroll said that night.

What did he mean? Did it happen just once or is that the only time I can remember? Did he carry him before when he was lighter? Or heavier? Or not at all? Why did Ma pull Da's shoes off roughly, not caring whether she hurt him? Why did she slap his face and shout, 'Jimmy, Jimmy, can you hear me?' Why did she sound frightened and angry at the same time?

Through the bedroom window, I see Kate in the deckchair out the back reading her letter. If only she'd been born earlier or later or, God forgive me, not at all – I mean not to me, to someone else, to a better mother, a better woman – things might've been different. I might've been down here more. I might've been able to keep a lid on things, mightn't I?

Memory and fantasy are fusing so that neither is pure. Why did I have to come across that bloody diary, a container of words that can't be unwritten? Why did I not write my own version of the truth?

I need to talk to someone, someone other than Joan or Ma or Bo or Tommy or the Powers, someone who knew me back then.

'Call me,' Arthur had said. He'd said it for a reason.

We used to take evening walks along the Bosphorus when we first arrived in Istanbul, watching the boats go from West to East and back. Voices around us were frenzied and urgent but we spoke quietly then, taking the time to recall every detail, minute for minute, of our lives before we'd met, filling in all the jigsaw pieces. We had had all the time in the world back then when it was just the two of us, before Arthur had met the others, his 'kindred spirits', as he called them, and started disappearing on me.

I told Arthur all about my father on those walks. I spoke more about him than anyone else. Arthur said so.

'Call me,' he'd said. I hadn't thought I'd ever have the nerve.

His card has been in the pocket of my blazer since that night. Packing the blazer spared me from packing the card. That would have been too deliberate. I glance out the back. Kate's still engrossed in her letter. I go to the wardrobe.

A. H. DELANEY
ARTIST

the card says. There's a mobile-phone number with an international code. Arthur Delaney is an international brand. I try to imagine him as he is now – pacing across a bleached-out studio, downing an espresso with a dead-beat curator, all in black. He'll be too busy, too preoccupied.

There comes a point when you've nothing more to lose.

Ma's phone wasn't made for global communication. It takes an age to push the dial around to all of Arthur's digits. I should have a cover story in case Kate reappears. The dialling tone is unfamiliar. It's giving long, purring noises. I don't trust my nerve.

''Allo?'

It's a woman's voice, a confident, sexy one. I recognize it straight away. It's the woman with the black hair and dangerous-looking cheekbones from that night in the gallery. I hadn't expected this.

'Hello?' I sound like one of the mothers who used to phone up the school I worked in, wanting to talk to me about their little Emma, one of those for whom the cut and thrust of the working world was alien territory. The phone intimidated them. The school receptionist would smell their fear and lick her lips.

'Could I speak to Arthur, please?'

'Hold on, please.' Her 'please' has too many *e*s in it.

I breathe heavily into the silence and balance myself at the edge of hanging up, but I tell myself that Arthur might be the only independent witness I have left so I keep on standing there, looking at the tail ends of Mossie Keogh's cows through the front window as they leave the yard above, their hips swaying provocatively from side to side.

'Arthur Delaney speaking.'

'Arthur, it's Sylvia.'

'Sylvia?'

One of the cows stalls at the back of the herd.

'Keane.'

'Sylvia. How are you?'

'Fine. I'm fine.'

'Good. That's really good.'

'And you? How are you?'

'Good. Er . . . very good.'

'Arthur, I'm sure you're busy. It's just that . . .' I turn, and through the window into the kitchen I can see out into the orchard. Kate is putting the letter back into the envelope. '. . . I'm sorry, Arthur. Really.'

'Sylvia, what is it?'

'Father. My father.' Such a momentous word.

'Is he okay?'

'Arthur, he's dead.'

It feels good, no, necessary, it feels necessary to be able to say it as if it happened yesterday so that in this moment, at least, someone else can share the enormity of it.

'I'm sorry to hear that. When did it happen?'

She's pushing herself out of the deckchair.

'Sylvia? Are you there?' He sighs. 'Sylvia, you really need

to talk to someone about this.' The 'someone' is someone else, not him. 'The trouble with you, Sylvia, is that you bottle it all up. I know you. You need to open up, really engage with it.'

He's right, of course. The trouble with me is . . . the trouble with me is me.

'I'd love to be able to do something to help but I . . .'

'Yes. Yes, I know,' I mutter, as I click the receiver back into place.

I remember now what it was my father said about Arthur. He said he had very clean hands.

20

There is something of a medieval St Stephen in the torso, with the sinuous white flesh and the twist of the body to make a dramatic line. He always knew how to get a good effect, did Arthur.

I peel the drawings away from each other, one by one. A drawing of a crumpled coat slides by. It took three hours one sticky afternoon during an entrance exam for college. I vigorously blended charcoal from dark to light and back to dark, stealing glances at the drawing of the boy opposite me as I worked. His was good, really good. It was Arthur's drawing I fell in love with first.

It's hard to believe that, after all this time, I'd dared to seek him out. What did I expect from him? Did I really think he could back up my story, tell me it was I who was right, not Joan, or was I somehow looking for my old self back, uncrumpled by loss, at a point in my life from when the script could be rewritten?

It's absurd. How could I overlook those chaotic weeks from long ago, before I got away, when he used to warn me? They were his words. 'I'm warning you, Sylvia.' He warned me I was not to hold him back. I was not to get in the way. His pupils were dilated and filled with intent before he headed out into the night. Later, when he returned, when we'd made up and he held me close, he warned me that he could not keep going without me. I lay awake caught between his need and my fear.

It doesn't take long to relearn lessons I learnt the hard way first time around. The taste of hurt is familiar.

And so, still in pursuit, I turn to this archive of drawings, and view each one from inside and out, flitting from one to another, praising a confident line, frowning at a weak one, forgiving myself for the naïvety of the effort. They're different from how I remember them, not better, not worse, just different. But, then, everything now is.

I used to try so hard back then. It was important that the drawings were strong, that they said something about the human condition. They had to move the viewer to look inside themselves and feel. Oh, God, the arrogance of it all. Now, nearly twenty years on, they lie here uselessly gathering dust under the bed, nothing more than a set of obscure references to the past.

I carried a bunch of drawings down to Da in his workshop when I was putting together my portfolio for art college. I defended each one at a hundred words a minute, but still he did not smile. Instead, he sighed heavily when we got to the ink drawing of him and said he had to let the cows out. After that, he was gone. I brought them back up here, shoved them under the bed, as if in disgrace, and refused to look at them for a week.

He dropped me off at the railway station on the day I moved to Dublin. He kissed my forehead on the platform. 'Do your best,' was all he said. I wrapped up those words with emigrant purpose and carried them with me through college and beyond, always trying to do my best. For him.

Kneeling on the floor, I sift through the drawings again, to track down that one of him, but he's nowhere to be seen.

'Sylvia? Are you up there?' Ma's back so I shuffle the pieces of paper together into piles and begin to slot them into the portfolio case. There, stuck to the back of one of the piles, is a small piece of airmail paper. I pull it carefully away. It's my father, mapped out with a minimum number of lines.

'Sylvia?'

The marks are fluid, moving from heavy and ink-filled to barely there, but the likeness disappoints. The eyes are dead and the mouth is inert. It's not how he was.

'I don't know what you do be doing up here like this all the time' – she's in the room now – 'and it a lovely evening outside, and what for Heaven's sake are the curtains doing open when the lights are on and people can see in?'

She's pulling over the curtains on a still bright evening. 'Kate's downstairs and the poor child hasn't eaten a thing since breakfast. I found her out on the street with Fred what's-his-name eating his crisps of all things.'

She turns on me suddenly. 'You look a bit peaky. Are you feeling all right?'

'Fine.'

'Come down for your tea now.'

If what Joan says is right about my father and I am wrong, why did no one ever tell me?

'Sylvia?'

Joan used to say that sometimes I'm not here, not really, not paying attention. She used to say that half the time my head is in the clouds, filled with notions, notions that will get me nowhere.

'Sylvia.'

The kindness has gone from the drawing. Joan has ruined it all.

'Sylvia. I'm talking to you.'

'What?'

149

'What is it? You look like you've seen a ghost.'

'Did you love him, Ma?'

'What did you say?'

'Da. Did you love him?'

Love. It feels like a word from science class that you nod along to but don't really understand. I scan Ma's face. I want her to exclaim, 'Yes, yes, yes. Yes, I loved him with all my heart, my soul and my body. I loved him every minute of every day from the moment we met until his last breath, and beyond.'

And yet I don't because I would be jealous of such passion. I don't know what I want. It's stupid of me to ask, so bloody stupid.

Ma sighs. Her knees creak as they bend and arrive on the floor opposite me. Her fists curl into the rug, bearing the weight of her, white behind the brown patches of her hands, and her cheeks hang loose from her skull. She sits back on her haunches and faces me. 'What is it, Sylvia child?'

'Did you love him? I just want to know did you love him.'

'Why, of course I did,' she says, with a tenderness that makes me squint. 'But he wasn't an easy man, Sylvia.'

'He loved us.'

'Yes, yes, he loved us. But it's easy to . . . Oh, Sylvia, he wasn't a bad man, far from it. But he had his own pain. It was hard.'

'What pain?'

'Well . . . there was his mother. He was only six at the time it happened. It must've been a terrible shock, God love him.'

I struggle to understand, to connect what she's telling me with what I think I know and with what the diary said.

'Sylvia, I tried to make him happy. God knows I did. But in the end there was not much I could do about it.'

We kneel facing each other, arms hanging uselessly, like actors in an amateur play who've forgotten their lines. I'm tired now and want this to be over. I should not have spoken.

'Come down and have your tea.' She sounds defeated. 'We can talk about this another time.'

'I'm not hungry.'

'But, Sylvia, you have to start trying to get yourself together now for the sake of . . .'

I put my hands over my ears and switch into the white noise of my brain. 'Don't.'

One Christmas, long ago, Joan and I were decorating the Christmas tree. It was our first real tree. We hauled kitchen chairs into the parlour to reach the upper branches and top it with the fairy. We fought over that job, me claiming the youngest child privilege, Joan the oldest. Da stepped forward, took the fairy from my podgy hands and placed her on the highest branch. We looked on silently, not daring to point out that she was crooked.

I asked Da then did he like Christmas. He was meant to tell me how he loved it. He was meant to regale us with tales of Christmases from his childhood, candles in windows, Wren Boys, presents of oranges in the toes of his Christmas socks, warmth and love.

'No,' he said. 'No' can be a long word.

'Why not, Da?' I was meant to make him like it. It was meant to be warm and snug for him, now that he had me.

He smiled his half-smile. 'Too many memories.'

Christmas was never the same after that. Da had a history, a life before us, a life that he carried around with him still, in his waking, in his sleeping, in his farmyard rituals, his visitations to Manning's, his knowing half-smiles, his half-knowing smiles, and there was nothing I could do about it.

But he had his own pain.

His mother.

It must have been a terrible shock.

This is the prologue of our family that has been buried over the years. Whatever it is, it has always been there and I, cosseted, head-in-the-clouds youngest one, I the baby, I didn't know it.

Did I?

21

Once Ma is gone, I dig out the diary again, the diary that I'm learning to hate, and wedge myself between the bed and the gable wall for as long as it's going to take. It doesn't take that long – just August in fact.

Aunty Sheila arrived last night (she's really Da's aunt). She seems really nice. She works as a nun in Sierra Leone. I only ever met her once before, around the time of my Holy Communion – she gave me rosary beads instead of money. This time she brought Miraculous Medals on chains for Sylvia and me. It took her three days to get here and she was really wrecked when she arrived. So after tea Ma brought her up to the gable room for an early night.

On the sideboard in the parlour, there's a framed picture of Aunt Sheila standing in front of the apple tree in the orchard with arms open like Mary in the Miraculous Medals she gave us. I never took much notice of it before.

She's one of those modern-type nuns that don't wear a habit. Her hair is so white, as is her skin. I don't know how she can be so pale when she lives under the African sun.

Aunt Sheila's skin was lightly lined, like tissue paper that had been scrunched up and smoothed out.

Ma said she thinks she is about eighty years old but no one knows for sure. This morning after breakfast, Aunty Sheila said that just the two of us should go for a walk on the beach.

When we walked with her, she'd try to get us to slow down, saying, 'If you knew what it felt like to be living in this decrepit body, you wouldn't walk so fast.'

She leaned on my arm all the way down the beach and told me about her life on the Missions. She built a hospital and tried very hard to get the African Chiefs to help her.

After Aunt Sheila died, we received a letter from a doctor at the hospital in Sierra Leone. Ma read it aloud at breakfast. The doctor wrote that Sister Sheila was 'one of the few unsung heroes of our time'. I remember thinking it was disrespectful that the table was covered with crumbs and rasher rinds while she was being commemorated.

She kept on making a great fuss about Sylvia and me being 'little women'. She said I take after Ma and Sylvia takes after Eithne, my father's mother. She died when Da was very small. Aunty Sheila said Eithne was a saint even though the Catholic Church might disagree. She could not cope after Da was born and everyone was very worried about her. Aunty Sheila had to go and help out even though she was only my age at the time. She cooked, cleaned and looked after the children. Eithne told her about a black crow that sat on her shoulder. She would walk for miles and miles cross-country on her own to shake him off but he always came back. After a year, she was more or less back to normal and Aunty Sheila could go home but Eithne got pregnant again a few years later. When Eithne was five months pregnant, she got up before dawn one morning, went out, put loads of stones in her pockets and walked into the sea. She drowned. It was nearly a week before her body was found.

The story gave me the creeps but of course I didn't say that to Aunty Sheila. She said it wasn't Eithne's fault and we shouldn't judge her, but to be honest I didn't really understand why she had to drown herself like that. It just didn't make sense. I began to think it wasn't true but when I told Ma about it, she said it did happen and made me promise not to tell Sylvia because we all know what she is like.

22

I lie buried in the darkness. The sea is a brutal blue-black force. It is groaning in my ear. The wind judders my bones, threatening terrible things. If I move, they will crumble, slowly falling in on themselves, like the skeleton of a city in a silent earthquake. I lie preserved by the night, waiting to be brought to the surface. I am tired. I've been here before, and now there is nowhere left to turn. Not to JP, high in the sky astride his big bridge. Not to Arthur, watertight in his white cube. Not to my father. Now, not even to my father. They have taken him from me too. I am nothing. I cannot move, strait-jacketed as I am by this stillness. I cannot shake the exhaustion, or the darkness. When I sleep, my dream is as empty as my awake. When I'm awake – or is it asleep? – the dark eyes in the ceiling regard me sadly. I am disappointed. I disappoint. I am nothing now.

Smoke rises from the bowl they left beside me. Funereal smoke. I watch it curl through the dimness, like the pain through my bones, until it is no more. I am tired. I have been here before. The sea is moving towards me, like a slow heartbeat. I wait for each wave. The spaces are long between them. The muffled hum of life goes on outside. People are talking out there, loosened up by drink, talking, talking, talking. Bells toll. On and on they toll. On and on they talk. Mossie Keogh's cows are treading over me towards some end point. I am tired in this darkness, tired, still and fatherless. Breathing is dragging its heels. The spaces are long and getting longer. The sea deepens its call.

She walked into the sea, merged herself with it and took on a wisdom that belongs to another place. The tide is approaching. I close my eyes and her body is there, polished by the water. Cows graze on the cliffs above. Clouds move in from the west and a crow has landed on her.

23

The fly on the ceiling is staring down at me. He doesn't move. Not even the white mist that covers every bit of the bathroom, making me the same colour as the water, can erase him. He is persistent, and procrastinating, like me. I am submerged. Only my breasts break the surface. I lie still for a long time to see which one of us will break first, the fly or me. In the end, I give in and move my legs to wring the last warmth out of the water. It clings to my thighs, like a stream over stones, and the scar on my belly skims the surface.

After the birth, they stitched me back together. I lay there listening to the sound of metal instruments. Then they washed me down the way you'd clean a corpse. Part of me got washed away that day and was never replaced. Later, long baths were my hideout. When Kate cried, I'd whoosh the water up with my legs to drown her need and the pain in my groin.

I pull myself out of the water, smashing through the stillness, and wrap a towel around my body. The water gurgles down the plughole. I head for the gable room. I step over drawings of the sea bookended by cliffs, the charcoal moving in motion with the waves more and more noisily with every drawing, until they no longer read as anything more than hopeless, deranged scribbles.

Ma and Kate are in bed. It's late, so late it's early. The morning air seeks out my nakedness until each hair is erect from cold, or is it fear?

I get dressed, thoroughly. Knickers, bra, T-shirt, jeans, jumper, socks, shoes. I name each item in a loud whisper so that I won't forget to put it on.

The house smells of freshly washed linen. It hardly dares to breathe. Downstairs in the hall, I reach for my coat from the stand. JP's anorak snuggles under it. I put that on instead, absorbing the smell of him. I wrap my scarf around my neck several times.

The bolts on the front door are stiff. Impatience wrestles with caution. A cool sweat gathers on my forehead. The door moans on opening. The morning enters the house and I enter it.

Outside, the sky is vast. A band of white light is pushing clods of dirty cloud up and out of the way. My shoulders rise and flesh hardens against the morning cold. I make my way down the road, up the steps, across the common land, where neighbours hang their washing on lines, and down on to the beach, to the point where water meets land, but it feels not far enough so I move down the beach, away from the stare of houses. Rocks, doubled in size by their reflection, sit at a distance. I must be careful. Reflections reveal some truths and hide others. The lighthouse on the horizon winks at me, promising to keep watch.

She stood at a shore out west, weighed down by the life in her belly. I must have known it.

I jerk off my shoes with my toes, just as I did when I was a child. The laces are too stubborn to open. They're not unlike my first walking shoes. My father, the father I knew, chopped the toes off them after four months of growing so that they'd see me through the summer.

I peel off my socks and take small, child-like steps into the water. The cold moves into me, seeping up through my jeans. Stones hurt my feet. I stand there like a new-born creature opening my eyes in a familiar world, until my legs are out for the count. A dog barks in the distance. A pink light glows in the east, like the last embers of a fire.

I move forward breaking up the appearance of reality with my steps. The cold massages my legs. The soles of my feet slip off the rocks they land on. Waves are approaching me, each new one slapping the old one on the back.

I brake suddenly. The water whips the shore impatiently.

Was this how it was for her? Did she hesitate? Was she afraid?

Water splashes my groin. I taste salt on my lips. This is far enough. Just here. No further.

My next step slides and twists. The pain of knee on rock takes over and I am down in the water, my arms, my body too. My feet have lost the feel of the rock beneath them and I strain my head towards the sky. My fingers are splayed and wild and my face smashes through the surface of the sea. Water is flooding around me, noisily leaking into my ears and my nose.

But I said, 'No.'

I begin to gag. Travelling across the fields on my father's shoulders.

Not yet.

My arms beat the water. JP's sideways, hopeful smile. The sea is dark and smooth and infinite. There's no beginning and no end. This is another place – a heaven, a hell, an afterlife, a before. 'I love your stars,' he said.

No.

So this is it. This is what it feels like. How long does it last? We stood on top of Croagh Patrick. Do you know when it's over or do you move seamlessly through so that before you know it you're viewing yourself from the other side? Breathlessly together we stood.

No.

Not yet.

Not now.

I'm not ready to go, to join the past – my father, my grandmother. They have all of eternity. They can wait some more for me.

No. I won't go. I will go back. I must go back.

It's darker here now. The sun has disappeared. It's too late.

Two large hands with splayed square-tipped fingers are coming towards me, entering this dark womb. They seem to take for ever. The water is trying to lull me to sleep but I force my eyes open for fear of losing sight of his fingers. He is here now. I knew he would come.

PART TWO

24

'And you were thinking what exactly, Sy?'

My sister fills the room like a Herculean monument, absorbing all the light. The bronze arms span the top of the dressing-table and the fingers stretch in a most impressive way. She takes to pacing the room, fanning her fingers as she speaks. The nails are of record length.

'There's Kate to think about for a start.' She swivels towards me. The eyebrows arch into sharp angles. The dark hair is lacquered and thick, the cheekbones are polished and the flesh is not quite flesh.

'It's not just about you any more, Sy. You're a mother now, and being a mother, well, it's a non-negotiable.'

It feels as though I'm watching afternoon TV, in which self-styled shrinks in brightly coloured suits set out to save unfortunate mortals like me.

'I thought you'd moved on. I really did.'

She's facing me now, hands on hips, as though she's expecting an answer, but my brain isn't working like hers. Hers is a well-oiled machine, logical and efficient. Mine can barely turn words into meaning.

I've been in a sleep, a deep fairy-tale sleep that separated and categorized everything into the correct compartments. 'Going under' went into 'then', and 'waking up' into 'now'. Life has a way of sorting itself into different chapters at significant moments: life before I married and life since, life before my father died, before JP left, and now life before I went under.

A small cast of characters appeared in my sleep – my grandmother, my father, my daughter, my husband, myself and the sea. My father as I knew him, with flat cap and dog, found my dead grandmother on the beach, not on the beach out west but on the beach at the end of this road. But it wasn't my grandmother who was dead, but Kate, her body rigid and pure like marble. But no, it was Kate, not my father, who found my grandmother's body, but when she rolled it over, it wasn't her body but mine and it was JP who found me. On and on the images revolved on a loop, each contradicting the previous, each character changing roles apart from my grand-mother, who was never anything but dead in the dream, always stone dead, all of the air in her expelled by water.

The bells for Mass told me I was awake, but I kept my eyes closed and worked hard on staying asleep. I needed more time.

And so I crafted a new dream, a waking dream built up of memories, layers and layers of memories of my father – fall-ing asleep on him during Mass, his night-time stories told slowly and carefully, one word at a time, the sight of a stooped back as he herded the cows, massaging his hands in a soapy lather, leaning on his stick as he read the evening sky, the light in his shed late at night, lacing up his boots in the hall, adrift in the yard in his shiny black suit, 'Do your best,' as I boarded the train for Dublin, late-night gravy sliding from his mouth, Ma tugging angrily at his boots, Tommy Carroll's 'Good man, Jimmy.'

With each picture came an impossible ball of grief, roll-ing up through me and exploding into the pillow. I gave myself over to them this time.

166

Then suddenly there was a new image: it was Da under the crimson glow of the Sacred Heart. His eyes were in shadow, his knees bent, his arms hanging like a puppet's. He swayed and Ma and I circled him, a circle of anxiety, ready to spring away from him should he swipe, and ready to jump forward should he fall. We weren't autonomous, Ma and I. We existed merely in relation to him.

'Why didn't you call me, Sy? I should've known something was up when I didn't hear from you, but I guess I thought you were in a better place now.'

Where had my sister learnt to speak like this? Has she been reading those self-help books or attending support groups? 'Hello. My name is Joan Keane and I am a control freak.'

Ma must have interrupted Joan's impossibly busy schedule for emergency talks. Clearly she had decided that things had 'got to that point' and she 'should've done it ages ago' and that Joan is 'the only one who can get through to her'. I'm happy for my sister. She'd have loved getting that emergency call in the early morning, before anyone else was awake. It would've penetrated her booked-up life in the most satisfying way. 'My sister needs me,' she'd have told her editor, in an early-morning call made from the car, followed by assurances that all deadlines would be met in total and on time. Far be it from my sister to let a little family crisis get in the way of her deadlines.

Something enters Joan's face, prompting a change of course. She forces a smile, revealing each one of her whitened teeth. Then she perches on the side of the bed, clasping an American Tan knee into place, and begins to stroke the quilt. Close up, her perfume is breathtaking.

'Sy? Do you remember the time we went to the amusements in Tramore?'

I wriggle further down into my bed.

'It was the day you got your Leaving Cert results. Bo drove us out. Remember?'

I shake my head petulantly.

'We dragged you on to the roller-coaster. You were screaming your head off and laughing and crying at the same time.'

I don't know what she's getting at, why she's pulling up this stuff to use against me. 'So?'

'Whenever I think of you and me, I think of that day. Oh, Sy, we had such a laugh back then, just the two of us. We were always egging each other on. And we used to talk about everything. You used to come to me with stuff, Sy. You used to trust me.'

'Did I?'

'Look, I know we're different. I'm seen as bolshie and all that and you, well, you're more sensitive.'

'You say it as if it's some kind of incurable illness.'

This makes her smile. 'No, I'm just saying you've got to get help. Professional help.'

'You mean drugs?'

'No. Well, maybe. If that's what you need.' She means drugs. Just like the last time. 'For God's sake, Sy, all anyone wants is for you to be happy.'

I heave myself up in the soggy bed. 'What time is it anyhow?'

'I don't know. Why . . .'

'Where's Ma?'

'I don't know.'

We both know Ma's in hiding. She sent in the big guns and retreated with her hands over her ears.

'Yes, you do. Stop treating me like some kind of kid, Joan.'

'No, I don't. Sy, can we talk about –'

'How's Brian?'

'Brian's fine. Francie's fine. Everyone's fine. Now, Sy, we're here to talk about *you*.'

'What about me?'

She's back on her feet. 'What about you? What about you fucking topping yourself?'

'I didn't top myself,' I say, with a pitch-perfect note of injury.

'You tried to.'

'No, I didn't.' I fold back the quilt and feel the cold of the lino on my feet.

'Sy, you can't even swim, for God's sake.'

'And is it any wonder?' I'm on my feet now and gaining ground.

'What do you mean?'

'When were you going to tell me, Joan?'

'Tell you what?'

'About Eithne.'

'Eithne?'

'Our grandmother.'

She's flicking through the files in her brain, trying to recall what she knows, what I don't know, what I'm supposed to know, what I'm not supposed to know. She turns to look out of the back window into the orchard in which once, as very small girls, we made apple-blossom bouquets for each other and used them to practise the Bridal March, taking turns to be the bride.

'When were you going to tell me about our grandmother drowning herself? That's what. Don't you think that's something I might want to know, Joan?'

'How do you know?' This is a different voice, a voice that sounds like it's breaking into little particles.

I go over to the dressing-table and prise open the top drawer. Inside, crouching under my underwear, lies the diary. I tap her arm with it. She turns and looks at it in my hand, hesitating. To claim it makes everything undeniable, but she takes it anyway.

'I don't need drugs,' I say, leaning into her. 'Just the truth.'

I wrap a dressing-gown around me and leave the room for the first time since I didn't die.

25

I take refuge in a bath, yet another. The fly is gone. Maybe he drowned.

Ma took me and put me in a bath of hot water after I was pulled out of the sea, washing every bit of me as if I were newly born. 'Oh, sweet Jesus, Mother of God. Oh, sweet divine mercy,' she muttered, over and over, in a gentle lament above my head. When she was finished, she opened the door to where Kate was standing and told her to keep an eye on me as she pulled some things out from the back of the hot press and brought them downstairs.

I could not meet my daughter's eyes so I kept my head bent as I listened to the words passed back and forth between my mother and the man who had brought me from the sea. They were sparse and low, but I knew the tone. A verdict was being reached. I was alive. God had spared me.

Strange how the water feels more like home now. I sink down into it until it strokes my chin. I need more time. Everything's happening too fast now that Joan has arrived. She and Ma are in the kitchen, discussing my case over mugs of cold tea. Poor Ma. What did she do to deserve this, she's asking.

My sister is down there telling Ma how I need to be thinking and feeling from now on. Ma is nodding along. How Joan must be loving it. I wonder is Kate with them or has she been set some task to make her disappear for a while? It's the kind of thing my sister does.

I take a nailbrush and begin to scrub my body, starting with my feet and moving upwards, covering myself with small, circular movements until new, raw skin is born.

Da used to warn me not to go too near the sea. He said that it lulls people in, they fall under its spell. 'It can turn on you at any moment,' he said. 'It's not to be trusted.'

But below the surface there was a different kind of place, unlike anywhere I'd ever known. Silent shafts of sunlight danced before me and through them came the hands. JP's name rose to the surface as mute bubbles. It felt safe in a bizarre way, terrifyingly safe.

It was a brief moment of insanity. It's hard to know what I was looking for. Some kind of serenity, maybe, like returning to the womb before the madness began. Or maybe I was just curious. Or maybe I was trying to understand.

I scrub my body until the red flesh overtakes the white. I know I should be thankful now for the hands that reached through the water to pull me out in those seconds before unconsciousness, and for the slaps on my face that opened my eyes and showed me the astonishing blue sky with swallows darting in and out of my frame.

But it was not JP who rescued me. It was old man Thady Walsh, spitting, cursing and muttering about the damned sea. He had pulled his dead son out of that water ten years ago, and today I had dragged him back in. I'm no compensation for his loss. He was angry, God love him, angry it was me, and I was disappointed he was not my husband.

I scrub myself even more vigorously, but the shame won't go away.

He hauled me on to my feet. His stubble grazed my face.

It was hard to stand up. It was the shock of it all. I faltered on the first few steps, and when I looked up, Kate was standing before me in her pink jacket, looking like she was dressed for school, right there, staring at me with her big, soft eyes.

There's a knock at the bathroom door.

'Sy?'

'What?'

'Will you be long?'

'For ever.'

Joan stomps down the corridor and I whoosh the water up over me, wincing at the sting of it on raw flesh.

Kate must've seen it all – me, her mother, sitting like a rag doll on the beach, convulsed by coughing, my wet hair falling over my face, making wet patches on the sand. She must've known how close I'd come to blackness. God forgive me. I never meant this legacy to be hers.

She'd followed me all the way up from the beach. Later, after my bath, when Ma brought me down to the gable room, having towelled the life out of me and dressed me in one of her flannel nightgowns all ready for bed, Kate was there, rummaging frantically through JP's wet coat, which lay in the middle of the floor.

'Kate, what are you doing?' Ma shouted at her.

'They're not here.'

'What's not here?'

'There's only Dad's mobile and this.' The wet green-blue button lay on her palm, like a rare insect smelling of the sea.

'Kate child, what in God's name are you looking for?'

But before Kate could answer, Thady Walsh was calling a

goodbye from the bottom of the stairs and Ma was asking God to bless and spare him as she headed down to him.

'Kate, what is it?' I hardly dared ask.

'The stones. There were stones in her pockets when she walked into the sea.'

26

From where I'm sitting on my daughter's bed, I can see my sister gesticulating her way around the orchard while talking on her mobile phone. I wonder what she's trying to get the caller to understand. It can't be easy for her living in a world of people so much less intelligent than herself. But for now I'm grateful she's preoccupied.

She'd sprung on me, like a wild animal, earlier, once she'd finished with the diary.

'Did you read this?' she'd demanded, holding the book high in the air, when all I'd wanted was to know where Kate was.

'Kate is downstairs. Did you read this?'

'Who's she with?'

'Why are you interested all of a sudden? She's with that mutt of hers, teaching him his bloody alphabet for all I know. Now, did you read this or didn't you?'

'Of course I read it.'

'Well, you'd no right. Where did you get it?'

I shrugged. Shrugging drives my sister crazy.

'Sy, will you leave your nails alone and tell me where you got it?'

'It just sort of turned up.' God knows what Joan would do if she knew Kate had read it too. 'Besides, what's the big deal? We all knew you couldn't wait to get away from here. I just don't know why you had to go on about Da like that.'

She laughed her mean little laugh. 'Oh, my dear Sy. You

would say that, wouldn't you? You were always Daddy's little girl.'

I struggled between wanting to cry and wanting to slap her.

'You were there, Sy. You know how it was.' She squinted at me closely. 'Or don't you? God, you don't, do you? You don't remember. You're so in denial. No wonder you're the way you are.'

I'm at the top of Kate's bed, near the window, with a bowl of stew in my lap and Kate's backpack at my feet. Comfort food. I stole it from a pot on the stove while Joan and Ma were busy in the back kitchen. Joan likes being busy down here. She likes to think that we can never really cope without her. Her busyness makes up for the loss of chaos that's so much part of her city life. She regularly has to take a call out in the orchard and she returns huffing and puffing with a work problem that is 'too complicated to explain'. I kept away from her after the diary exchange, hiding out in the gable room with my watercolours, painting pictures of a baby Kate from a curled-up photograph, avoiding questions I cannot yet answer.

When Joan and I were young, we used to share this room that Kate now sleeps in, until such time as my sister insisted on getting a room of her own. We called it 'the blue room', but as an adult, I can see that it's more grey than blue. The window comes up from the floor, and beyond the orchard you can see the sea. At night-time, we would stare really hard to find the line where the sea started and the sky ended. There are still two single beds in the room and a narrow space between them, and we used to hold hands across it. Not often, mind. When the moon was out, it shone through the curtains, illuminating the blue and white pattern of a cottage in the woods and Joan would scare me with stories about things that happened in that cottage. Joan was always good at making up stories.

The pile of drawings at the end of Kate's bed has grown. When I look at them closely, they're all of the same four figures, five if you count the dog. A tall man in the middle is flanked on each side by two little girls, one with long yellow hair and the dog and the other with glasses and freckles. I'm the only one who changes position. In some drawings I'm in the middle, right up close to JP. In others, I'm at a distance and smaller than everyone else. Sometimes I'm holding a paintbrush. Sometimes I'm not.

I stir the stew aimlessly around the bowl in my lap while waiting for Kate, picking up a spoonful of the goo, complete with carrot, meat and spud, and watching it plop back down. I make myself put some into my mouth and pull out the spoon. The food lingers behind my teeth, waiting to be admitted, until eventually I swallow. My throat tightens around it on the way down.

Steam clings to the window, and through it, I see Kate holding a washing basket up for Ma in the evening sun. The steam condenses into drops and my daughter crystallizes into a sort of mosaic, standing there, waiting patiently for Ma to drop the last peg into the basket before they head inside for dinner.

I look at the drawings again and realize that the small figure in the corner is in fact Ma, with her soft curls and apron, not me. There is no me.

A picture of a wide-eyed girl is on the front of Kate's backpack – huge head, tiny body. Her cuteness is a kind of deformity. The bag has been sitting here since it came up from the beach with Kate yesterday morning, all packed and ready to go. I saw it last night on my way back to bed. It sat staring up at me, a riddle that needed to be solved. I had seen it before, of course. I know what it contains. Clothes neatly folded for the journey ahead. Toothbrush and pyjamas and clean underwear, each item packed with detailed anticipation. I lay awake last night, wondering how she was planning to travel. By train or bus? Did she have a lift to the station? How much money did she have? Did JP know she was coming, or was she heading blindly into the day? Is she still planning to leave?

I am tempted to open the bag, understand the specifics of my daughter's plans to leave me, but I don't. I will wait. I can guess at much of the story. The clues have been there all along.

My stew is thickening. I should try to eat some more but I'm too nervous. I'm not sure what I'm going to say. I don't want to interrogate her. I don't want to scare her. I drove out JP and now I may drive her away too. Who could blame her? I would've upped and left here long ago if I were her. No, I have no right to point a finger. It's me that's to blame. I gave her no choice. It's time to try to put things right, if it's not too late for that, but I don't trust myself. I'm emptied out in every way. So I just sit here stirring my stew, waiting and hoping that some-how something happens before the pink bag in front of me detonates into little pieces.

I straighten at the sound of the fifth stair. Kate stalls in the doorway on seeing me.

'Kate?'

She closes the door slowly behind her and glues her back to it. Maybe she thought that I as good as died back there. Maybe she figured she'd never have to deal with me again, her inconvenient burden of a mother. I take a breath.

'Hi, Kate. What are you up to? Have you been helping your gran?'

Her palms are flat against the door. She's looking at the girl with the oversized head on her bag.

'Your bag's packed. Were you going somewhere?'

Her eyes are shiny.

'Kate, were you going to . . . Were you planning to leave?'

She nods slowly at the girl.

'Was it because of me, because of what I did?' I know this is wrong. This bag was packed before I ever walked into the sea, but the sequence of things seems immaterial now.

Kate shakes her head and continues to stare at the bag.

'But . . . where were you going? Were you going to Dublin?'

She shakes it again, forlornly. I want to prise her open, but I must wait.

'But where were you going, Kate?' I'm pleading now. 'Kate, please.'

Her knees hit the floor and she crawls over towards the bag on all fours. The zip growls on opening. She searches between the clothes and pulls out a brown envelope with 'Miss Kate Larkin' and Ma's address in capital letters on it. She hands it to me, without looking at me, or it.

'Are you sure?'

She nods and sits back on her heels. It's just one page, handwritten on a pristine piece of letterhead from JP's company. I can see JP writing at his desk at home in Dublin. He takes pleasure in his handwriting, and when he finishes a word, he goes back to lovingly cross the *t*s and dot the *i*s, as if he's icing a cake. I swallow and prepare to read the letter aloud. Kate seems to expect this.

'My dearest Kate,

 I'm writing this note from Drogheda. I came up here to build the Bridge Man. It's really taking shape and will be the most beautiful bridge in Ireland once it's finished. I'm sharing a flat with two men I work with, just for the time being. They are good company but I miss you very much indeed.

 I'm sorry I had to leave in such a hurry without saying goodbye. I hope you will forgive me. I think of you every day and try to imagine what you are doing. I imagine you are helping Gran in the garden and that Monty is getting good long walks. I hope that you are being a good girl for your mother. She needs you to be good and strong now and I know that you will be that for her.'

Kate's head is gently tilted to one side, as if she were listening to a piece of exquisite music. Her eyes follow mine as they move across the page. The words are becoming hazy.

'I don't know how long this job will take or when I will get to see you in Dublin. Let's hope it won't be too long. Perhaps you could write me a letter to my address in Drogheda which is: Flat 1, 5 Oliver Place, West Street, Drogheda.

 It would be lovely to hear from you. I love you very much and I look forward so much to seeing you again.

 Your loving

 Dad'

A drop lands on the page, somewhere between 'loving' and 'Dad'. I read the letter again, this time to myself. JP misses Kate. He loves her very much and he needs her to be strong now. Why now?

'When did you get this?'

An image of an empty bed lands before my eyes, a kitchen

table with just the two of us sitting at it, Kate and me, a garden with no JP in it, and I am sick with the impossible fear of it.

'Tommy gave it to me.'

Their little secret.

'I see.'

It was JP who had written to Kate, not Brigid. JP misses Kate. Of course he does. And he isn't at home in Dublin. He's in Drogheda.

Kate gets up and brings herself to the other end of the bed. Nothing is as I thought. Life has been moving on, away from me, without my knowing. Everything has changed.

'The Bridge Man,' says Kate.

And it is all my own doing. 'Sorry?'

'I was going to go to Dad at the Bridge Man, the one he told us about, the most beautiful bridge in Ireland.'

'How were you going to get there?'

'By bus, then another bus, then a train and then a bus.'

'And nobody knew?'

'I couldn't tell you. You wouldn't have let me go. And Gran would just keep on sighing and crying and stuff. I couldn't tell Dad because he said I had to take care of you.'

'He did?'

'He said you needed me. Same thing. I tried to phone his office this morning, when they were in the orchard.'

'You did?'

'Well, I had to do something. If I didn't, something really bad was going to happen, just like in the little blue book. I had to tell Dad. I had to phone him at work because his mobile phone is here.'

'But where did you get the number?'

'It's on the top of the letter. I know it off by heart.'

'And what did he say?'

'I didn't get to talk to him. This man answered the phone. He was really cross. I said, "Can I speak to my father, please?" really nicely, and he just said, "And who might your father be?" I told him it was Mr Larkin, and he said he was off out on site, these days, and he'd tell him I called and then he just hung up.'

'And did Dad call you back?'

'No. Not yet. I wanted to phone back the cross man and say, "You don't understand. I have to talk to my dad now because there's been an accident."'

'An accident?'

'Fred said that's what people say. They say there's been an accident because an accident can mean anything. It can mean that someone has fallen off their bicycle and hurt their knee, or it can mean that your mother has nearly drowned for good. Actually, I really wanted to say, "My mother could die and we really need Dad," but then they came back in from the orchard and it was too late.'

'Why was it too late?'

'Aunty Joan watches me all the time, like she's a hungry dog. She's always telling me what to do. "Sit up straight, Kate. Don't drag your feet, Kate. Finish all your corn flakes, Kate." And when she's not telling me what to do, she's up here telling you what to do. That's what Gran says anyway.'

'And you didn't tell Gran what you were doing?'

'No. I didn't. That's my thing. Well, it's our thing now.'

I smile and hold my arms out, but this makes Kate more agitated. 'No, Mam.'

'No what?'

'No, it's not funny. We have to do something. Fred says we have to do something.'

'Fred? You told Fred?'

'I didn't tell anyone. Only Fred.'

'What's Fred got to do with it?'

'I had to. He got me the bus times and the train times and he lent me the money. We have to go. Don't you see?'

'See what?'

'The accident was a sign.'

'A sign of what?'

'We have to leave here. If we don't, it'll be just like in the little blue book.'

I hold my arms out for her again and this time, unbelievably, she enters them and places her head on my shoulder. Her bones feel so small under my hands. I pull her nearer to me and feel the bowl of cold, wet stew leak into my lap and spread out between us.

27

We're going to find JP. For whatever reason, love or guilt, hope or fear, want or need, I promised Kate that I would drive us to him and, with that, I stepped over to the other side, to a place there's no returning from. I sat on her bed and promised her we'd be a proper family again. I hesitated on the 'again'.

In the dim evening light, her face blossoms into a smile, a smile that binds me to my promise, a promise that now overrides everything. In years to come, that smile will be yet another milestone to catalogue all life events into befores and afters. Now I'm in the after of my promise to Kate, my first promise since she was born. Her birth was a sort of promise in itself, a promise I could hardly take the weight of.

I sleep the sleep of the dead after that and dare to dream of JP. I lie hammocked in his arms, and let him breathe for me. The longing wakes me, but when I open my eyes, the dark, breathing mound is missing. It's somewhere in a narrow bed in a bachelor flat in Drogheda. I must find him.

'When?' Kate asks. The word is as soft as the wind.

'Sorry?'

'When will we leave?'

'Friday.'

'That's ages away.'

'Kate, I need that time.'

'For what?'

'Well, I need to learn to drive better for a start. It's a long journey and I've never done any long-distance driving before. I've never even driven on my own.'

'But you'll have Monty and me. You won't be on your own.'

'I've never driven without someone in the car who knows how to drive. I've got to practise so that I can get us there safely.' I need to learn to drive without believing that every corner could bring death. 'You understand that, don't you?'

She nods, barely.

'Besides, Gran has been very good to both of us. We can't just run away suddenly without explaining to her and saying a proper goodbye.' I need to be able to come back. 'Please be patient with me.'

She nods again. 'Okay then. Friday.'

And, with that, she presses an invisible stopwatch. If we're not out of here by Friday, we could implode for good – Kate could kick off or run away, or I could come up with all the reasons why it's just not possible, reasons that become part of my history and my future. I could lose my nerve for good, and there goes the happy family ending.

I need something to do between now and Friday, something to focus on, to quell the fantasy I don't dare have of my husband at the end of a long bridge with arms outstretched, saying, 'I always knew you would come,' as he combs my hair with his fingers, or the fears that he and Kate will join hands and go home together, shutting the front door in my face. There can be no room in my head for what may happen.

Bo gives me a hard time when I phone him.

'I thought you wanted me to piss off,' he says, with mock injury.

'Look, Bo. I need your help. I've got to get out of here by the end of the week.'

'Intriguing. So what's brought this on all of a sudden?'

'I have to find JP.'

'JP? The husband? Why? Did you lose him?'

'Don't let on to me you haven't heard, Bo. JP left going on two weeks ago.'

'And what makes you think he wants to be found?'

'I don't know that he does but that's the chance I have to take.'

'Do you know where he is?'

'He's north of Dublin, working on a bridge.'

'I see. And how are you going to get there?'

'Well, this is where I need your help. JP left his car behind and I need to drive it to him.'

'And?'

'Well, as you know, I'm only learning to drive. I need a bit more practice. I wonder could you bring me out in JP's car a couple of times?'

'My dear, are you out of your sweet little mind? Look, I'll drive you. I've nothing else on other than Project Grandma.'

'No, no, no. I have to do this on my own. Me and Kate. I promised.'

The knock on the front door makes Monty bark.

'Oh, bless us and save us. Who is that now at this hour?' Ma blesses herself three times in a frenzied formation. Joan is at the door before me.

'Well, well, well, if it isn't the beautiful Bo. What a sight for sore eyes. Come in, come in.' She drags him by the sleeve

186

as far as the kitchen table. 'Mother, you remember Robert Quirke, don't you?'

'Ah, Robert, of course I remember you. I'm sorry to hear about your poor father. He was a true gentleman, so he was,' says Ma, half standing and fumbling at the strings of her apron.

'And this is Sylvia's only child, Kate. Kate, say "hello",' says Joan.

'Hello.'

'Hello, Kate. Pleased to meet you.' Bo holds out a hand with silver rings wrapped around each finger. They shake hands.

'So sit down, sit down,' sings Joan, as if she has called a meeting and needs to press on. Everyone obeys.

'Now, Bo, it's so good to see you after all this time. You haven't changed a bit – well, apart from the hair.'

'Joan!'

'Well, you know what I mean, Sy.' She sounds only mildly embarrassed. 'You had such gorgeous blond curls, Bo. We used to call you our little Cupid.'

'I remember.' Bo grins. 'So what brings you back to base?'

'Oh, you know how it is, Bo, family stuff. Sometimes I get called in. But we're all doing okay now.' My sister smiles a wide anchorwoman smile around the table. Kate tries to rub out what's left of the ducks on the oilcloth with a wet middle finger and Ma chases the teabags around the teapot with a spoon.

'Bo, we're being very rude altogether. Won't you have a cup of tea?'

'No, thank you, Mrs Keane.' He stands up and slides his chair back under the table. 'I'm just here to bring Sylvia out for a spin and a bit of a driving lesson, I believe. Sylvia, are you ready?'

'Sylvia girl, you're not going to drive, are you?' says Ma.

'I hope so.' I slide my chair under the table to meet Bo's.

'As if things aren't bad enough as they are. Sylvia child, you don't drive.'

'Yes, she does,' says Kate. 'She's learning. She's very good. I saw her. Fast. She's very fast.'

'God almighty. Since when did this happen?'

'Ma, it's all right. She's been learning for a while,' says Joan.

'Well, no one told me anything of this. What car are you taking?'

'She's going in Dad's,' says Kate.

'But, Kate child, she's not insured.'

'Of course she is,' I say. Somehow it's easier to lie in the third person.

Bo turns to Kate. 'Kate, would you like to come with us?'

'Sylvia, no. Leave Kate here,' says Ma. 'Things can always –'

'Did JP put you on his insurance?' asks Joan.

'I know, Ma,' I say. 'But it's okay. Bo'll be doing most of the driving and he's an outstanding teacher, aren't you, Bo? Really careful.'

'Can Monty come?' asks Kate.

'That's up to Bo.'

'Is he a good traveller?'

'Outstanding.'

Kate grabs Monty's lead from the coat-stand, I swing open the front door and, before Ma and Joan can protest any more, all four of us are out on the street.

*

JP's navy Volvo has been sitting glumly outside Ma's house since the night he left, abandoned, like a child that somebody forgot to pick up from school. It is evidence for the village, if evidence were needed, that something happened that night, something against the natural order of things that made everything stand still for a while.

I pass the car keys to Bo but his hands stay deep in his pockets.

'You must start as you mean to go on, Mrs Larkin.'

'Aw, come on, Bo, it probably won't even start for me. And if Ma sees me getting in behind the wheel, she'll have a bright yellow canary.'

'She's going have to get used to it if you're serious about doing this.'

Kate stands beside him, ears wide open.

'But what'll the neighbours think?'

'Fuck the neighbours.'

I dart my eyes sideways towards Kate to warn Bo – *No 'fucking' in front of the child, please* – but there's a wide grin on her face. She likes Bo Quirke.

Getting started is a palaver, making this machine fit me, adjusting the seat, the mirrors, finding the levers, the wipers, the lights, the horn, shit, that's the horn, rehearsing with the gear stick, tugging on the safety-belt, introducing the pedals to my feet. It feels as if I'm breaking into a stolen car. The windows fog up and I wipe a view with my sleeve. Throughout all this I ignore Ma, visible as a shadow through the net curtains in the parlour.

At last I turn the key and the engine begins to hum.

'She's happy,' says Bo.

'Glad someone is.'

I press pause on my breathing and lift my foot slowly from the clutch. Amazingly, the wheels turn and we pull away.

'There's Fred,' calls Kate, from the back. The boy's sitting on the Powers' wall, kicking his heels against the pebble-dash. I accelerate away from him.

Once out of the village and past the first few bends, at which I brake and jerk us all forward and back, muttering apologies and curses, I begin to breathe normally. A car overtakes from behind, unannounced, and skims past me.

'Where the hell did he come from?'

No one answers.

We take the coast road, the same road Bo and I drove not so long ago, past the stone walls, the cattle chewing on the horizon and through the tree tunnels. That was when JP was around, Kate was taken care of, Ma wasn't on my case and I, looking back, I had it easy.

We pass the graveyard and the big, beckoning blue of the sea. After a while, we approach the viewpoint where we stopped that day. The dark cliffs drop down to the sea, pro-tecting the beach, shielding its secrets.

'Sylvia.'

A car is coming towards me. Its lights are facing mine.

'Sylvia.' Bo's hand is on the steering-wheel. I brake and swerve back to my side of the road. Its horn is shrill as it passes.

'Are you all right? Do you want to stop?'

'No, no. I'm fine.' I'm going to puke.

Bo turns around. 'Are you still alive back there, Kate?'

'Yes, thanks.'

'Are you sure you don't want to stop, Sylvia?'

'I'm sure.'

After a while the countryside becomes cluttered again with man-made stuff – signs, bungalows, sheds, fences, garages, shops, roundabouts, paths, more signs. A dolly-mixtures row of houses appears at the water's edge in the distance.

'Fancy an ice-cream, Kate?'

'Yes, please.'

Ice-cream means stopping. That means braking and gears and things I can't be dealing with right now. There's space on the side of the road. I brake, pull in, brake again and tug up the handbrake. We jerk forward as one.

'That was quick.'

'She wants an ice-cream, doesn't she?'

'Yeah, but we could've –'

'What?'

'Nothing.'

Bo presents Kate with an ice-cream shaped like an Olympian torch.

'Now, my dear, get your delicate little jaw around that.'

'Thanks, Bo.'

Then he sits on the bench beside me and takes out a cigarette.

'Sylvia?'

The cliffs are still hanging before my eyes, like curtains. It feels like they've been there all along, but I can't recall. 'Can I have a cigarette?'

'I thought you didn't partake?'

'I do now.'

I suck my cheeks in as Bo lights the cigarette and soak up the smoke floating through me. There's a boy on the beach below the cliffs. He's not alone.

'Kate, please don't tell your grandmother about your mother smoking, or your aunty Joan, because they'll only blame me,' Bo's saying to Kate, who's staring at me over the furrows of her ice-cream. Monty sneezes in disapproval.

'What about Dad?'

'Especially not your father. Just don't tell anyone. Ever.'

'Monty knows.'

'We trust Monty,' says Bo, patting Monty's head.

Kate and Monty walk to the edge of the water to look at the boats in the harbour.

'Feeling better now?' asks Bo.

I nod.

'God bless nicotine. Works every time. So, tell me this. What do your mother and Joan think about you going after JP?'

'They don't know.'

'You're going to have to tell them.'

'They're going to kill me.'

'Why so?'

'They just will. They think I'm losing it. They think JP has left before. They think he makes a habit of it.'

'And does he?'

'No. I told Ma that just to get her off my back. Besides, Joan's not talking to me at the moment.'

'Oh, I wouldn't mind Joan. She was always a bit volatile. What's her problem this time?'

'Long story.'

We sit and watch people walking by in ice-cream-licking fleshy packs.

'It wasn't meant to be like this, Bo, was it?'

'Like what?'

'You and me, stuck here at home with our mammies.'

'And is that so bad? Our mammies are the place we land, Sylvia. They save us from falling off the earth completely.'

'And they scrutinize your every action. They try to tell you how to live your life when you don't know what the hell you're doing yourself. They add to all the confused, contradictory voices when you just need them to be quiet. They can't help it, I know. They're made that way.'

'But you're a mammy, Sylvia.'

'Your point is?'

'They're just looking out for you, that's all.'

'But don't you get bored, Bo? Frustrated? Sneaking out of the house for a breather. You should be out there in the world, doing your thing.'

'I'm alive,' says Bo, chin into chest.

'It's just you're such a talented designer. There's a million things you could be doing.'

He turns to me and I could swear his eyes are wetter than normal.

'Sylvia, this morning I brought my mother up a cup of tea in bed, sweet and milky, just the way she likes it. She said to me, "You're a good son." That's what she said. I'm a good son, just because I gave her a cup of tea, I who robbed from his friends to get a drink, who woke on a different carpet every morning and drank out of half-empty glasses with cigarette butts floating around in them for a cure. If she only knew. I'm thirteen months sober today. Ma doesn't know that when my brother clicks open a can of beer during the nine o'clock news headlines, as he does every single night, I have to rally whatever is left inside me not to get wasted. Sometimes I just want to toss over the table I laid beautifully for our tea, go out and get hammered, but I somehow manage not to. I'm terrified that some day my granny will die or Ma will make me cry again or whatever, and there won't be any more self-control to be found. These days, Sylvia, I aim to be boring. As for being a good son, that's more than I could have dreamt of. But, you know, I'm sober, not for my mother or my granny but for me, because at the end of the day, I know I want to live.'

'I'm sorry.'

'Don't be.'

I inhale on my fag all the way up to the filter and twist my foot over the stub.

'Come on,' I say. 'We'd better head back before they lock me up like Mr Rochester's mad wife.'

28

The suitcases sit beside each other on the bed, like a couple who have not spoken for a long time. Joan and Ma don't yet know about us leaving. Kate and I avoided the question again today by driving with Bo up the mountains to a long white ribbon of a waterfall that divided them in half. It was Bo who drove us up the steep, winding roads, not me. Once there, he and Kate set off on foot towards the waterfall. They tried to get me to go with them but one glance upwards at the stone wall of mountain before us made me feel weak. I waited for them stretched out on an earthen table, looking at the clouds skirting past the sun.

I made Kate promise she wouldn't let Ma or Joan know anything about our plans and told her to leave the talking to me. It won't be long, however, before the dam against her excitement bursts. I'd planned to tell them over dinner this evening, with all four of us around the table. I was going to say it out straight, 'We're leaving the day after tomorrow,' just like that, followed by a big full stop to block any blabbering or backtracking. I was going to have to be firm to deflect their whys and what-ifs, their knowing looks towards each other and their superior common sense. But when it came to the time, one sigh from Ma, a simple sigh, not relating to anything that was said before it, just a stand-alone sigh filled with a weariness of its own, was all that was needed for my courage to leave the table.

I pile my unworn skirts and dresses into my case, followed by the staple jeans and T-shirts. I always pack more than I wear, or wear less than I pack. The anticipation is more expansive than the reality. I've never packed for JP before. It would've seemed too intrusive somehow. I bring a sleeve of his shirt to my nose. It smells of the sun. I pull his clothes down one by one and carry them over to his case just as Joan walks in.

'Well, well, well, what have we got going on here? Planning the great escape?'

'What's it to you?'

'What's it to me?' She lands on the side of the bed and we're in. 'I only had to put my life on hold, cancel assignments, farm out my son, because my kid sister decides to walk into the sea and you ask what's this to me?'

'Well, I apologize for the inconvenience but nobody asked you to.'

'Well, actually, they did. Ma did. She begged me to come down here. I don't think you have a clue what you put that poor woman through. As for your daughter . . .'

'You leave my daughter out of this.' I pull open the top drawer of the dressing-table.

'Are you going back to JP?'

I scoop up the last of my stuff in silence.

'Is he expecting you?' My socks and underwear rain into the suitcase. 'He doesn't know, does he? You haven't spoken to him, have you? Jesus, Sy, why do you always have to make things so hard for yourself? He walked out on you and now you're going to go running after him.'

'It's not like that.'

'It's just like that. It's just like Arthur all over again.'

'This has got nothing to do with Arthur.'

'I told you to get out back then. I told you he was bad news. But no. You had to follow him to the other side of Europe in search of some impossible romantic dream. He was the one who gave you that scar. Admit it. Well, very fetching, if you're into that kind of thing.'

'JP is not Arthur.'

'I know he's not but I just don't want to see you get hurt again. You need to be careful, protect yourself a little, take it step by step. I worry about you, Sy. I don't want you going back to that place you were in.'

'What place?'

'All I want is for you to be happy.'

'What fucking place?'

'You know, after Kate was born . . .'

I zip up my case in one swoop.

'You don't remember, do you? Jesus, Sy. Talk about denial.'

'Denial? What's this with you and denial? I'll tell you about denial, Joan. Denial gets me up in the morning. Denial keeps everything on a level, just like the drugs you'd have me take. Denial makes everything just about bearable. I don't even know what's truth and what's not any more – and you know what? I don't want to know. I envy you, Joan. I really do. You look at everything head on. You never flinch. You never waver. Well, bully for you.'

Joan's looking at me as if I were the climax of some kind of epic film and she's hanging on to see how it will end.

'Look.' I land beside her on the bed. 'JP didn't walk out on me.'

'But I thought –'

'I told him to fuck off.'

'Big deal. I tell Brian to fuck off every day of the week. I think he likes it, actually.'

'This is different. I made him leave.'

'And what? You thought he'd be back by now?'

'I don't know what I thought, Joan, but right now I have to try to make things right for Kate's sake, if not my own. Kate has to see her father soon and I have to see him too. Before it's too late.'

'Too late for what?'

'Too late for him and me. I never meant . . . I don't know what I meant but, yes, I'm going after him. And, Joan, I have to tell Ma myself, when the time is right.'

'All right. But she needs to know.'

'And I will tell her.'

Joan's arm is reaching for my shoulders. 'Why don't you just phone JP first?' She sounds weirdly gentle. 'What's with all this cloak-and-dagger stuff?'

'No, no, no. I can't. He won't talk to me.'

'You were the one who told him go. You just said it.'

'He hates me.'

'He doesn't hate you. He idolizes you. He always has, the fecking eejit.'

My head falls on to her shoulder, right up close to her neck. She manages to let me stay there, without talking or telling me what to do, until my breathing flattens out.

'What does "cloak-and-dagger" mean?'

Kate's standing in the frame of the door with JP's toothbrush and razor in her hand.

Joan rushes to take the razor from her. 'Kate, what are you doing here?'

'I wanted to help Mam pack. I didn't want her to forget anything. Mam, Dad's anorak is back down in the hall. Gran washed it after, you know, the accident. Will I go and get it?'

'No, Kate, we'll pick it up when we're leaving.'

'But what if we forget it?'

'We won't. I promise.'

Kate goes over to the dressing-table, pushes her whole body against the top drawer to close it and pulls out the bottom drawer where the rest of JP's clothes live. She piles pullovers and T-shirts into her arms without letting them unfold and lowers them into his suitcase. She sprinkles them with socks and underwear. She carries his sandals over from under the wardrobe. 'What do you want me to do with these?'

'We'll get a plastic bag for them.'

When she's satisfied that every bit of him is accounted for, she looks around the room one last time. 'What about your pictures?'

'What about them?'

'Aren't you going to bring them?'

'What's the point?'

Kate's thought becomes a smile. 'We could show them to Dad?'

'He wouldn't be interested.'

'Yes, he would. He loves your pictures.'

I go to roll up the drawings, if only to avoid the told-you-so look from Joan, and stall for a moment at the sight of JP's merry eyes looking back at me. Kate cries, 'No, you'll ruin them.' She reaches for my big sketchbook, which is propped against the wall, and opens it. We carefully lay the drawings in it and lay that on top of JP's clothes.

'What about your paints and stuff? Aren't you going to bring them too?' Kate asks.

'I won't be needing them.'

She's not listening to me. Instead, she's placing the curled-up tubes, jars of brushes, pencils, charcoal and pastels on another sketchbook and presenting them to me, like a special gift.

29

Mr Moriarty's horse has a way of looking at you. He closes his eyes and opens them again in slow motion. It's like he's trying to tell you something. It was Kate's idea to visit him. Apparently last year Ma caught her and Brigid feeding carrots to him and went ballistic. She told Kate that when she was a little girl a neighbour's niece had been kicked to death by a horse in England. The girl had been trying to plait its tail. It seems JP had promised Ma that he would accompany Kate to Moriarty's horse every time, so after he left, Kate had had no choice but to sneak out on her own to see him.

The poor horse must be wondering what he's done to deserve this delegation of four – Bo, Kate, Monty and me – five, if you include Joan, who's busy fighting with her husband on her phone in the car. Kate is balancing herself on the middle rung of the gate stroking the horse's nose, with Monty at her feet, circling the ground, lying down, getting up and circling again in an effort to get comfortable. Bo and I share a fag behind them and talk in low tones.

'So, what's the grand plan after the joyful reunion?' asks Bo.

'With JP? He'll probably want nothing more to do with me.'

'I mean with you.'

'What do you mean?'

'Well, you seemed to think I should be out there, doing my thing.'

'And?'

'Well, it seems to me, my dear, and I hope you'll forgive me for being so bold, that you've been driving around in second gear for some time now.'

'And you want me to step up a gear?'

'It's what you want that I'm asking about.'

'I don't know. I don't even know that I can.'

'Well, it's either that or stand still.'

'I suppose I should try to make myself more useful, and I need to start paying my way. God knows, I may have to soon enough. I tried to go back teaching after Kate was born, but . . .'

'But?'

'It didn't work out.'

'You could paint?'

'Could I?'

'You're a beautiful painter, Sylvia. You know that.'

'Do I?'

'Sure you do. You have a way of nailing it without killing it. I always wished I could paint like you.'

'But what use is that? How would that help things with Kate or JP or making a living?'

'Sylvia, they only want you to be happy.'

Happy. That word again. How does it work? Do you wake up some morning with the sparkling realization that you're happy, as if it's been sprinkled all over you in the middle of the night by a higher order? Thank you, God, for making me happy. I promise I'll be really good from now on and never do anything to jeopardize the happiness you have bestowed on me.

Or do you just snatch the moments when the sun comes through the trees over the road, a horse blinks at you or your daughter breaks into a smile because you promised her what she needed to hear, and do you wrap up those moments and put them in your pocket for dark times ahead?

We wind through empty country roads with the windows down and the wind forcing our hair to clump together. With each passing mile, I get a bit more confident and begin to think that maybe, in fact, I won't kill us all off in one great newsworthy car crash. Joan's questioning Bo about everyone we ever went to school with.

'I heard Douglas Chambers's business has gone down the tubes?'

'Really?'

'Yeah. He was never much of an architect anyway. All his houses looked like Lego. And I believe Sally Ann's around?'

'So Sylvia says.'

'And pregnant?'

'Apparently so.'

'At long bloody last. She must have got some help with it?'

'Joan.'

'What, Sy? I'm just saying . . .'

'Well, don't.'

'That's the first time I ever heard you stick up for Sally Ann Power. I thought you –'

'Give it a rest.'

Just then we come into view of the sea. Joan calls, from the back, 'Why don't we all go for a walk down on the beach, just like the old days?'

She means her old days when she and Seamus Manning

used to snog and fumble at the point in the distance where the beach turns the corner out of sight of the village, and he declared his undying love for her.

'*No!*' cries Kate.

The car wobbles and I glance at Kate in the rear-view mirror. She is looking straight ahead with her chin cocked and her eyes wide.

'I don't want to go back to the beach,' she says, in a sturdy voice. 'I don't want to go back, not with Mam. Not without Dad.'

We end up in the graveyard. Swallows swoop to greet us when I pull open the gate. Someone has mown the grass and left the grass cuttings in lines that are now turning into hay. Joan suggested we stop off to visit on our way back home. It came as a surprise. The bunch of sweet williams I left is rotting into Da's grave. I pick it up and spread it under a hedge. Then I pluck a couple of dock leaves and use them to scrub the gravestone, revealing the writing for my sister's benefit. I wonder when she was last here.

Joan's meandering around the graveyard, examining all the headstones one by one before she finally arrives at Da's. We all gather around it for a while, heads bowed in loving memory. When I close my eyes, Da is swaying under the Sacred Heart lamp but, unlike Joan, I still can't bring myself to be angry with him.

A sniffle ends the silence. Two black lines are creeping down Joan's cheeks. She blows her nose and mutters, 'Bloody pollen.' I squeeze her arm. 'It's okay, it's okay,' she says, dusting me away.

Bo places his hand on Kate's shoulder and guides her back towards the gate. Joan links me as we follow them. I nod a goodbye to the dead names around – I won't be back for a while.

Kate's telling Bo about the time JP brought her here. It was the same day they walked along the cliff's edge at the lighthouse, she's saying, and explored a huge dead house, only they couldn't get into the house and could only see around the sheds outside.

'So what do you think, Sy?' asks Joan.

'Think about what?'

'About coming back to Dublin with me. I've got child-minding till Sunday. We could leave then and you could stay with me for a few days until . . . Well, it would give you and JP a bit of time to work it out. Come on, you might need that breathing space and, besides, we never get to hang out like this any more.'

It could be tempting to loll about with Joan and the past for a while more, postponing the future and revisiting our air-brushed dreams, now that she's stopped fighting with me.

Kate is making Bo laugh. He's asking the odd prompting question to keep her going, just as JP used to do.

'Joan, JP's not in Dublin.'

'Where is he, then?'

'He's outside Drogheda, working on his bridge. That's where we're headed.'

'And how the hell are you going to get up there?'

'I'll drive.'

She pulls her arm out of mine. 'I don't bloody believe it. I thought you were taking the train.'

'No.'

'And I suppose you're going to drag that poor child up there in the car with you?'

'Keep your voice down. It's Kate who wants to see the bridge. I promised her I'd bring her there.'

'Are you out of your tiny deranged mind? You're only learning, for God's sake.'

'We're going, Joan. We're leaving tomorrow.'

30

'Ma.' Joan plonks the word rudely in front of my mother who is mashing potatoes on the kitchen table. 'Ma, did you know that your younger daughter will drive your only grand-daughter up to Drogheda tomorrow? Did you know that, Ma?'

'Actually, we're going to drive to the bridge that Dad is building,' says Kate.

Ma stops and looks at me. 'Is this true, Sylvia?'

The potato made little blond curls as it moved through the holes in the masher.

'Is it, Sylvia?'

'Ma, I was going to tell you.'

'She was going to disappear in the middle of the night. That's what she was going to do. She didn't want me to tell you, Ma.' Joan's arm is outstretched, pointing to a faraway place.

'Gran,' says Kate, 'it's the most beautiful bridge in Ireland. You should see it. It's got this big –'

'Kate, go to your room,' says Joan, barely looking at my daughter.

'No. I don't want to go to my room. I want to stay here. I want to tell Gran about the bridge.'

'Kate, do as you are told,' says Ma, quietly.

Joan waits until the door slams behind Kate. 'Ma,' she says, 'she doesn't even have a driving licence. It's complete madness.'

'Shut up, Joan,' I say. 'I have a licence.'

'A provisional one, I suppose.'

'Lots of people drive on provisional licences.'

'People who have been driving for a while do. And what about insurance?'

'And I'm on JP's insurance.'

'But you said . . .'

'Besides, you were with me in the car this morning. You know I can drive. Perfectly well. Ma, we're leaving tomorrow morning. I promised Kate. I would have told you. Of course I would. You see, she asked me to drive her to JP after he left and I refused to and then . . . Well, Ma, she nearly ran away.'

'When did this happen?'

'The morning . . . the morning I went under. I can't risk that happening again, Ma. She needs to be with her father. So do I.'

'"Go under". Is that what it's called now?' says Joan. 'You tried to top yourself. Remember?'

'I keep telling you, Joan, I didn't. It was an accident. I fell.'

'And you just happened to be standing in your bare feet in the sea at dawn. And you can't even swim. And now you want to drive up to Drogheda on some kind of Bonnie and Clyde mad expedition.'

'I promised Kate.'

'Well, unpromise her.'

'I can't. You don't understand. Ma, do you think I don't know what it looks like? I swear to God I never meant to go under. But now I've been given a second chance and I've made this promise to her. I owe it to her, to see it through. I've . . . I've never really been there for her. You know. When she was a baby.'

'You were sick, Sylvia.' Joan is shouting now.

'What do you mean "sick"?'

'You had post-natal depression.'

'Joan, there's no need for that,' says Ma.

'No, Ma, she has to know. I'm sick of tiptoeing around my little sister as if she's some kind of special case. I'm sick of her going on as if nothing happened, as if she's fine, just fine, we're all fine. Let's say it as it was. You couldn't get yourself washed or dressed. You couldn't have a conversation. You managed to feed Kate, I'll give you that, but come on, you were like a zombie.'

'Joan.' Ma is shouting too.

'We were always having to check up on you. Or get other people to check up on you. It was all "How is Sylvia today? I hope Sylvia is feeling better today." It was Sylvia, Sylvia, Sylvia, from morning to night. Poor JP. He used to bring Kate out for walks in the evening and phone me from the box at the end of your road. He was beside himself with worry. He thought that if he could get you painting again, or if he got a camper-van and brought you up to Croagh Patrick, that might cheer you up. It was me who told him you needed time, that's all. That's what I thought in the beginning. But how wrong I was.'

'Joan, that's enough,' says Ma.

'You know, it's the child I feel sorry for. No wonder she was wetting her bed.'

'She doesn't wet her bed,' I say. 'Not any more.'

Joan stops and is glaring at me through dark eyes and it feels like years of pure hatred are oozing out of her. I turn back to my mother. Her eyes are heavy with sorrow, my sorrow. I stop to prepare myself.

'I was there.' The words are dry and crackling. 'And I'm not proud of it.' I force them out one by one. 'Look, I know

I went off course back then. And I know you were all worried about me and I know now I should have got help sooner. I know I never really got back to being the person I was before, and then, last week, whenever it was, do you think I don't know what I nearly did to Kate? It could've been just like Dad all over again, losing his mother. The thought of it terrifies me and I'm not about to do something that stupid again.'

I stop to look from mother to sister, sister to mother, but they don't move. They are expecting more.

'It's . . . it's just that when I found out about my grandmother, our grandmother, I thought . . . Well, Ma, I thought that maybe that's why I was the way I was. I was her all over again. That that was my future in some way, me and the sea, because . . . because it was my past.'

Ma reaches up to push a loose hair back from my forehead just as she used to do when I was little.

'Ma, I was afraid to tell you I was leaving. I know I've been a disappointment.'

'Oh, Sylvia child, you get these notions.'

She looks behind her to find the nearest chair and suddenly Joan and I realize we have all been standing right up close to each other, a tight knot of shared pain. I sit on a low stool opposite Ma. Joan takes a seat in the distance.

'Listen to me now, Sylvia,' says Ma. My hands are between hers. 'You're not to be upsetting yourself with these notions. Your grandmother was a very sick woman and she'd been sick for a long, long time. She didn't get the help she needed, God love her. You were just meant to get on with things back then. You'd no choice. You had to look after the children and the house, and there might be an ageing relative or two. Her husband was out at sea for most of the time and she, God rest her, she had it very bad. No one talked about depression or that kind of thing back then. But you, you are not your grandmother, do you hear me? And you must remember that.'

'I know.'

'And despite what Joan is saying, and it's true we were worried about you for a long time, you've got a lot more fight in you than you think. I remember when you were little.' She turns to share the memory with Joan. 'The same girl who would cry and cry until she was about to break in two could turn and charge at you like a bull. I never knew what you were going to come out with next – and I suppose Joan is right. I used to find myself tiptoeing around you sometimes. I suppose you were like your father in that way.'

She rubs my hands between hers so that they are burning hot. 'Oh, when I think of your poor father and how you used to follow him around, longing for any scrap of attention. You'd be so excited when he brought you up the field to get the cows, and I suppose we were, well, jealous of that. No, it wasn't jealous so much as sad that you were so contented with so little from him. But no, Sylvia, you are not your grandmother and you are not your father. You are a mother now in your own right, and you must live your own life and do what you believe is right for your little one.'

'You're not going to let her go, are you?' says Joan.

'I've never been able to stop her once she puts her mind to something. But if anything happens to you or to that precious, precious little girl of yours, anything at all . . .'

'Oh, Ma. It'll be okay. I'll be okay. We'll be okay. Really.'

If I say 'okay' often enough, there is a chance that it just may be. 'I'm taking the back roads. I have it all worked out. Honest to God, Ma, I know what I'm doing.'

Ma smiles at me, a sad sort of smile. 'Phone as soon as you get there,' she says.

The cases are stacked in the hall. Kate's been in bed for hours, tucked up with a letter that arrived from Brigid and the promise of what tomorrow will bring. Joan is in the parlour working on an assignment. Ma is asleep in her chair in the kitchen, with the light from the television dancing across her face. Her fingers are entwined in a half-prayer on her lap. Her skin is soft and downy. It drapes in little pleats over her eyes. Sacks of flesh are spilling on to her cheek-bones. I think of what Bo said. Our mothers are the place we land every time when our feet lose contact with the ground beneath.

I take my father's chair on the other side of the stove and stretch my neck over the back of it. It won't be long before my eye sacks begin to swell like Ma's, until they're too heavy for my skull. Already I'm feeling these forces of nature, like the plates under the earth's surface, shifting and moving to an ageing pulse. My eyes run along the wallpaper all the way up to the ceiling. It's a brave, geometric pattern that JP hung in preparation for the last Stations while I polished every piece of cutlery in the house and Ma starched the net curtains. I bring my eyes back down to the kitchen table, laid for breakfast already, and see Ma and Da, Joan and me passing salt and throwaway comments to each other.

It's funny how this waiting room that Kate and I have occupied, driving aimlessly up and down the coast with Bo, became for a short time a sort of end in itself. The anxiety of the journey ahead and what lies at the end of that journey vanished for whole moments at a time, and now that we're on our way out of the door, now that the hours are numbered,

I wish I had more time to spend with my past, to find answers – to what I don't know exactly.

Suddenly there's a knock, a hard knuckle on a hard surface, tap, tap, tapping in relentless succession. Ma opens her eyes. It takes a few taps before I realize that the taps are coming from the other side of the front door.

'Is anyone going to answer that?' says Joan, who's now standing before us. She tugs open the door. 'Yes?'

'Is Sylvia there?'

I jump to the door. 'Fred, what are you doing here?' Even in the dark, I can see all the colour and poise is washed out of the boy.

'Sylvia, you've got to come quickly.'

'Why? What's happening?'

'It's Sally Ann. She needs you. She's having the baby. There's water all over the kitchen floor. It's a big mess. You've got to come to drive her to the hospital.'

'Water?'

'Her waters have broken,' says Joan. 'We'd better get her to hospital. Fred?' she shouts at him. 'Have you called an ambulance?'

He shakes his head.

'What is it, Sylvia?' Ma calls from the kitchen.

'It's okay, Ma, I've got it,' says Joan. 'Fred, where's your father?'

'On the plane.'

'And your grandfather?'

'Grandma says he's had one too many. You've got to come now, Sylvia. She says it's happening too fast.'

'But, Fred, you can't ask me to drive her.'

'Why not? You can drive Mr Larkin's car.'

'But I don't . . .'

'You were driving it this morning. I saw you.' Tears are popping out of his eyes.

'I'll drive,' says Joan. 'Sy, get me the keys.'

'No. No way.' Fred's fists are clenched. 'Sally Ann says it's gotta be Sylvia. She says only Sylvia understands.'

31

I'm swimming through the inky cold blackness with Sally Ann beside me in the passenger seat, pulling the white strips in the middle of the road towards us, one by one, faster and faster, so that they become one long strip, and I'm driving at a speed that I never knew I could. And praying. *Please, God, please don't let this baby come, not yet, not into my hands, not into this dark night, please.* Suddenly the moon appears from behind a cloud, full, fecund, plating the ground with silver.

'I can't believe this is happening. I can't believe it. I'm not due for another two weeks. Oh, Jesus, why did I leave it so late?' howls Sally Ann. 'It's all Bob's fault. I've been trying to get hold of him all day but he switched his phone off. Imagine – he switched his . . .'

She seizes my arm and I can feel her whole body harden in pain. Her cry is too big for the car and it propels us towards the other side of the road. I swing back and wind down the window. 'Breathe, Sally Ann, for God's sake. Breathe.' *That's what they say, isn't it? When in doubt, just breathe.*

'Are we nearly there?' she cries, once the contraction has passed.

'Yes, we're nearly there.'

'What if we don't make it, Sylvia?'

'We have to make it.'

'Imagine – he turned his phone off. He never wanted this kid. He said we were fine now that Fred was living with us. Fred . . . imagine . . .'

Only God knows why Sally Ann insisted it should be me who makes this journey with her. The world is overflowing with mothers armed with wet wipes, brimming with their nurturing supremacy, and I am not one of them. It's my own fault, of course. If you stand still in one place for long enough, you find yourself being signed up. I should have got out sooner. I should have gone to Dublin when Kate first asked me to.

The woman in A&E sends us down a long, dim corridor. 'Turn right when you get to the end and take the lift up to the second floor. Press the bell at the entrance to the ward. If it's not working, just holler.'

Sally Ann hangs on to my arm and I carry a bag that smells of talc. Her moans echo through the gloom. I walk as fast as she'll allow. We find the bell and Sally Ann presses it long and hard.

'Yes?' The midwife is small and tough, like a beetle.

'Sally Ann Larsson. I called.'

'Aye, you did. You'd better come in.'

I'm tugged forward, like a wilful dog.

'This is my birthing partner, Sylvia.' She offers me to the Beetle who turns away and leads us to a pinked-out room.

'Right, we'd better check on how this baby's doing,' she says, snapping on a pair of surgical gloves.

After the examination, she props Sally Ann up with gas-and-air on tap, places a jug of water on the table beside her and leaves us to each other with a smile that seems to say 'good luck'. The windows are high up and made black by the night. A small picture of a mother and child reflected in a bubble of sorts, signed by an 'A. Hughes', hangs alone in the middle of the pink wall. I study it closely and wonder if A.

Hughes is a mother or a father, or a nobody like me. There's a clock on the wall over the picture with both hands pointing to midnight. There's not much else to look at except each other.

'Breathe with me, Sylvia.'

Sally Ann's eyes fix on mine, and I mirror her breathing and her fear. She sucks deeply on the gas-and-air but it makes her sick. I hold a metal dish up for her to puke into, wipe her mouth with tissue and mop her brow, wondering if I'm doing the right thing.

'Open the windows,' she begs. I tell her they're already open.

'Well, give me some water.' She drinks greedily but it makes her sick again. 'Any word from Bob?'

'Not yet, Sally Ann. Not yet.'

The contractions attack like grenades, more and more frequently, so that there is no peacetime, only war. Sally Ann stretches her neck and bawls. A scream replies in the distance. I rub her legs, cautiously at first and then more vigorously. It's the only thing I can do, that and gather up the vomit in the metal dish. I remember JP rubbing my legs with gusto. He was good at this kind of thing.

'I want an epidural,' Sally Ann cries, when the Beetle reappears.

'I'm afraid it's much too late for that, Sally Ann Larsson.'

'What?'

'You're seven centimetres dilated, my girl. There won't be any epidural for you tonight. It won't be long more now. You're nearly there.'

'You've been saying that all along but I can't go on.'

'Of course you can. You're doing great. Not long more now.'

'It's Bob,' Sally Ann wails. 'It's all his fault. He promised on his life he'd be here and I was holding out for him. And now it's too late. Now I can't have the epidural.'

'You don't want an epidural, Sally Ann,' I say quietly.

'Why not? What makes you think I don't want an epidural?'

'Because you won't be able to feel anything, that's why.'

'Don't you think I'm feeling enough?'

She's right, of course. Who am I to tell her what she needs and doesn't, I who had epidural upon epidural? Not that I asked for it. Those decisions were made in hushed tones over my head. Now, looking back, I can't recall the labour pains, even though I'm told they lasted for a day and a night. It's as if I read about them later. Rushing through corridors on a trolley, crashing through double doors and more double doors, the bright lights, the numbness, the masked faces, the scared eyes is what I remember.

'Of course you'll make it,' I say. 'You heard what they said. You're nearly there. You're doing great. Now breathe with me.'

We continue that way for a while, breathing down into the contractions, Sally Ann in pain, me in the viewing gallery.

'Right, you're ready to go,' says the Beetle, on her next visit. They gather round and raise Sally Ann's legs into stirrups. Everyone takes their ringside place including me, up beside Sally Ann's head. My arm reaches around her shoulders.

'Breathe in, Sally Ann,' they say. 'Good. Very good. Now push. Push down. Down, down, down.'

Sally Ann grimaces. The red marks on her huge yellow watermelon belly inflame. With every push, I pray to God knows who – *Please. Please bring the baby.*

'I can't do it, Sylvia. I can't do it.'

'You can. You're doing great.'

'Now push,' calls the Beetle, from the other end. All the pressure of the world is on us. This could be the one. *Come on, Sally Ann. Push down, for God's sake.*

Something moves in the room. I loosen my hold on her and go to the other end, to another world entirely, another life. Something dark and slimy is lodged down there between her legs. *Oh, Jesus.*

It squirms.

'Push, Sally Ann, push down.'

The black thing stalls, between two minds.

'Push hard now, Sally Ann. *Hard.*'

Sally Ann's cry comes from the pit of her. The creature is swimming through the wave of pain, making the world spin faster.

Oh, God. So this is how it's meant to be.

The Beetle moves in, wraps her hand around the baby's head and pulls. *Be careful, for Christ's sake.*

A baby girl is hauled into the world, raw and smeared with blood. A shower of gunk whooshes out of Sally Ann, marking an end point just as the baby releases a wild, outraged cry. Everyone sighs as one. The baby is carried to her mother and I follow it, transfixed. It has nothing, no name, no identity, no personality, but it commands the whole room, the whole world, this little thing. It pushes back its swollen eyelids and looks at Sally Ann, dazed and knowing. Its mother looks back in awe.

Everything returns to normal after that. A new normal. There's a bustle in the room involving injections and stitching and weighing and cleaning and recording, but Sally Ann is oblivious to it all. She's cradling the new-born with tender disbelief. I'm back on the outside.

'I'm off now, Sally Ann.' I kiss her damp forehead. 'I'm off to find JP.'

But she's not listening. She's in a wide-eyed bubble with her child. She will never be the same again.

32

I stop the car at the outskirts of the village, at the point of change where the road, still holding a view of the estuary, is about to dip down between the houses. Dawn is creeping up the water, the light blue of a new day quietly overtaking the darkness. The birds are awake and elated. I think of the journey Sally Ann made for her child, full of pain and fear, courage and love. It takes courage to be a mother. Already the baby is older now, more dependent, more autonomous. Everything is changing, moving on, all the time. I think of Sally Ann and her baby, wrapped up in their perfect bubble. How lucky they are.

Kate and I – we were separated from each other with a knife. It was a shocking start to things.

Monty steps sideways to allow the back door to open.

'Monty, what are you doing up at this hour?'

His tail wags in relief and he leads the way to the front hall to where Kate is standing faultlessly still, facing the door. She's fully dressed and her pink bag is hanging from her back.

'Kate?'

She doesn't move. I walk around her to face her. She's staring straight ahead at something that's not in the room. Her lips are dark against her dead white face. She seems not of this world.

'Kate?'

She blinks and looks amazed. 'Mam?'

'Come on now, come back to bed.'

'Mam?'

'Yeah?'

'Today is Friday, right?'

'That's right.'

'We're leaving today, aren't we? You said . . .'

'Yes, of course we are.'

'That's okay, then.' Her shoulders lower.

'But it's still the middle of the night,' I say. 'We need to get some sleep.'

She follows me dutifully up the stairs but stalls outside her bedroom door, looking at me with those downward-sloping eyes that make her seem sad.

'Do you want to sleep with me tonight?'

She nods. Monty runs ahead to the gable room.

I take my seat in front of the dressing-table and click on the lamp. In the mirror Kate, peeling off her jacket and jeans to her nightie underneath, looks frail and alone. She slides into the cold bed. The light daubs dark marks under my eyes and beside my mouth that drag my lips down towards my chin.

Is she kind as she is fair?
For beauty lives with kindness.

I have aged since this morning. The passage of time cannot be denied in the face of a new life. We must all move on together. I push back my hair with a band, close my eyes and cover my face with cleanser, soaking up the coolness. Then, still with my eyes closed, I feel around for cotton wool, and remove the cream with long, upward strokes, as they advise, as if this choreography will counter the gravity of time. When I open my eyes, the whites of Kate's are visible in the mirror. I swivel around. She sits up. 'Did Sally Ann have her baby?'

'Yes, she did.'

'What did she have?'

'A little girl.'

'What was it like?'

I think of the slimy black head emerging into the hands of the midwife. 'It was beautiful.'

'Did it hurt?'

'Yes, it hurt.'

'Did it hurt when you had me?'

After they'd stitched me up, they lifted me legless on to the trolley. I remember feeling as if I had been attacked. I knew the knife had gone deep even though I was numb. I heard myself moan and realized I was still alive, although I didn't know whether I was glad of that or not.

'Not so much.' I pat the stool I'm sitting on and Kate takes her place beside me. Her eyes are deep and her skin is like porcelain in the light. I take some night cream and massage it slowly into her forehead. It smells of an old woman's perfume. She closes her eyes and scrunches them up as if anticipating pain. I lean forward and dare to kiss her. When she opens her eyes, I'm rubbing the cream into the worry lines on my forehead.

'Mam?'

'Yeah.'

'What do you wear makeup for?'

'Dunno. To rub out the mistakes, I guess.'

'How old were you when you started wearing it?'

'I put on some of your grandmother's lipstick one day

before I went to school. Sister Assumpta went mad when she saw me and sent me home. Then Gran went mad and made me take it off and go straight back to school.'

'How old were you?'

'I was about eleven.'

'But that's my age.'

'I didn't really wear it again until I was sixteen. Gran used to watch me like a hawk and wouldn't even let me put Vaseline on my lips. She said I'd mortified her that day.'

'Brigid wore makeup once.'

'Really?'

'On the bottom of her eyes.'

'Did it make her look nice?'

'No, just dirty.'

She studies me as I massage a different cream into my crows' feet.

'Mam?'

'Yeah?'

She brings her index finger up and places it carefully on the scar beside my right eye. The warmth of her finger is like a soldering iron, smoothing out the bumps and ridges of the mark.

'Where did that come from?'

I smile and tell her it was just one of those things.

The waiting room has high ceilings. A number of people are sitting upright in a circle, their backs to each other. I am among them with a crying baby on my lap. I bob it up and down but it doesn't stop crying. Two antiquated desks sit at the top of the room, facing the group. A neat woman in a tweed suit and a pillbox hat sits at one. A man sits at the other. From time to time, he calls people up to the desk. I stand up, leave the baby on the chair behind me and go to the man. 'I need you to help me find my way out of here,' I say. He leaves his desk and walks down the long room, with its flocked wallpaper and fussy carpet, past the waiting people towards an emptiness and a closed door at the end wall. I follow him. The baby's cries get louder as I move away from it. We walk for some time. I recognize the man's movements. When we get to the door, he opens it and I step inside. It's dark in the room, dark and musty. There are no windows.

'No,' I say. 'This is where I was before.'

I open my eyes just as JP leaves and locks the door behind him. Kate's standing in front of me, dressed again in her jeans and her bright pink jacket. At first I think she's in the room I've just entered. Then I sit up, look around me and remember.

'Kate? What time is it?'

'Ten minutes to nine.'

I close my eyes in a time-buying blink.

'It's Friday. We have to go now. You said . . .' says Kate.

'I know. Friday.'

Joan and I load up the car in silence. Then she lines up with Ma inside the front door for the goodbyes, safe from the eyes of the village.

'Goodbye, sis.' She pulls me close to her in an awkward clutch. 'Sylvia, I didn't mean what I said yesterday. I just get so . . . Well, I just get frustrated sometimes. I don't mean it. You know that, don't you?'

'I know.'

Ma holds Kate's head against her bosom. 'Oh, sweet child,' she mutters. 'Come back to me soon, won't you?'

Then she lowers her voice even further. 'And you take good care of your mother for me.' She slips some money into Kate's pocket. Monty wags his tail. I wait my turn.

The soft sacks below Ma's eyes are more bloated in the cold morning light. She hands me a bundle of sandwiches that I know will never get eaten and blots her sadness with a barrage of instructions. 'Drive carefully. Take the road easy. Phone when you get there. Tell JP I was asking for him.' Then she leans into me and grips my hand tightly. 'Don't expect too much now, Sylvia. Marriage, let me tell you, is hard work.'

'I know, Ma. It's love that's the easy bit.'

She opens the door for us. 'You'd better get going. I can go and change the sheets at last now that you're gone.' Her laugh is an effort.

I take my time getting into the car, putting on my safety-belt, making sure Kate has hers on and that she has a good hold of Monty on his short lead. Finally, when I run out of excuses, I switch on the ignition, check all three mirrors, look over my right shoulder, before turning the steering-wheel, taking my foot off the clutch and pulling away, like an orchestra playing the first tentative notes. I lean into the wheel, willing the car forward. When I look in the rear-view mirror, Mrs Power and Fred are crossing the road towards Ma and Joan. A red Mini is pulling up in front of Ma's house and Bo Quirke is scrambling out. He raises his hand in a half-wave. I don't stop. The wheels are going round and round, and stopping would mean starting again. I have to keep going.

33

So here we are, mother and daughter, on our Mad Expedition, in search of the Holy Grail, my husband, her father. The wheels are going round and round. I feel them touching the road, as if it's me who's on the road in my bare feet. This time feels different from all the others, different from driving to the hospital, from driving with Bo and, of course, different from the lessons with Roger. This time it's me who's the grown-up on the grown-up roads, feeling the full weight of my small passengers.

Kate and Monty don't comment on the grinding gears or yelping of the engine. Maybe they don't notice the flashing lights and beeping horns when I find myself driving at thirty miles an hour in the fast lane, too petrified to move over to the slow one. With every car skimming past me, I sink further into the seat, until I'm wholly under siege. Bo had said the first leg would be the hardest.

Voices come in and out of my brain, like radio interference.

Why do you always have to make things so hard for yourself?

Why don't you just phone ahead first?

What makes you think he wants to be found?

Loudest of all is my own voice.

Are you mad? Driving without a licence or insurance? Lying to your mother? Putting your daughter's life at risk like this? Hasn't she been through enough already? What are you going to do when you get there, when you see him? What are you actually going to say?

I try to soundproof myself against them with the memory of Kate's smile and the touch of my lips on her forehead. I repeat in my head my words to Ma. I can drive 'perfectly well', 'honestly'. I am 'okay'. 'Really.' And then there's the sound of Sally Ann's baby's first cry. This is not about me. This is what childbirth is all about, giving birth to a greater need. This is – what was it Joan said? A non-negotiable.

On the outskirts of town, a group of boys are messing beside the road. They're kicking a football between the cars and shoving each other off the pavement. One of them pushes a boy with bright orange hair right on to the road. I beep the horn at him, with a bit too much zeal. He jumps back on to the pavement, but when we drive by, they run after us, yelling and holding two fingers up in the air.

'Arseholes.' Then I remember Kate. 'Sorry.'

She says nothing.

'Are you okay, Kate?'

'Uh-huh.'

'Are you missing your gran?'

'I guess.'

She's not missing her gran. Rather, she's wound up tight with longing to see her father.

In the early hours of this morning, as we lay parallel to each other in the darkness of the gable room, she asked me how I met JP.

'Kate, what's with all the questions tonight?'

'Did you meet him at a dance? Brigid's mother met her father at a dance. Brigid says that's where couples met in those days.'

So I told her the story of how I met JP, not at a dance but in Dublin airport on my way back from Istanbul many years ago, how I pulled a rucksack from the carousel on to a trolley, how I veered it in the direction of Customs, how I felt a light tap on my shoulder, how I assumed it was a Customs officer, but instead it was a man, not in uniform, about my own age, tall, tanned, with eyes slightly too close together. He was leaning on two crutches. His right leg was in plaster and bent and his foot hovered over the ground.

'I think you may have my bag,' he suggested. A balding koala bear with frizzy ears was hanging from the rucksack in my hand. I blushed and checked the label – 'JP Larkin', with some address in County Tyrone.

'I'll help you find yours,' he offered. 'What's it look like?'

'Like yours, without the marsupial.'

His smile revealed the gap at the back of his mouth where two teeth had once been.

'JP Larkin.' He held out his hand. 'JP as in James Patrick. My parents could never agree.'

'Sylvia Keane.' His handshake was secure.

He was on his way back from Australia. He'd spent four years out there, working with an engineering firm, until one day his motorbike had spun out of control and he'd ended up under a lorry. He had a degree in engineering and a willingness to talk, and was coming home to convalesce before heading back out. He asked me where I was coming from. I gave him the edited version as we waited in vain for my luggage to appear.

I told Kate the kind of story I'd have told Joan way back when we used to share a room, lying in our separate beds in the dark, savouring the detail, crafting the comedy with images and dialogue, repeating myself for effect, taking artistic licence. I didn't tell her how all the rucksacks merged into one for me that day, how I was a dazed war veteran returning home, grateful for the kindness of a stranger, any stranger, so grateful I'd have followed them home, like an abandoned puppy. I didn't tell her of my relief that he never once asked me about the stitches around my right eye or that I, in return, didn't ask about the missing teeth.

I didn't tell her that he felt sorry for me – he must have – and that in those first few coffees we shared after the airport encounter, breaks from our busy unemployment, coffees that became short walks and long sits by the canal, when we shared our notions about the future and he gradually stopped talking about returning to Australia, I couldn't see what was going on, that he liked me. He actually liked me. I couldn't see this because my heart was still in Istanbul, and, like my lost luggage, it was some time before it was returned to me.

Once out of town, the fields merge into each other, like a quilt draped over hills. In the distance, fields of pale gold, brushstrokes inserted by the artist at the last minute to lift the scene. The villages unfold before us, revealing the sets of local soap operas. But this is no drive in the country on a Sunday afternoon. Everything is a hazard: the other cars, the bewildered cows – even the unending hedgerows can't be trusted. I think of that day Joan talked about when I got my Leaving Cert results and we went to the amusements with Bo. We spent ages on the dodgem cars, swerving and crashing into each other with accelerating force. I was off to art college and life was going to be exciting.

Kate looks straight ahead for the most part, coiling and twisting Monty's ears. Monty keeps his eyes on me, egging me on. He has always been on my side, I think, willing me to do the right thing, forgiving me when I screw up. He looks at me with gentle benevolence, his eyes permanently set at sad. During those explosions of crying on the sofa while the baby Kate screamed for her feed, he'd lay his moist chin on my lap and gaze up at me. 'I know it's hard,' he'd say.

I turn a corner and end up in the middle of the road. I swerve back to the left-hand side. I hear Bo's voice: 'Keep to the left. Down into second gear for corners. Don't coast.' Roger's too: 'Do you know who's behind you now? Mirrors, mirrors, mirrors. You should be in fourth.' Every man in my life has taught me something. The car wobbles slightly. Roger again: 'Concentrate.' My own voice now: 'I can drive perfectly well.'

Then there's another little voice, a quieter voice. 'I want to go to the toilet,' it says.

I can't stop the car. If I switch off the engine I may not be able to get it started again. Ridiculous, I know, but there you go. Besides, where could we piss at this hour? All the pubs are shut. In a field? In a shop? It's too much to work out at thirty miles an hour.

'Didn't you go before you left Gran's?'

'No.'

'No? Okay, let's just see if we can find somewhere to stop.' I sound vague. I am vague. The wheels are going round and round, past rolling hills, trimmed with lace horizons.

'Mam?' It's a faint whimper this time.

'Yes, yes, I know. Toilet. We must find a toilet. We'll find a toilet soon. I promise.'

Where had JP stopped when we needed to go to the toilet? Where had I been at those times?

'Mam, it's too late.'

34

The next village is the kind of one-street place where houses line up and gawk across at each other and young people dream of an early escape. I pull the car into the side of the road, slam my foot on the brakes and cut out.

'We'd better walk from here.'

'Where are we going?' asks Kate.

'To the nearest toilet.'

I take JP's jacket out of the boot and hand it to her. She looks at it glumly. 'It's too big.'

'I know but it'll cover you up. I'll get some clean clothes out of your bag.'

A drop falls from her nose on to the jacket.

'Kate, I'm sorry.' I reach out my hand but she steps away. *Why the hell isn't JP here when I need him? He'd know what to do.*

We find a place called Rosie's Diner. The big glass window is frosted over with condensation. Inside, two customers are sitting facing it, as far away from each other as possible, as though they're the only people on a bus. The man in the corner is placing a small packet of butter on the teapot to make it soft, just like JP used to do. An old woman in a pink fur coat with a tiny head and tiny hands is struggling to cut through the bottom of her apple tart with a fork.

I approach the woman behind the counter who looks like she could be a Rosie. Her complexion is fat and smooth and her boobs and belly roll like hills under her apron. Even her earlobes are swollen.

'Excuse me, do you allow dogs?'

Kate had insisted that Monty came with us.

'Let's have a wee look at him here,' she says. Her boobs land on a plate of fairy cakes as she leans over.

'Ach, isn't he a lovely wee thing?' she says, to the two people in the café. They don't turn around. 'Of course we'll allow him. Would he like a bowl of water?'

'Well . . .'

'Yes, he would, thanks,' says Kate.

'No problem at all.' She's out from behind the counter and is scratching Monty's head with her fat fingers. 'He can have Henry's bowl.'

'Won't Henry mind?' asks Kate.

'Of course he won't. Sure isn't Henry dead?'

'Dead?'

'We had to give him the injection in the end. It was a mercy killing, God rest him. He didn't feel a thing. Cancer, the vet said. Riddled with it. But his kennel and things are still out the back, just where he left them.'

'Could you tell me where the toilet is, please?' I ask, before she leaves in search of Henry's bowl.

'It's not working.'

'Oh.'

'Is it for yerself?'

'No. My daughter.'

'Well, she can use the one out the back.'

She pulls aside the long strings of beads hanging from the arch behind the counter. 'Paddy Joe, do you have the key to the toilet? There's a wee girl out here who wants to use it.'

Paddy Joe appears at the arch holding a monstrous key attached to an even bigger piece of wood. He's about a hundred and toothless.

'You follow Paddy Joe,' the woman says to Kate, 'and he'll show you where to go.'

Kate takes the plastic bag of clean clothes from me and follows the old man out of a back door, head hanging, down a dark corridor with empty bottles on both sides and out of another door into an unknown.

'Maybe I should go with her.'

'No, no. She's in the best of hands with Paddy Joe.'

I order a sandwich for Kate and a cup of tea for myself and pay before taking my place on the pretend bus equidistant between the Butter Man and the Fur Coat. The smoke from the man's cigarette releases a craving in me.

When Kate returns, her eyes are lined with red. I lower my cigarette under the table but the smoke gives me away. I lean forward and touch her arm with my empty hand. 'I'm sorry, Kate,' I say again. She waits until I take my hand away before she picks up the sandwich.

'Kate? I know I should've stopped sooner but I didn't . . .'

'It happened before.'

'What happened before?'

'I wet myself.'

'You did?'

'I wet myself in Gran's. Gran had to change all the sheets, the bottom sheet and the sheet underneath it, and give me a clean nightie and she had to wash them all and dry them out in the orchard.'

It was JP Kate had gone to when she'd wet her bed first time around – she was six or so. Every few mornings she handed the wet sheets to him. I put clean ones on her bed. And so it went for a few months. The doctor said it was just a phase. She'd probably grow out of it by herself, he said. And she did.

'But why didn't you tell me?'

'Gran told me not to.'

'But . . . ?'

'Because you were in bed, sick. She said we shouldn't disturb you.'

'When was that?'

'Before. Before the accident. Before you didn't drown.'

Rosie arrives at the table. 'Are ye feeling better now?' she asks Kate, stroking her hair and pulling her ponytail up through her strong hand.

I have no sense of how long I spent in the darkness of the gable room, before the accident. The clock said it was no more than a day and a half but time was a relentless loop, like the tide coming in and ebbing out, not going forward or back. Babies were born in that time and people died, but I had no interest in the living, not even in my own daughter, who was wetting her bed again and moulding conspiracies with my mother, just as my mother had with my sister years before, tiny conspiracies, like stitches, to keep me for ever in the cocoon that is my life. I look at Kate nibbling at the edges of her sandwich and wonder how long more it will be like this.

I stub out my half-smoked fag and turn to Rosie. 'Excuse me?'

'Aye?'

'I wonder could you help us?'

'If I can I will, surely.'

'Could you tell us the way to get to Drogheda? We'd like to take the back roads, avoid Dublin if possible.'

She grabs a chair from the Butter Man's table and slides it

under her bum. 'Oh, I never go through Dublin. No, no, no, I avoid Dublin like the plague, like the plague I do.'

She starts talking about roundabouts and forks in the road and fourth right turns and third left turns, sketching each one in the air. She says things like 'It's easy to miss it' and 'You can't miss it' and 'If you see the handball alley, you've missed it.' From the corner of my eye, I see Kate feeding the limp crusts of her sandwich to Monty under the table.

'My twin sister Dora lives in Drogheda. She's married to a Hodge. A Mrs Hodge she is. She runs a B&B there. You might come across her.' She laughs aloud. 'You won't get fed there like you do here. Her husband is a terribly mean man, so he is.'

The Fur Coat pushes away the crust of her apple tart and makes her way to the counter to pay.

'Excuse me a minute,' says Rosie, getting up from the chair and heading back to the counter. I signal to Kate and we leave.

35

We're driving against the grain. Every second sign points towards Dublin and to our lonely house, vacantly staring ahead, with its white kitchen table, bare apart from the coffee-stains and the empty fruit bowl; the blinds are pulled right down, maintaining our discretion. JP's strawberries must have ripened and rotted by now, unless he has gone there and tended them. I don't imagine so. I don't imagine he wants to be reminded of our failure any more than I do. So I keep driving north, hugging the hedgerows, easing through the bends, the endless bends, and ignoring the signs for Dublin. We travel in dismal silence, with only the sound of Monty's panting and a happy engine for relief. Humiliation and guilt fill the space between us.

Rosie's directions reveal themselves one by one – the fork in the road, the dried-up petrol station – like clues in a giant game. The next clue is a grotto of the Virgin Mary. Apparently her halo is lit up night and day and we can't miss her – *Hail Mary, full of grace.* I get stuck at 'grace' and start again: *Hail Mary, full of grace.* Villages come and go and still the Virgin eludes us. I switch on the radio to distract me from my unease.

I don't register his voice at first, his deep, slow tones. It's only when he says, 'Absolutely, absolutely,' that rapid succession of affirmatives, that I tune in. He's been short-listed for a major international art award. I listen to his breathing, the way he inhales quickly between sentences. I can see him now in the radio studio, body slumped to one side over the arm of the chair, while one leg is buttressed by the other. His forefinger crosses his lips, forcing his silence while he earnestly listens to the interviewer's earnest questions about the earnest issues of the artist's practice.

Arthur Delaney can be so bloody earnest. And when he isn't being earnest, he's spectacularly mocking. He plays the game and makes fun of it in one. Oh, he was full of games, with his talk of living like poor aristocrats, when really he wanted to be a rich one.

When I think of how it was back then, the passion, the rows, the silences, the derision and the punch that finally drove me back to Ireland, did I believe it was love? Maybe. Or perhaps I was flattered that this young, brilliant artist – his words, not mine – had taken an interest in me, Sylvia Keane, who, like a naïve Sunday painter, painted nothing less obvious than the clouds and the sea.

'The trouble with the current discourse is that we're accelerating towards an ideological cul-de-sac referencing previous inconsequential nuances within art and ignoring the social and political responsibilities of our practice.'

He's seducing the interviewer with his mellifluence but for me there's nothing left except the dry taste of cynicism. Was it ever any other way?

Oh, yes, he was exciting once. He was fervent. He could think at a level that would shrivel the minds of others, couldn't he? He could confer significance on the insignificant, juggle with notions – oh, the notions they were endless – but ultimately, at the heart of it, he was flawed. He was disappointing. He was cruel. He was deliberate.

He sat on me when he hit me. I didn't see it coming. That was what I told myself all the way home.

But that was then.

Kate looks ahead, vanished into her own thoughts and oblivious to the radio voices. Her hands hold each other gently in her lap, in the manner of an old lady whose life has taught her patience. I think for a moment of Sally Ann's baby. Everything's changing around us, all the time. Then I think of the first time I saw Kate, the baby I gave birth to, when they held her high in the air with her bloodied scarlet head and her soft grey body for me to see. I switch off the radio. This is now.

'Kate?'

'Yeah.'

'We need to find the Virgin Mary grotto.'

'I know.'

We turn a few more bends and soon we see nothing but a fog rolling over the fields towards us, making everything even vaguer.

'Look, Kate. A cloud has landed.' She stares at it, mesmerized and lonely. 'What was that game you used to play with Brigid and Dad?'

'I don't know.'

'Yes, you do. The one where Brigid and you used to guess what was around the next corner?'

She continues to stare ahead as if her thoughts are wrapped up in the fog.

'Kate? Come on. Do you think we could play it in the fog? What do you reckon we'll see when we turn the corner? What would Brigid say?' I slow down the car to give Kate a chance to come up with something and give me time to adjust to the strangeness of my voice.

'Kate?'

'Brigid . . .'

'What about Brigid?'

'She's in love with her cousin,' she blurts, as if dropping a heavy weight.

'I'm sorry?'

'You can't be in love with your cousin, can you? Not your first cousin?'

'Well, it depends.'

'No, you can't. He's her dad's brother's son. His name is Danny. You can't be in love with your dad's brother's son.'

'And where did she meet him?'

'He lives at the farm she's staying on. He's fourteen and she says his eyes look like huge pools that are really dark. She says they're so huge she's going to drown in them. I mean, I wouldn't want eyes like that. Would you?'

'I guess not.'

'They go for walks in the woods together in the evenings and he takes hold of her hand when they go over the stile.'

'I see.'

'Yeah, and he dries his hair by sticking his head into the stove before he goes out to milk the cows. The first time he did it, Brigid thought his head was going to explode.'

'And did it?'

'I suppose not. He never speaks to her in front of the others but sometimes he looks at her over the breakfast table with his eyes, and once he said out loud, when they were clearing up after lunch, "Does the O'Sullivan lass want to come down the field to help with the hay?" And then, before Brigid could say yes, of course she wanted to go down the field and help with the hay, he was gone.'

'I suppose he's shy.'

'I think he's weird. He doesn't like books or words or any of the things Brigid likes. And they don't talk much because they've got that special connection, which is what love is, Brigid says, and you don't have to talk when you have that special connection. I've never heard Brigid talk about saving hay and milking cows before, even though we helped Mr Power catch his hay last summer. And she didn't ask me what I'm doing, apart from the polite bit at the beginning of a letter that you have to write. Is that what love does to people, Mam? Does it change them? Were you a different person before you fell in love with Dad?'

'Well . . . it's hard to say.'

'Brigid's changed. I know she has, even though I haven't seen her. She wouldn't want to guess what's around the corner any more. I wasn't sure in the first letter but it was for certain in yesterday's one. You can tell, you know, even though it's only in letters. Yesterday's letter went on and on about Danny and her and that special connection and I wouldn't understand.'

'Does he love her?'

'I don't know. She didn't say he did and she didn't say he didn't, but what does it mean to be in love anyway?'

I smile.

'No, Mam. It's serious. It's really serious. I might never see Brigid again because of Danny and his eyes. Her dad already got to keep her for the summer holidays. Now Brigid might never come back to me.'

'Kate. There are many types of love. Even with boys, you can love in different ways at different times in your life.'

'I know that.'

'You do?'

'Well, it's like Cathy and Heathcliff and Edgar, isn't it?'

'Heathcliff and Edgar. That's it. Exactly. Passion and steadiness.'

'Brigid says a whole new world has opened up and she can't think of anything else. She's only happy when she's with him.'

'Oh, Kate. She's just going through a phase. She has a crush. People get very silly when they have a crush. You'll know what it's like soon enough.'

'That's what she says. "You don't know what it's like, Kate, but some day, if you are very lucky, it will happen to you too." That's what she said in her letter. I don't want it to happen to me if it means I go like her.'

'So did you write back to her?'

'No.'

'Why not?'

'Well, she wrote to me the first time after Dad went away and I wasn't going to write back then.'

'No?'

'No, because I didn't want to tell her what happened. She'd just say that because Dad went away that makes him the same as her dad, but he's not. My dad's *not* the same as Mr O'Sullivan. My dad went away because he had to. He had no choice. I didn't want her to say, "I know how you feel," or something like that because she doesn't know. She can't know.'

We continue around a few more bends in silence.

'Mam?'

'Yeah?'

'What was it like when you met Dad?'

'JP? Didn't I tell you all about that in bed this morning?'

This morning feels a long time ago, last night longer again and my body has only just remembered that it needs to sleep. Every bit of me is deflating like a balloon.

'No. What was it like when you fell in love? Did a whole new world open up for you?'

'Sorry?'

'Like, could you think of anything else?'

'Could I . . .?'

'Besides Dad,' she says impatiently. 'You know – the way Brigid said that when you fall in love a whole new world opens up and you can't think of anything else and you don't want to be with anyone else. You're unhappy if you're apart. Is that the way it was for you?'

How was it for me? It's hard to recall. I was so busy, back then, shutting down one world that I didn't notice a new one opening up. It seemed to happen almost despite me.

Then a fresh image slots into the projector of my mind's eye, an image so immediate and strong it makes me veer towards a ditch.

There was a river, or a lake maybe, and we were lying on the grass beside it and I could hear the sound of a passing train in the distance. Our bicycles were abandoned not far away. There was something about his smell, as if it came from generations ago. I remember the red glow of the late summer sun through my lids. When JP leaned over and kissed my right eye, I could make out the shadow of his lips on my eyelid. My ribcage swelled and it was at that moment that I realized this was more than a refuge: this was, in fact, love.

36

It's not the Virgin Mary who directs us in the end, but a hooded youth leaning against a pub door. He pulls a finger from deep in his pocket and points it towards Drogheda, without lifting his head. From then on it gets easier. Country roads unfold revealing signs for our destination, like origami creatures becoming undone.

Kate's excitement grows with every mile. 'How long more will it be?'

'Not long now.'

As for me, I could meander indefinitely through this rural hiatus, full of curious cows and fields glowing in the afternoon sun, taking the bends carefully, playing second fiddle to a tractor or a herd of cows. Now that we're close, I don't want the journey to end. The villages become more frequent and are fortified by apartment blocks, some partly constructed, some partly lived in, looking as if they don't belong. We enter one with an antiquated core, where ivy is pouring down stone walls and hedges are cut into neat boxes, and we fall into step with a funeral procession. Somehow we are trailing the chief mourners' car. Through the back window before us, we see the widow flanked by her two daughters, heads down, merged in grief.

Joan refused to wear black at my father's funeral and I, weighed down by the new life inside me when I had not let go of the old, was too tired to argue. It all happened too quickly.

It began with a phone call in the middle of the night. JP went to answer it. I remember the chink of streetlight through the curtains, enough for me to find my slippers and dressing-gown. I tied a double knot over my kicking belly and padded down the stairs to take the receiver from JP in those last few moments of my innocence.

'Hello?' The receiver was heavy in my hand. 'Sylvia, is that you?'

'Ma? Is everything okay?'

'I think you should come now.'

Those who led more interesting lives than us were heading for bed as we made our way out of Dublin that morning. I sat in the passenger seat, bent over with fear, my face sinking into my scarf, the cold eating into me.

The hearse in front of us turns right, followed by the swell of mourners on foot. I stop the car in the middle of the road and let them pass.

'Where are they all going?' asks Kate, making a hole in my thoughts.

'It's a funeral procession. They're following the hearse, that big black car over there that's carrying the coffin. The long windows are so people can see inside. They're bringing the body to the cemetery to be buried.'

'Why are they having a funeral procession?'

'They follow the corpse, the dead body, to show their respect and their love.'

'Did Granddad have a funeral procession when he died?'

'Yes. Yes, he did.'

'What was it like?'

'Sad. Very sad.'

'Was Dad there?'

'Yes. Dad was there.'

The car wobbles against the push of people.

'What was Granddad like?'

Surprised, I turn to Kate and see my father's sad eyes looking back at me. A surge of love rises up and expands at my throat. 'Oh, Kate, you'd have loved him. He had a dimple here' – I press my finger gently to her right cheek – 'when he smiled. And he had your eyes. And he was kind and gentle and funny.'

So what if I'm selective? So what if I'm in denial? So what if I try to keep Kate out of the shadows and reverse the impact of Joan's diary? That's what you do, isn't it? You protect them from the dark, right?

'So, he was like Dad, then?'

'Yes. I suppose you could say he was like your father.'

Somebody taps on the roof of the car as a signal to move on.

'So what did he die of?' asks Kate, as if kindness buys immortality.

The tail end of the crowd is turning right towards the cemetery. An old woman in a purple coat with a stick pulls her dog into line. The dog looks older than her. He doesn't like walking. Someone taps on the roof of the car again.

'Kate, your grandfather had a very heavy heart,' I say at last, in a whisper that doesn't want to be heard. 'I suppose in the end he died of that.'

37

The car clock says 15:37 when we cross the bridge into Drogheda. We began our journey over six hours ago. It has taken three hours more than Joan predicted yet still feels too quick. Now that we're near the end, I want to close the book and put it away until a time when I'm ready for what is to come.

Kate's excitement, on the other hand, is willing us on. 'This isn't the bridge we went over when we were on the school trip. Look, Mam, there's the old gate into the town. That's the kind of gate towns have when they've got walls around them. Brigid says walls are good 'cause then you can be sure who's a townie and who's a culchie. She said that long ago culchies could come into the town during the day to shop and stuff but they had to go home at night. It's funny. Drogheda looked old and dark last time. Don't lick the window, Monty. Dad says we won't be able to see out if you lick it.'

There's something too final about the sight of the city gates, a clear demarcation between the outside and inside, between travelling and arriving, that makes going through them so frightening. What the hell do I think I'm doing? Do I really think I can turn up at JP's flat as if all the parts of our marriage have been sent to the factory, fixed and reassembled, ready for use, good as new, as if nothing has happened, as if JP doesn't hate me?

'Oh, we're back here beside the river. Mam, we were here

before. There's the gate again. We went through that a minute ago.'

I allowed myself get carried along by the force of Kate's determination and that was a mistake. This is Kate's story now, not mine, and, as if knowing that, she pulls JP's frayed letter out of her jacket pocket.

'The address is flat number one, number five Oliver Place, West Street, Drogheda. That means we have to find West Street first. Mam, we've been here before. Why don't we just stop and ask someone where West Street is?'

'But it isn't even five o'clock.'

'So?'

'So your father won't be home yet.'

'Yes, he will. He always comes home early on Fridays.'

'Not when he's working on site he doesn't.'

'Yes, he does. If he's not there, we can wait for him outside and he'll see us when he gets home. He'll be so surprised. I wonder what he'll say. Let's get out and find West Street.'

'West Street is just straight ahead.' My finger points over the steering-wheel to a crossroads clogged up with cars.

'Let's get out and walk, then.'

I pull the car towards the kerb, switch off the engine and look out at the people walking up and down West Street.

'Mam?'

There's a trough on the bridge of Kate's nose where her two brows come together.

'Kate, we . . . we can't turn up at your father's flat, not just like that.'

'Why not?'

She's right. Why not? JP's my husband, Kate's father. Doesn't that give you certain rights? The right to order him out of your life for ever and the right to say you didn't really

248

mean it? In fact, you didn't know what you meant. Isn't that what marriage is all about? Isn't it meant to withstand the emotional tides of the mere mortals involved? Isn't it meant to laugh off their whims? Isn't it meant to say 'This is me, marriage, sticks and stones, I'm stronger than that'? Isn't that why I signed up? Wasn't it one big mad adventure in security?

No, not security. Belonging. Love, even.

We were going to be best friends, JP and I, exchanging trivia from the day as I rubbed cream into my hands and he scanned the paper in bed at night. That's what marriage was going to be for us. We were going to trade our repertoire of stories and jokes so that after a while we could talk in shorthand, and by the time we were in our rocking chairs, we'd get by with an economical grunt at each other and we'd understand.

We were going to be lovers. We were going to find each other with caution and certainty in the dark. And the next day we'd kiss each other lightly on the lips when JP dropped me off at work, as a postscript to the night before.

'Why not?' Kate's pushing the red button on her safety-belt.

'Maybe he doesn't . . . I mean it's just not so simple . . .'

'It is so simple. It *is* so simple.'

Kate finds the handle on the car door and pulls it. The door falls open and she jumps on to the only space on the pavement, between a bin, a pole and a briefcase. She slams the door shut on me calling her name and doesn't look back.

She runs towards West Street, hopping and skipping between people, dodging contact for fear she'll be stopped by them. I step on to the street, followed by Monty. A car squeals behind us. I grab Monty's lead. Up ahead, Kate's in the middle of the crossroads, surrounded by cars. Horns are honking at the top of their voices.

'*Kate.*'

Everyone looks around, everyone apart from Kate. She's on the other side. She's on West Street now. Monty drags me forward, sniffing the air in every direction.

'You're not going to leave your car parked like that, are you?' some suit barks at me. Kate's a blob of intense pink in the crowd ahead, running, stopping, looking up to read the name of every side-street off West Street. But none of them, it seems, is Oliver Place.

People are staring at me.

You're not going to leave your car parked like that, are you?

You're not going to let your child run wild like that, are you?

You're not going to run after your husband like that, are you?

Then, suddenly, the pink blob runs across the road towards a jewellery shop that's selling engagement rings and romantic dreams sitting on pink velvet cushions. Next to it a church sits on top of a pile of steps that draw your eyes up in reverence. Monty pulls me towards it just as its door closes over the pink and he drags me up each step. The door is heavy and inside the smell of spicy smoke makes him sneeze.

We stand at the bottom of the aisle. Everything in this church is dark – even the stained-glass window behind the altar doesn't want to let light in. Three or four people are kneeling in the pews. Kate's nowhere to be seen.

It was an aisle like this that my father walked me up to hand me over to JP. I was all wrapped up in ivory silk and grinning loudly, wanting to laugh at it all, laugh at the panto-mime of it, corsages, pillbox hats with net, tears smudging makeup, and JP grinning back at me. It was hilarious. A window of merriment in my life between one thing and another. That's how it was in the beginning, JP and me. We found the absurd in the everyday and saved it up to share with each other. We took trips to the tops of mountains and the tips of land sticking into the sea, giddy with the excitement of our adventure together. It was standing breathless on Croagh Patrick that he asked me to marry him. The sun was high in the sky and shadows were nowhere to be seen. They fell later when the laughing faded and was replaced by fear and a scrutiny of every look, every word, every silence as if we were rehearsing a play, always wondering how we were doing.

Halfway up the aisle, Kate comes into view, off to the left, alone with the residue of Oliver Plunkett's head. She looks frail in the hugeness of the space around her. Her head is bent in prayer, for her father, for Brigid, for the people she loves most in the world whom she has lost, albeit only for a while, but that's all it takes. Tears are trailing down her face, disproportionate with the smallness of her cheeks. She struggles to keep her lip in.

'Kate?'

'Brigid said he was hung, drawn and quartered just like a cow you'd see in the butcher's.'

Poor Oliver is encased in an ornate casket under a spire that's almost reaching the heavens. His head looks like nothing more than a wizened lump of sealing wax, but his pain is preserved in his grimace.

'She said that he offered it up for what he believed in.'

'Offered it up?'

'Back then people who had mean things done to them offered them up to God instead of doing mean stuff back.' She sighs heavily. 'It's hard to explain.'

'I see.'

'Mam?'

'Yes, Kate?'

'Why did Dad never come to get us if he really loved me as much as he said he did in the letter?'

It's a question that brings me to the edge of a massive plain, a life without JP, which is too vast and frightening to consider. It's been loitering on the outskirts of my brain since he left, coming with time into centre stage, and I'm afraid to look for the answer. It's easier to stay in this limbo where everything is undecided and anything is still possible.

'Maybe Dad is just like Brigid's dad after all,' says Kate, in a hushed voice. 'Maybe he doesn't want to be with us any more. Maybe he's gone away to get a new child and a new family. Maybe he'll go to Australia and send a Christmas card every year that says "Love, Dad" on the bottom of it, just like Brigid's dad, and he won't be able to write more often because his new wife won't let him.'

'No, Kate, you mustn't think like that.'

'I know it's my fault.'

'Kate, it's not your fault. It could never be your fault.'

'No, Mam, I know it is. I've thought about it. I'm not a boy. I don't build bridges and know about the Enigma Code and all that. If he had a boy and a girl, that might be okay but because it's just me . . .'

'Kate, your father loves you with all his heart.'

'He said that he wanted to go back to Australia. He said he loves the big open spaces there. There's millions of stars in the sky at night in Australia and there are lots of brilliant animals, like wombats, and people who lived there for millions of years that go on long walks singing.'

'The Aboriginals?'

'Yeah, them. I've tried to offer it up. I've tried to say that some people get the bad luck and that's just how it is. Look at Brigid. Her dad went away and she never said anything. But I can't. I can't just offer it up to God and not know. Besides, there's the dog to think of.'

She steps forward and takes Monty's lead from me. 'Monty would really miss Dad and he's done nothing to deserve that.'

The tears are flowing down her cheeks but she sounds strangely calm, almost resigned. It's like meeting someone new, someone who opens up the concealed parts of their mind and in so doing gives words to your own unutterable thoughts.

It's like falling in love.

'I'm going to find him,' says Kate. 'I'm going to tell him that even if he is going to Australia, I'm his daughter and I'm coming with him.'

38

Kate's shoulders judder up for three and down for three as she marches up West Street. At first, I try to keep up with her and Monty, but when she hears my quickening steps, she quickens hers too, and when she stops to ask a postman for directions, I stop too.

Finally, all three of us converge outside an anonymous-looking apartment block, a few steps back from the main street, the kind occupied by people on the move. Curtains are drawn over most of the windows. A menu of eight doorbells sits beside the front door. The bottom one is neatly labelled 'Creative Solutions'. Kate presses it long and hard.

'Hello?' says a girl's voice. She sounds young and worried.

'Hello,' Kate shouts into the bell. 'Is that number five Oliver Place?'

'No,' says the girl. 'This is number one.'

I lean in and press a higher bell.

'What did you press that one for?' Kate asks.

'Well, if that one was the first, this one must be the fifth.'

We listen to the silence that follows. JP may have headed straight for Dublin after work for the weekend, if indeed he lives here at all. I press the bell again, longer and harder than before. Kate stares intently at the door, willing her father into existence. I'm about to turn and leave when a man's voice growls over the airwaves.

'Yeah?'

'Hi,' Kate shouts. 'Is my dad there?'

'Come again?'

I lean in. 'We're looking for JP Larkin.'

'He's not here.'

'Do you know where we might find him?'

'He's still at work, at the bridge.'

'The bridge.' Kate lights up. 'Where's the bridge?'

'Who's this?'

'Kate.'

'His daughter,' I explain. 'I'm Sylvia, his wife.'

'And Monty,' says Kate.

'Who's Monty?'

'The dog.'

'My, my, it's quite the family outing. You'd better come up.'

A loud buzz opens the front door. Kate and Monty are halfway up the stairs before I cross the threshold.

The owner of the gruff voice looks like he hasn't shaved in three days and hasn't slept in as long, except we've woken him up. One arm wraps around his skull, the other stretches over the opposite shoulder to the unreachable itch on his back. A tattooed dragon is creeping around his upper arm and under his vest. He's still in his boxer shorts.

A sickly smell fills the room, the smell of sweat and sleep and stale drink. His bed, a nylon sleeping-bag on a couch, is tossed to one side. We're imposing.

'I'm sorry to impose,' I say.

'No need to be sorry. Like, haven't I had three hours' kip? That's one less than Maggie Thatcher.' He offers a hand to Kate, then me. 'I'm Hugo,' he says, in a way that suggests we should've heard of him. 'Hugo Delamere.'

'I'm very pleased to meet you. This is Monty,' Kate says,

pointing to the dog, on a strained lead, who is busy hoovering up every scent of the carpet around him.

'What kind of a mutt is that?' asks Hugo.

'It's a basset hound.'

'So it is.'

Hugo Delamere is about forty. His chin is dimpled and his eyebrows are colliding with each other in the middle. 'Beware of men whose eyebrows meet,' Joan would say.

'So, like, you're looking for JP?' he says to me, folding his arms across his chest.

'Yes.'

'And you're the wife?'

'Yes.'

'And you're the kid?'

'Yes,' says Kate.

'I didn't know he, like, had a family,' he says. Then, on seeing Kate's face, 'Not that I know him very well, like. He's more a friend of Kent's,' gesturing to a shut door out of which someone had taken a lump. 'We pass like ships in the night. I'm on the night ship.'

'Where's the bridge?' Kate asks.

'What bridge?'

'The bridge Dad's working on.'

'Oh, that bridge. Well, it's a few miles from here.'

'How do we get to it?'

'Oh, you can't go there,' says Hugo. 'You need the gear, the hats and the boots and stuff. Not to mention the Safe Pass.'

'We've got to go there.'

Hugo registers the pitch and looks to me for direction.

'It's important,' I say, with as much implication as I can manage.

'Okay, okay. I'll show you where the bridge is.' He reaches over to grab a pair of jeans from the back of a chair. He drills one leg into them, then the other.

'You'll have to drive,' he says to me. 'I can't risk it, not after the week I've had.'

I don't know how we get to the bridge. One minute we're in the town, driving from red light to red light. Next, we're going along a motorway, with cars speeding past us on both sides and signs with arrows telling us what lane to be in and what lane not to be in. The horn of a jeep screams at me. I curse. The driver overtakes with an erect finger. A sign with arrows appears out of the blue. Bollards rise up before me. I have to change lanes. I hate changing lanes. What if the car behind me is going too fast? I almost crash into the bollards. I shift into the next lane with eyes not quite closed but not quite open. Next up, a roundabout. We've to go right, according to Hugo, over a bridge, over the fast-moving herd of commuting traffic below, like a massive waterfall that could carry us away. Another roundabout. Then, without warning, Hugo reaches over and turns the steering-wheel in a massive arc. We swerve up a dirt track lined by bollards and potholes and find ourselves in God-knows-where. Dust is all around us. We brake in front of steel barriers.

Reaching up into the air is the tower of the bridge, legs spread wide and arms stretching high, like a powerful king surveying all that he rules. There's something ominous about him. I can't tell what.

'Look, it's the Bridge Man,' says Kate, pushing her face forward between Hugo and me and stretching her eyes all the way up to the top. 'The force pulling inward is the same as the force pulling outward.'

'Come again?' says Hugo.

Kate points to the bridge. 'But the strings aren't on it pinning him down.'

Hugo's looking dazed. He raises his brows towards me but I let Kate do the talking.

'He's bigger and more powerful than I ever imagined,' she says.

'He's big, all right,' murmurs Hugo.

'I wish Fred could see him.'

'Fred would love him.' He nods.

'You know, Hugo, my dad built that.' Love and pride for her father are puffing Kate up, making her taller so that her head is scraping the ceiling of the car.

'Did he now? Isn't he a great man altogether?'

'Let's go in,' she says.

Hugo turns in his seat to face her. 'Do you see that sign over there?'

'Yes.'

'What does it say?'

'"Trespassers will be" something. What are "trespassers"?'

'That's what you'll be if you go through those barriers and they catch you.'

'What will they do if they catch me?' There's a thrill in Kate's voice.

'Well, you'd better stay here and let me do the talking.'

'Okay, but you'd better let Dad know that we're here. He'll arrange it all. He won't let them catch us.'

'You should go,' I mutter to Hugo.

We watch in silence as Hugo strides towards the gap in the barrier. A short man with a yellow jacket and yellow hard hat comes out and folds his arms over his yellow belly. Hugo gestures towards us in the car and the man squints in our direction. He shakes his head, unfolds his arms, puts his hands on his hips and opens his legs wide. After a bit more pleading and head-shaking, Hugo turns to walk back to the car.

Kate's trembling behind me, like an elastic band that's pulled tight. On seeing Hugo's face, the band snaps. She climbs into the front seat, finds the door handle and the door pops open. Monty jumps out after her. Amazingly, he gets to the gap before Kate and runs between the legs of the yellow-bellied man, his ears slapping the insides of the man's legs. The man jumps and shouts, 'Shit,' as if he's been stung. 'It's a fucking dog,' he roars.

He runs into the site after Monty, followed by Hugo. Kate goes after them through the gap and disappears into a maze of giant containers.

39

Stillness fills the car. This is the end of the journey. Kate is gone and I am alone now. I could feel it coming on, gathering strength like distant storm clouds, but I did nothing to stop her. I couldn't keep her. It was bound to happen, sooner or later, ever since the day she came out of hospital, newborn and hungry, ever since we were flung together by virtue of birth.

That time from long ago still hangs like a picture carved into my mind, not always visible but always there. I choose to think of it as a coma, but I was awake throughout. People came and went, calling with forced cheer from a distance, 'Only me.' Only me. Only me. Only me. They made me endless cups of tea. They put sugar in though I didn't ask for it. They even stirred it for me. 'How are you feeling today, Sylvia?' they'd ask, looking Kate over for signs of . . . what? I didn't know. They spent ages talking at the front door to people with briefcases, letting all the cold air in, asking the Briefcases was it normal, was *I* normal? Then they'd ask questions that began with 'Sylvia, would you not . . .?' Would I not what?

It's never really gone away.

I could turn the car around now and drive in the opposite direction. I could travel this life alone, unaccompanied and unaccountable. I could let Kate go, into the void before me, to be reunited with JP, unfettered by me. I have delivered her to her father, again. I have done the right thing. Maybe this is how it was always meant to be. I could absolve myself at this point. I could pick my way out of this place for good, and would it make any difference to anybody? Would it? JP and Kate would stitch themselves together into one neat unit, no loose threads or frayed edges, and they could do that without me, without conflict or compromise, somewhere on the other side of that barrier.

But somewhere in my depths another voice is humming, quiet but insistent, like a soft bass drum, a voice that is only now being heard.

I crank open the door of JP's car and, under the shadow of the Bridge Man, stumble over the grating landscape towards the site entrance that swallowed up Kate, Monty and Hugo. There's no sign of them anywhere. There's no sign of anyone but a lone man in a distant field digging a trench. Large containers sit in an arrangement before me. Diggers vibrate at a distance. The voice beckons me on.

'Can I help you?' a man is shouting in my direction, like the one Hugo spoke to, small-eyed and stroppy. Stubble covers his double chin so that the short hard hairs are attacking their own flesh. My father used to scratch my forehead with his sandpaper chin under the light of the Sacred Heart lamp when he told me my night-time stories.

I look up. There's something about the Bridge Man's menacing presence over us that's calling up a story from long ago. I look down. The man's steel-capped boots are rooted in the lunar rubble beneath us. His left leg is straighter than the right. Then they alternate. I'm not sure if he's moving, or is it me?

Then, it comes to me, as if an out-of-focus image I'd been carrying around with me is suddenly pulled into focus.

Once upon a time, a long time ago, my father told me late

one night when I was fighting back sleep that a beautiful creature was washed up on a beach far away. She was wrapped in seaweed and all wet from the sea and her hair was running down the sides of her face as far as her waist. She lay perfectly still, sleep-like, as the sea pushed her, bit by bit, up on to the sand, and all around were these enormous black cliffs, looking over her like guardian angels. Nobody knew she was there, apart from a little boy who found her when he was playing on his own on the beach. In fact, nobody knew he was there because he had never before played on that beach. In her pockets were shiny magical stones to keep her safe, and around her neck was a medal of Our Lady. He held her cold hand and told her stories of things that happened in his home, everyday things, things that only she would understand, all the time trying to get her to wake up. The boy lay down beside her and fell asleep, and when he woke up, she had disappeared.

The spot where my father's stubble had pricked my fore-head was wet. I had wiped his cheek dry with my small hand. It was my job to look after him.

'Can I help you?' the man asks again, unhelpfully. I take a step forward and stagger. 'Are you okay, love?'

The earth slides away from under me and everything turns black.

'Sssylvia!'

A slap vibrates in my ears and I open my eyes. JP's face is shaded by his hard hat. Random bits of his cheeks are lit by the sun.

'Sylvia, what the hell are you doing here?'

'I came to find you,' I say, closing my eyes and heading back towards the cliffs. I need to know how the story ends.

He burrows his hands underneath me and gathers me up with impatient effort, one arm under my back, the other under my knees, quivering under my weight, then steadies himself. My head falls back and I let myself be carried, until something catches up on me – shame, I think. I force my feet down on the uneven ground, like a child who no longer wants to be carried, toes first, stabilized by heels, and hastily brush myself down. A couple of hard-hatted men look on, like extras in a movie.

'How did you get here? How did you know where to find me? Did you phone the office? You know you're not allowed on this site.'

He sounds perplexed but, then, he wouldn't know, would he? In fact, come to think of it, he knows nothing at all.

The noise of boots on rubble brings another man, dressed in the classic hard hat and luminous jacket. This one is short and snappy, a thorough Jack Russell.

'Larkin,' he barks. 'You'd better get your bony arse over here to supervise this pour if we've any chance of getting out of here tonight. If it's not started in the next five minutes, it'll be sent back, and on your head be it.'

JP swears something I cannot hear and turns towards the bridge. Then he's gone, not before ordering a Hard Hat to bring me up to the office.

I'm marched to a pair of Portakabins, one on top of the other, and up rickety steps to the upper one. The door is opened for me and the locks turned behind me before I can explain about Kate and Monty and Hugo. I stand for a while, adjusting to the coolness and darkness of my cell, in which two cluttered desks sit facing each other.

He was the one who found her.

I sit on the black swivel chair and study the dirt all around me, the dirt on the computer mouse, the dirt on the keyboard, the monitor, the desk itself. It's like someone has rubbed tiny balls of murky dough into selected places. He knelt beside her and arranged her hair around her face. I begin to scrape them off with my thumbnail and carefully place them on a yellow delivery docket, like laboratory specimens. He called her 'Mother'. I open up a random paper clip and use it to shovel the dirt and fluff out from between the letters on the keyboard. I swivel as I work. I keep going as far as the monitor. Did he call her 'Mother'? It's decorated with a garland of yellow Post-its. What did he call her? Numbers and measurements are written in JP's careful hand. I look around. A phone number in his handwriting is on a notebook beside the keyboard. This is JP's desk.

I stand up and look it over, opening and closing the drawers, lifting and placing back down meaningless papers. Did he know who she was? He must've known who she was. On the back of JP's chair is his navy fleece, the one he wore on that last night when he told me about wind-loading tests in Manning's, when he wanted to be let in, when I told him to go. I rummage through the pockets. I don't know what I'm looking for, something of me, I think, or of us. But there's only a crumpled tissue. I pull his fleece off the back of the chair, scrunch it up and hug it close to me, searching for the warmth of JP in it.

Through the window the half-built bridge deck reaches into a vast emptiness, not looking to the future or to the past, just suspended and waiting to be brought bit by bit to the other side, to a state of completion. JP's out there, overseeing the concrete pour. Kate's out there, telling Hugo all about her father, and Monty's out there, having the adventure of his life. And I, I'm banged up in here, I who drove them all away. And now it may be too late.

The door of the Portakabin opens abruptly. It hadn't been locked. JP's standing there in the frame.

'Kate? Is she okay? Is she with Hugo?' I ask.

'What would Kate be doing with Hugo?' He sounds cold. I can bear anything but cold.

His arms are wrapped tightly around his torso and I want to unpick him, to open him up. I must speak up. All words have consequences but silence does too.

'JP?'

It's hard to say everything that has to be said. It's hard to find the first word, the first point in a story that is beyond my knowing.

'I am sorry.'

He is gazing down at me with a strangely calm look of hate or love or something in between. But there is nothing in between.

'I was scared,' I say.

He does not speak.

'I was scared for a very long time.'

The silence is torturous.

'He found her, you know.'

'Who?'

'My father. He found her body washed up on the beach. To think that I nearly . . .'

'Sssylvia . . .'

He says my name in that slow way of his as if it is a long story full of twists and turns, too difficult to tell. His face is pixellated by my tears.

'. . . I should never have left, not for a day.' He moves towards me and I feel a cry rise up through me, like an oncoming train. If I start crying, I may never stop this time. I try to steady myself with my breathing but it's making me shake all over.

'I was a coward,' he is saying. 'There isn't a minute of the day when you're not with me, Sylvia, in my head. I talk to you all the time, out loud, up there on that bridge. It's like you're never not there.'

He reaches for me but I'm not ready for that, not yet. I fling my arms forward, dropping the fleece, and my words are spewing out, all over the place.

'But you don't see, JP? I must've known. I must've known all along.'

'Known what?'

'Everything. My father. My grandmother. She's in me, JP. She's who I am.'

'No. She's not who you are.'

'JP, you think I don't know, but I do.'

'Know what?'

'Know what? Know what?' I'm circling around in the only spare space in the Portakabin, around and around with my arms flung wide, like pure madness itself. 'I know my father was a drunk and that he loved drink more than he loved us.'

'That's not true. It was hard for him.'

'I know that too. I know he never had a chance. I know his mother filled her pockets with stones in cold blood and walked into the sea. Did you know that, JP? Did you? I think I did. I think I knew that all along and I couldn't bear to know it because that's the very saddest thing I know.'

His arms are around me and my words are gnawing his chest between the cries and moans.

'And, you know, there's no end to the story. It goes on, in me, in Kate, it keeps going on.'

He tries to shush me but I can't stop.

'I loved him so much, despite everything.'

'I know you did.'

I push my head further into his chest and barely say the words. 'I blamed Kate for . . . for him dying, for taking his space in the world. I know that's lunacy but, God forgive me, it's true.'

He tightens his arms around me so that it feels I'm no longer standing by myself but am being held up.

'Something happened to me, JP. I lost my nerve.'

'I know.'

'I was running from you.'

'I know.'

'I was so full of guilt for . . . for not loving as I should.'

'Ssh.'

I step out of his arms and smear the tears around my face. 'It's easy for you, JP. You're not afraid to love.'

He smiles at me, a warm, idiotic smile.

'No, JP, it's true. Kate idolizes you.'

He holds his hand up to my cheek and I lean my head into it. 'Kate loves you too, Sylvia.'

'How can she, JP? After all that I did? After all that I didn't do for her? You were there.'

'You know she does. You're her mother. '

'And soon she'll be a woman and it'll be too late. She'll be wrapped up in her own story and she'll be lost to me and I know this is my only chance but I don't trust myself . . .'

'You're her mother, Sylvia, and that's all you ever have to be.'

Something in his words or the way he says them, like a soft bass drum, soothes me and I let myself enter his warmth again. His tears are on my forehead.

'I miss you, Sylvia Larkin.'

'*I* miss me, JP.'

The door opens again and men's voices are filling the cabin. The Jack Russell's rises above all the others.

'*Larkin.*'

'You can go fuck your concrete pour,' shouts JP.

'Larkin, there's a kid on the bridge.'

We spring back and stare out of the window, our eyes running along the bridge, taking in the black plastic that billows from its edge, the loose rope, the spikes of metal, the raw fragmentation of it all.

You don't always know what danger looks like. You just feel it running through you. You want the moment to stay still. Awful as it is, it's better than what the next one may bring.

We keep scanning and there, at the point where the bridge stops and drops into the dark river below, is a bright pink speck.

40

A mass of yellow-coated men split in two when JP and I get to the stump of the bridge, breathless. Everything goes quiet apart from my mind.

Please, God, please keep Kate there, in that spot, right there, God. Don't let her move. Keep her there.

The men close the circle behind us. JP takes my hand. We tiptoe our way along the bridge, over the new man-made terrain towards the pink speck. I am cold. The bridge is shaking and a sickness is sitting in my throat. I swallow. I'm afraid to look up, because I know the horizon is spinning around me, faster and faster, like a lasso being whipped through the air. I feel the heat of JP's hand and concentrate on my feet landing on the hard surface. The ball of my foot goes down first. Every contact with the ground is a relief. Any moment now, the world could turn upside down and we could fall into the abyss, all three of us.

When I look up, I'm nearer the end of the half-built bridge than the beginning. The pink speck has grown into a wet blur. Kate is waiting for us with Monty beside her, stomping on the last piece of ground, up and down in the same spot. They're just one step away from infinity.

'*MAAAM.*'

The cry echoes through the valley around us, through the bridge and through me. It's a cry like her first, raw, primal, expelled by her lungs into the world, giving nothing but the brutal truth that she needs me.

JP lets go of my hand. 'You go.'

I'm on my own again and all eyes are on me.

This is no time for stalling. I have to keep going, to the beat of the soft bass drum – *you're her mother, the only mother she has* – step by quaking step, all the way up to the mark, moving faster than the unknowable time it takes for death to arrive. This is our last chance.

Don't move, Kate. Stay right there. I'm here. I'm right here. I promise everything is going to be okay.

When I look up, Kate's standing right in front of me, wide open. I kneel before her so that I'm at eye level with her golden, sloping eyes and wrap my arms fiercely around her for the first time. She lays her head on my shoulder and we stay like that, suspended in mid-air. I am made breathless by the flawless beauty of her trust. Fear is in every bit of me, but it's a beautiful kind of fear.

At last, I lift my head and return her smile.

'Kate, we have to . . .'

'Ssh. Look.'

With one arm still over my shoulder, she draws a circle with her other arm around her, like a conductor applauding his orchestra, and presents to me the glory of the day. Space is all around us, wide-open space wrapping around the corners of the globe. Fields of different colours are almost within reach and hills fade into the distance. Birds weave paths through the blueness above. The Bridge Man looms over us. Below, the river is a deep darkness. There's nothing holding us in place but each other. If we fall, we plunge straight into it, down into the silence.

I reach into my pocket and pull out the grey pebble with the white streak. Kate stares at it on the palm of my hand.

I let go of her, crouch on all fours and extend my hand shakily over the water. I stop to taste this meeting point of past and future before I tip my hand over. The pebble slides away and down, down through layers of history and the milestones of the past, through the door slamming behind JP, through the incision in my belly, my father's last breath, the hello at the baggage carousel, Arthur's goodbye punch, and through the day my grandmother walked into the sea.

We wait for the splash and when it doesn't come, I stand up slowly, looking straight ahead at the huge, frightening, beautiful world around us. Then I take my daughter's hand in mine.

'It's time to go home now, Kate,' I say.

It feels different when Dad drives. He hardly touches the steering-wheel. His elbow sticks out of the window and his left hand just pushes the wheel up or down, but not very much. Now and then he lets his right hand touch the wheel so that he can change the gears with his left, but he does this without thinking. His hands have a mind of their own.

Dad said to Mam that she should drive us back to Dublin. He said he'd like to see her drive because she drove us all the way up from Waterford in one piece, but she didn't want to. She said she was exhausted after everything that had happened. She promised to start driving again as soon as everything gets back to normal. Tomorrow, maybe. Dad said that was okay, he understood. Then he kissed her right eye, as if it was a really precious thing, and it made her close her eyes and smile.

I don't know what Mam means by 'normal'. I don't think things will ever be normal again. Already they're different, I don't know how they are, they just are. Mam and Dad are different, and I think I am too, different but the same. So maybe Mam means things will just be a different type of normal.

It was brilliant to see Dad again, better than I imagined in all my daydreams. I stuck to him, like a baby monkey. He smelt just the exact same, apart from the smell of the bridge that was in his clothes. He didn't let me go, not for ages. That was when I knew that he wasn't like Mr O'Sullivan. He didn't leave us. It wasn't his fault and I'm sorry I thought that. I'm sorry I thought it was my fault because I'm not a boy, because that's just stupid, anyone can see that, but sometimes your head tells you things that aren't true and sometimes you listen even though you know it's not true. It was just one of those things, like what Mam said about the scar under her eye. Just one of those things.

I wanted to tell Dad about the huge trip Mam and Monty and I did together to get to the bridge and to him, but really I wanted to tell him about everything that had happened since he left, because when you leave, you can't know what happens when you're not there. I wanted to tell him how I planned to take the buses and the train to find him, but I didn't want to have to tell him how Mam walked into the sea on the morning I was going to leave, just like the woman in the little blue book, only that woman died and Mam didn't, and then I couldn't leave because it was like all of a sudden I was in charge. I didn't want to have to tell anyone that, not even Dad.

But anyway I couldn't tell Dad any of this because all these men in yellow coats were standing around us saying I should never have been on the bridge, and they were asking each other who let me up there, as if someone had actually said to me, 'It's all right, you can go on up now.' So then I had to explain to Dad really quickly that going up on the bridge wasn't my fault and that no one let me go up there either. It was because of Monty, you see. I got lost in a maze of giant boxes and after I got out of the maze, Monty was up on the bridge, sniffing all over, although there was nothing for him to smell up there but new pavement. No dog had ever been up there before. Monty was the first. I had to go after him because I'm the one in charge of him and that's what you do when you're in charge. But when I got hold of his lead and looked around, I could see we were right up there in the sky and I could see the way the world curves at the edges and something made me want to walk right to the end of the bridge. I had to see as much as I could see.

When we got to just before the end, everything was so far away from us and there was nothing to hang on to. The Bridge Man was standing in a river and there was this huge gap between his legs and us, so there was no way we could touch him. This ladder ran up the side of him leading to a sort of nest for humans on top, and when I looked up, I could see men in it but they were tiny. Behind them were lots of cotton-wool clouds, like the ones in Mam's painting from long ago. I thought that maybe Dad was up there in the clouds, looking down on Monty and me, and that's when I thought that maybe he'd be angry with me. Dad doesn't ever shout at me. If he's annoyed, he just says, 'Kate,' with a longer than usual *a* sound. Only I understand the *a* sound. I hate myself when he says it. It means I've disappointed him. It makes me want to hide away and not come out again. I don't ever want to disappoint Dad.

It turned out Dad wasn't up in the nest after all. He was halfway down the bridge deck, but I didn't know that then. So Monty and I were stuck there, we really were. We couldn't go forward and we couldn't go backwards and it suddenly felt like we were hanging there in the middle of the sky and that was when I started to cry. I know it's stupid but I did. I cried because I thought Dad didn't love me any more and Brigid only cared about Danny and there was only Mam and Monty. I cried the way you cry when you're little and you get lost in the supermarket, because you think you'll be lost for ever and will never be found again. That was why Mam had to come all the way down the bridge to bring us back, even though everyone knows that she hates being high up. It makes her really sick. But she came right down to the end of the bridge to get us and we threw this stone she had into the water together and she didn't get sick so maybe she's not afraid any more. Maybe it's me that's afraid now.

I fall half asleep in the back of the car on the way to Dublin. Mam and Dad are talking in low voices. It's hard to make out what they're saying and who's speaking. It's strange. They sound like the same person. When I open my eyes, the moon is up high, even though the sky is still blue, and Dad's turning the car and we're going down our road. Mam's messing with her hair, putting it up on top of her head in a bun and letting it fall again like she does sometimes. She's smiling. She's beautiful when she smiles.

Acknowledgements

Many thanks to all those who helped me with my research – Douglas Baxter, Michael Durand, Layla Hughes, John Iliff, Sinead Lawlor, Sarah Malin, Martin MacGuill, and Grace and Zoe Staunton.

Thanks to my readers – Dr Nick Bankes, Derek Flynn, Susan Gallwey and Juanita Wilson – and to Vanessa O'Loughlin, Mark Roper, Grace Wells, Margaret Organ and the Waterford County Council arts office for their guidance and support. Thanks also to all the staff of the Tyrone Guthrie Centre, Annamakerrig.

I am particularly grateful to my agent Ger Nichol of The Book Bureau who championed this novel so enthusiastically, as well as Michael McLoughlin, Cliona Lewis, Hazel Orme and all the team at Penguin, especially my astute and generous editor, Patricia Deevy.

Finally, special thanks are due to Susan Cowman, Aiden Lloyd and Pete Smyth.